Of Knives and Night-blooms

The River Divine

Book One

Tansy Rayner Roberts

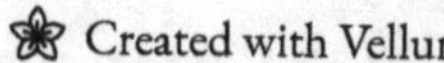
Created with Vellum

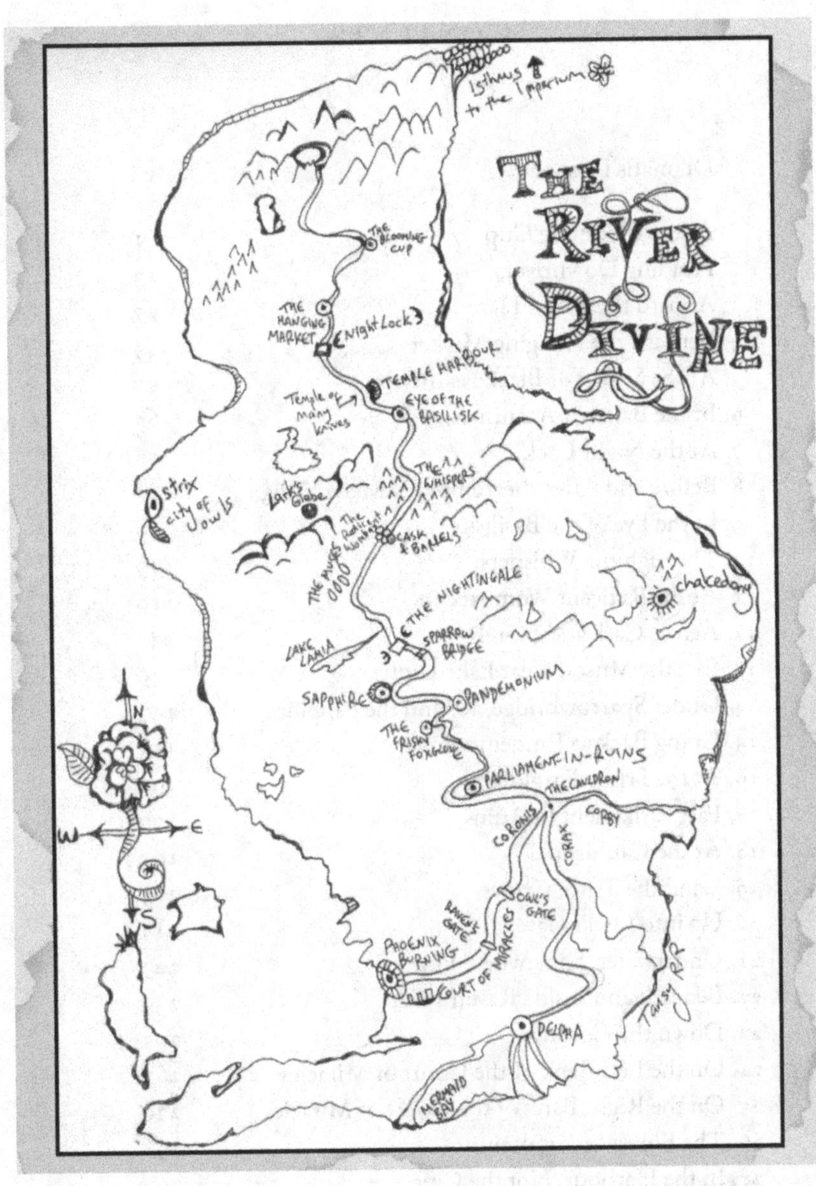

THE RIVER DIVINE
Isthmus to the Imperium
THE BLOOMING CUP
THE HANGING MARKET
Night Lock
TEMPLE HARBOUR
Temple of Many Knives
EYE OF THE BASILISK
Strix city of owls
Lark's Globe
THE WHISPERS
The Reticent Wombat
CASK & BARRELS
THE MUSES
THE NIGHTINGALE
Chakedony
LAKE LAMIA
SPARROW BRIDGE
SAPPHIRE
PANDEMONIUM
THE FRISKY FOXGLOVE
PARLIAMENT-IN-RUINS
THE CAULDRON
CORONIS
CORAX
CORBY
OWL'S GATE
RAVEN'S GATE
PHOENIX BURNING
COURT OF MIRACLES
DELPHA
MERMAID BAY
Tansy
N
W
E
S

Contents

Dramatis Personae

- DIO TAURUS: a river rat with aspirations
- IKAROS SWIFT: a priest of the Black Raven, the Hand
- VALERIA SWIFT: a priest of the Black Raven, the Blade
- MARDI MORENCY: a priest of the Black Raven, the Needle
- NIMUE: daughter of the Imperium, student of the House of Velvet
- CALYX: daughter of the Imperium, Petal of the House of Flowers
- BETO: hostess of the Blooming Cup tea house, Dio's auntie
- CAPTAIN OF THE *SILKEN HARE*
- YEONY: handmaiden at the Shrine of Black Feathers
- AODHAN: a mystery
- SHANITH: another of Dio's aunties
- DAPHEEN: and another
- JANNA: innkeeper of the Reticent Wombat

- EMBERLEY: barmaid at the Reticent Wombat, Janna's daughter
- LAYLA: former innkeeper of the Reticent Wombat, Janna's mother
- PERAYA: one of Janna's friends, much-married
- REYNARD KALDORAN: a priest of the Black Raven, the Bow
- BORS: deceased priest of the Black Raven, the Stave
- LANYET: hostess of Pandemonium
- KALISTA: one of Dio's many former employers, manager of a discreet escort agency
- ULWEN: knight of the Bright Owl
- ZENOBIA, ARTEMIS, ATTICUS: owls
- MAVADIAN: head priestess at Raven's Gate, aunt of Yeony
- YAIN: ink-speaker, abbot of the Blazing Phoenix
- CAPTAIN OF THE CITY GLADII: has helmet with plume
- NINIANE: Empress of the Imperium, Calyx's sister
- THE THIRTEENTH TREASURE: heir to the Divine Kingdom
- THE DIVINE KING: king of the Divine Kingdom

CURRENT GODS OF THE DIVINE KINGDOM

- The Black Raven: god of death
- The Bright Owl: god of healing
- The Silver Hawk: god of war
- The Grey Lark: god of the hearth, fertility and protection
- The Blazing Phoenix: god of the creative arts
- The Divine King: would have put himself at the top of the list, actually

1. At the Blooming Cup

Dio Taurus knew this taste. Shaderoot and honey; his tongue was sticky with it. He woke slowly, becoming aware of the cloth stuffed thickly into his mouth, and the sweet, herbal scent that had forced him to sleep too long.

(He had trained himself on potion after potion, tasting tiny doses of the fifty most common criminal concoctions until he knew them cold. If the examination was only based on things he could remember, he would have qualified as a gladius years ago.)

Ridding himself of the gag was easy; Dio bit and chewed at the cloth, stretching his jaw until the cloth slid free, smearing his chin with the same tincture that had kept him drowsy. His wrists and ankles were another matter — leather cuffs bound him to the bed.

"You made neat work of that," said a dry voice, nearby. "I almost wish I'd let you keep the wire you sewed into your cuff. Nothing like an amateur escapology trick to brighten my day."

Dio tipped his head back. In the low light he could see the intruder: a man in black standing at the window of the little room in the Blooming Cup teahouse, where Dio had been staying for the last few weeks (family discount, only two crows a night with meals thrown in if he helped out around the place). There were worse places in the world to be broke and waiting for his next opportunity.

He didn't have to be a gladius to know that the man at the window was dangerous. Dio was at his mercy. It might take two, three hours for the shaderoot to clear completely from his system. Until then, Dio would remain clumsy and slow. Sluggish of movement. Compliant.

It took him several minutes of wriggling to confirm that the lockpick wire he usually kept in his left sleeve (a gladius is always prepared!) was gone; nothing but threads rubbing against his wrist.

He should be afraid. But through a glazed shaderoot fog, he found it hard to care that he was trapped. Fear would come later, he supposed.

"What do you want?" he asked.

"Nothing from you, boy," said the intruder.

There was only one window, facing into the shaded courtyard, so it took forever for the morning light to slide in here. Still, by the sounds rising from below, breakfast was well underway. Dio should be working already, earning his keep. Auntie Beto was going to be pissed off that he had slept in.

The man was all shadow and black hood. Dark on dark on dark. Dio could see the faint line of a bearded jaw, but little else. The man was so still, it would be easy to miss his presence altogether.

Once he started paying attention, though, he knew the shape of that long, tailored jacket. *Featherbrace*. Black patterns embroidered on light black fabric. Black feathers at the collar and cuffs. Twisting sigils market the tailored black cloth: scythe-knives and feathered wings, woven together. The threads were thin so that they could barely be seen. In the low light of the room, they glowed faintly purple.

An elaborate sketch of that particular pattern had featured in four of the examinations Dio had failed in the last year; it was a favourite question to test the arcane knowledge of the applicant. Not that it required any specialist knowledge to recognise a featherbrace at a distance.

"You're a priest of death," he breathed.

"Don't worry," said the stranger in that deep, thrumming voice of his. "You're not my mark, Dio Taurus."

Dio hadn't imagined that he was. The priests of the Black Raven didn't turn out for any old random citizen. You had to be important to warrant that kind of attention, and Dio was... well. He hadn't got started being anybody yet.

He was twenty-two years old and had still not managed to convince anyone in authority that he was competent enough to do the one job he had always wanted. The only way he was getting assassinated was in a case of mistaken identity.

"Why drug me?" he demanded. "If I'm so unimportant." Blame the shaderoot for making him brave; this was the most interesting conversation he had had in months.

The man at the window made a movement that might have been a shrug. "I like your window. Good line of sight. Minimal risk of being thwarted in my sacred duty. No offence, but you're less of a threat than the old ladies in the room next door. They sleep lighter, and their yarn is full of needles."

Dio made a noise of protest. His throat was recovering, at least.

"A word of warning, Dio Taurus," said the intruder, still calm and friendly, for a killer. "I don't want to leave my post right now, which means that I prefer not to stroll over and replace that gag. However, if I suspect for a moment that you are going to make a sound any louder than that chicken squawk you just uttered, I will end you from here. Without hesitation."

Dio lifted his chin at that. "Isn't it against your code to kill someone whose murder hasn't been bought and paid for?" he challenged.

The man in the black featherbrace turned slightly, enough that Dio could see one glittering eye as well as the sleek crossbow he had resting on the window sill. "You make a good point," said the assassin. "Such an act is frowned upon by my god. I would have to do *weeks* of penance. And yet. Without hesitation."

Under normal circumstances, Dio was excellent at knowing when to shut his mouth. The half-dozen aunties responsible for raising him over the course of his childhood had ensured that, if nothing else. He knew when it was a bad idea to keep talking (even if, more often than not, he did it anyway).

He managed silence for several minutes, counting his heartbeat and watching the figure at his window. A cramp twisted in his calf, and he wriggled a little to settle it. "I'm a gladius," he tried finally. "My team will come looking for me if I don't check in."

This only provided entertainment for the priest of death, who huffed a laugh. "I know you've failed the exam nine times this year," he replied. "Under six different names, across multiple provinces, because there's actually a limit on how often the system allows you to embarrass yourself like that. The only person likely to come looking for you, Dio

Taurus, is your Auntie Beto. But there's an important visitor at the Blooming Cup today, and she'll be distracted for a while yet. I don't need much time."

"How —" Dio's voice cracked on the word. No one knew about all the failed exams. Not his aunties, not *anyone*. He'd been so careful. "How do you know all that?"

"I needed to stand at your window," said the assassin. "I always do my research."

They both gave up talking after that. Dio slumped back on the bed. Shame overwhelmed him, cutting through the shaderoot daze. The illusion that no one knew about his evergreen humiliation was all that had kept him going through all the failures. And here was this complete stranger — a professional killer with a delicious, growly voice who took one look at him and saw everything he had worked so hard to hide.

Dio's only consolation was that the priest of the Black Raven was almost certainly going to kill him to tidy up the scene after he finished his work. And if not, he cared so little about Dio's existence he was unlikely to gossip to his friends and family.

The water clock on the dresser dripped its way past a whole hour. The priest at the window barely moved.

"Who are you here to kill?" Dio asked finally, when he could take the silence no longer. The shaderoot must be wearing off, but he still felt weirdly relaxed, as if he could drop off into sleep.

The assassin laughed; an odd, pained sound. "That's a complicated question," he said. "Getting more complicated by the minute."

"Is something wrong?"

The atmosphere in the room had changed; he wasn't sure how he knew that, but the reason Dio kept failing his gladius exam had everything to do with how words and letters jumped about on the page, and nothing to do with his crime-fighting instincts. The priest of death had been cool and confident before; now he sounded rattled.

"You might say that." The assassin stepped back from the window, his gaze fixed on the square below. His hand never strayed far from his crossbow. "I was paid to kill a foreign royal, visiting from the Imperium. I'm looking at her right now — she is currently drinking tea with your auntie in the shade of a rather spectacular peach tree."

"The Petal," Dio moaned. "Oh, *hell*." Auntie Beto had been prepping for this honoured visitor for days, ever since she got word from the Northern Gate. A Petal of the House of Flowers visiting her teahouse was the most exciting thing that had ever happened around here. It was going to be so embarrassing, if the guest was killed in Auntie's courtyard.

"You've heard of these Petals?" snapped the priest.

"Ladies who work magic." Women born with magical abilities in the Divine Kingdom were rare, and their powers were tightly controlled or repressed. Over the border in the Imperium was another matter. They had actual colleges, and women studied there as well as men.

"Luckily for me, this one does not," said the assassin. "It's a cover story, and a weak one — as if any woman with half a spark of magic would set foot in this benighted country. Our so-called Petal is the widowed sister of the current Empress of the Imperium, travelling to Phoenix Burning with her daughter for a wedding."

Dio had heard stories of the Imperium from his aunties, who took a close interest in the magic that women were allowed to possess in other lands. He was confident that the First Family of the Imperium had magic in their blood. An Empress' sister could easily be a priestess and a magician *as well as* a royal. Still, there was no reason to volunteer that information. This assassin claimed to do his research.

Also, he had a point. A magical woman would have to be very sure of her powers and protections, to travel through the Divine Kingdom. She'd bring armies of banshees and sprites to keep her safe. Dio would definitely have heard about it if Auntie Beto had to turn out a dozen rooms for an army of banshees.

"Why haven't you shot her already?" he asked. "If she's right there. What are you waiting for?"

"As it turns out," said the man in black. "My client has hired more than one priest of the Black Raven for this job. A colleague of mine is currently sharing tea with the Petal and her daughter and your auntie, right below this window. Another is working undercover in the laundry — I caught sight of her a few moments ago."

"But that's —" said Dio, frankly astonished.

"Fucking outrageous, yes. I agree."

Dio was no worshipper of the Black Raven, or any god beyond the Divine King. Born unmarked, he had the freedom to choose. He chose nothing. His plan was to devote his life to national service, and the gladii preferred their cadets to start out with as few religious obligations as possible. (They weren't soldiers, after all, to follow the Hawk of War.) Still, Dio paid the usual tithes every new year to each of the gods, and he knew the basic tenets of the Black Raven's service.

Religious doctrine was easier to access than most of the material covered by the gladius exams. All you had to do was attend the right temple services, listen to the right sermons. No books necessary.

"Isn't it an abomination, to contract more than one servant to the same holy quest?" Dio blurted out now.

"That's one of the twelve abominations, yes? It stains your soul to kill another priest's mark."

"Yes," said the assassin between gritted teeth. "Well done. If only those exams you keep failing only required you to know things."

"Perhaps they're here to kill someone else?" Dio suggested. He had no idea why he was trying to make this man feel better about his disaster of a mission.

The assassin rubbed between his eyes as if he was getting a headache. "Is the Blooming Cup commonly the site of a sacred killing? Let alone a messy massacre?"

Well, no. They were right on the River Divine, in the foothills of the Iron Mountains. The occasional corpse washed up here from time to time. That was to be expected. But no one who knew Dio's Auntie Beto would dare murder a guest under her roof.

Except, apparently, a cluster of death priests. *A murder of ravens.*

Dio answered the question with another question: "Is it true you sense each other's presence — that you can recognise another servant of the Black Raven by their aura?"

"Sure," said the assassin. "But in this case I also have eyes, and I know these priests personally. The one sharing tea with your auntie is the Needle. The one in the laundry is the Blade."

"Does that make you the Crossbow?"

"Blood and endless, do you ever shut up?" The assassin raised his weapon, aiming down into the courtyard. "Brace yourself, Dio Taurus. The world's about to end."

Dio had promised himself he would not cry out, but as he saw the bolt loosed, he could not help but open his mouth to bellow a warning to the priest's victim.

The room blazed with a blinding light. Dio's stale

mouth filled up with a syrupy gunk, so thick and plentiful that his body revolted against the intrusion. It was sweet. Sweet like rose petals. Light seared his vision until it gave way to darkness.

Magic, magic, magic. He could taste it on his tongue, even as his mind fought against whatever was happening to him. To his blood, his body.

Sleep took him back.

When he next awoke, Dio was tied to a different bed, in a different room — no, not a room. A cabin in a boat that rocked and bobbed gently beneath him. A river barge, by the feel of it: low and slow.

He was not alone.

This was a wide bed, large enough for several people. A man sat opposite him, tied to the foot just as Dio was tied to the head, propped up on pillows.

This was the death priest from his room, younger in appearance than Dio first thought, though that meant little. The Black Raven was known for keeping his servants youthful for decades or even centuries of service.

The priest had high cheekbones, and long lashes. He was scarred across one of his thick eyebrows. A pair of dark eyes bore into Dio from this short distance; a scowling mouth twisted beneath a dark, close cropped beard. In full light, the priest looked even more likely to murder Dio for being in the wrong place at the wrong time. His tailored featherbrace was loosely buttoned at the front. His wrists, bound to the bed, were wrapped in long pink ribbons.

He was far more attractive than Dio was prepared to deal with right now; that inconvenience could be put away in a box and never examined too closely. Dio had figured out long ago that the type of men and women he was most likely to fall in love with were also the type most likely to step on him from a great height.

Dio opened his mouth to speak and spat out fleshy petals: river lilies, chewed up and sour. He could feel the ghost of the shaderoot still in his system — at least, if that was the reason he was not screaming in panic, he was grateful for it.

"Well," said the priest of death, spitting out his own mouthful: bright pinks and oranges, the remains of a tiger-orchid that would cost a mint at the Hanging Market. "This is just *peachy*."

They were not the only occupants of the bed. A woman beside Dio was still unconscious: she had a mass of black curly hair spilling over her shoulders, and her body was all curves. One curve in particular called attention to itself: a pregnant belly, swathed in layers of soft larkflax in dark colours: blue, layered over plum. She was also tied to the bed by pink ribbons looped around her wrists.

She looked soft, but she had a harsh past; there were long, rough scars on both arms, and others near the upper swell of her breast. Her brown hands were calloused from needlework, not the soft skin of an indoors lady.

The other woman was narrow and angular, her dark hair pulled back in a practical series of braids designed to stay the hell out of her way. Her scars were on her face, two by her hairline and another down by her jaw. She wore a plain dark dress and soft grey apron, exactly like every laundress that Auntie Beto had ever hired. She strained against the ribbons as if she expected to be able to break out with willpower alone. Her whole body vibrated with fury as she stared at Dio's death priest, who glared right back at her. The air crackled between them; two damaged, powerful people seething with rage.

Simultaneously, they both snapped: "This is all your fault."

And Dio, fool that he was, blurted: "Do you two know each other?"

2. Heading Downriver

A priest of the Black Raven had many rules. Ikaros Swift was born with a scythe-knife burned into his left palm, and he had chased his fate for years before his god allowed him, at age fourteen, to take the oath of a priest. From that moment, he had been beholden to a long and complex system of list and conditions.

- One did not speak the true name of the Black Raven aloud. (Death, his true name was Death, no matter what else one might call him on any given day.)
- One did not steal or share the mark of a fellow priest.
- One did not fail one's sacred duty.

There were other abominations to avoid, but those were the important ones, most relevant to his life.

Ikaros also had his own rules.

- One did not play games of chance with Mardi Morency.
- One did not drink anything named for its colour, or for a mythical creature.
- One did not trust magic, in any of its forms.

In recent years, he had added another: *one did not travel on the River Divine*. This was a rule that only he seemed to believe was a good idea, but he had never been proved wrong. There were many ways to get from province to province. Anyone who told you that the river was the shortest path from one end of the kingdom to the other was lying. And, most likely, planning to rob you blind and leave you dangling from one foot in the Hanging Market.

The River Divine was nothing but trouble.

The flowers currently filling Ikaros' mouth tasted like the river. The scent in the air smelled like the river. They were on a boat. Heading downriver on the bloody River Divine, of course.

Captured by his own mark, if he was reading the situation right. Abandoned by his god. And, oh yes, tied to a bed with a failed gladius, and the two most dangerous women in the Divine Kingdom.

"Well," Ikaros said aloud, spitting petals. "This is just peachy."

Of course it was Valeria's fault. It had to be. Who else would be ruthless enough to take a mark that was already assigned elsewhere? Valeria had been around too long; she thought herself above the rules.

Mardi, Mardi had done it as well, that didn't make as much sense but Ikaros wasn't thinking about her right now. He was thinking about Valeria the Blade, and how those ribbons tying her to the bed were probably the only reason she hadn't slit his throat.

Speaking of ribbons... but no, he was not about to free himself. He did not want to free himself. That was an odd thought, alien in his mind. Ikaros was not yet willing to challenge it.

This wasn't anything like the shaderoot he had given to the boy. It wasn't a drug that kept him compliant. Magic, he recognised. Magic was keeping them here, forcing them not to fight their bonds.

Fucking magic.

He saw Valeria realise it at the same moment; she did not *want* to escape. Her body would resist any attempt to do so.

"Ikaros, what have you done?" she breathed in her usual murderous tones.

"For once, dear heart, this isn't down to me."

Whatever had been used on them; it had Mardi out like a light. She lolled on the pillows, her feet tucked comfortably into Valeria's lap. Valeria was strangely accommodating about this: perhaps she was bottling up her vengeful spirit for later. Perhaps she drew the line at kicking a sleeping, pregnant woman. Or perhaps, friendship had finally worn her down...

Mardi was getting big, blood and endless, surely she was running out of time? Ikaros had lost count of the months. Motherhood beckoned, and with it Mardi's retirement from the priesthood. Which would come first? Assuming they found a way out of these pink ribbons before her water broke.

Valeria turned her scorching gaze on to the stranger in their midst. Young Dio sat staring at them all like he was in a private box at the opera, and they were the show. The lad still wore his rumpled sleep clothes, a soft grey larkflax tunic and baggy black pants. He looked like a startled dormouse in a bed full of vipers, which wasn't an unfair comparison.

"Who is this?" Valeria demanded. "Has the Black Raven been recruiting?"

Dio blinked. "I'm not a —" he stumbled.

"Use your senses, Valeria, he's not a priest," Ikaros cut in. "I don't think gods take them this young these days."

"I'm twenty-two," protested the boy, which had to be a lie. Ikaros had never seen such a fresh, innocent little face.

"Why is he here?" Valeria snarled. "Why is he our fourth?"

A good question, certainly. They knew who to expect as an obvious fourth in their group: either the Stave, who was dead, or the Bow.

In an insane scenario where four priests of the Black Raven were paid to take out the same mark (if that were even possible, Ikaros had not yet wrapped his head around the *how*), surely Reynard the Bow would be included? Suspicious, that he was not here to share their fate.

Instead they had Dio: a wet-behind-the-ears orphan lad who had spent the last several years pouring all his funds into fake identification papers in the wild hope of serving a city, any city, as a gladius. Anyone else would have accepted by now that he was completely unable to pass the written tests. An intriguing example of youthful spirit and a can-do attitude, but hardly what one wanted in a trained killer.

The lad would trip over his feet the first time he needed to hold a knife to a throat.

(*Not that we're recruiting*, Ikaros reminded himself.)

Mardi awoke. It was strange to see her in layered colours instead of her usual featherbrace and blacks. Perhaps the featherbrace didn't fit any more, over that belly.

Ikaros spotted the exact moment that Mardi realised how close she was to Valeria; she went still, holding her breath, and then drew back her feet, putting an inch of distance (the only distance possible) between them. "A nightmare, then," she muttered. "Here we go. One more pregnancy symptom. Come back, heartburn, all is forgiven."

"Hello, Mardi," said Ikaros. "It's been a while."

They were a study in contrasts, these two women: Valeria was narrow-boned and angular, all sharpness and pale skin, her hair as black as her long eyelashes; she was dyeing both again, no doubt. Her scars, as ever, made her look more fierce and beautiful than any unmarked woman half her age. Mardi was all warm shades of deep brown: skin, eyes, hair. Valeria looked like the evil stepmother who would seduce you and cut out your heart, possibly at the same time. Mardi looked like the friendly innkeeper who always remembered your birthday.

Ikaros loved them both. They were the two people in the world most likely to be the literal death of him; the only ones left he would ever let that close. It was a long time since the three of them had been in the same room together.

Had it happened since Bors died? Ikaros could not think of a single instance.

"Ikaros, I'm assuming this is somehow all about you," said Mardi. She wriggled her fingers against the ribbon ties. "Pissed off any mountain sprites lately? Fucked a dragon?

Declared a side in the war between the nixies and the dryads?"

Ikaros smiled at her with all his teeth. "I'm not the one who accepted a mark already issued to another servant of our god."

Mardi glared at him. "Neither am I."

"Introductions," interrupted Valeria, looking at Dio as if she wanted to eat him. "Ikaros, you know this young man?"

Playing at tea parties, were they? "This is Dio Taurus," Ikaros said reluctantly. "Nephew to our hostess at the Blooming Cup. He's nobody."

The young man arced up at the insult. "I'm not nobody!"

"For the sake of this conversation you are," Ikaros replied. "Settle down, sprat, your elders are speaking."

Dio gave him a scornful look. "You can't have more than a decade on me."

"Oh, you'd be surprised." Three decades or more if the lad was telling the truth about his age; the Black Raven was kind to his servants. Didn't like to leave them too worn about the edges.

Valeria (who was at least two decades older than anyone in this room; she'd recently passed her seventieth birthday without comment) preened. "Dio, please ignore my husband, his manners are such a trial to me. Valeria Swift. Charmed."

"Mardi Morency," put in Mardi. "The Needle of the Black Raven, to give you my formal title. She is the Blade," she added with a fond look at Valeria. "Because she's a back-stabbing, vicious creature who cheats at cards."

"Oh, I'm sorry," said Valeria. "Am I the only person on this bed who cheats at cards?"

Dio looked sidelong at Ikaros. "I didn't think priests were allowed to get married?"

Ikaros indicated his wife with a thin smile. "We're the reason they brought in that law."

Young Dio darted a cautious look at Valeria, like he thought she was the person in this bed he should worry about most. Good to know he wasn't entirely stupid. "Why do they call you the Blade?" he asked.

Valeria smiled, and shifted one arm. The right sleeve of her plain dress unrolled, revealing an array of knives, razors and a very tiny rapier, all arranged in thin pockets of taut black leather. "We each have our specialty. The arts of the Black Raven are many and varied."

"Okay," said Dio, his eyes taking in the weapons, and then returning to her face. "So why haven't you cut yourself free from these ribbons?"

Oh, this kid was going to get himself *murdered*.

Valeria's whole body stiffened as she considered the question. "I don't know," she snapped, and swished her sleeve so that the blades rolled up again, out of sight. "I don't want to."

"I don't, either," said Mardi, shifting uncomfortably on the pillows. She had been given longer ribbons than the others, so she had a little more freedom of movement — enough to move from side to side. "But we'd better figure it out fast. I reckon we've got about fifteen more minutes before I have to pee, and that's being generous."

Ikaros eyed her expanding waistline. Anything he said about her condition was bound to be wrong; he'd learned that lesson already. "Mardi. Show me the mark on your hand."

She gave him a quick, confused look and then raised her right hand. Like him, she was marked there with the seal of those in service to the Black Raven: the scythe-knife's blade curving around her index finger and thumb, its handle running down the inside of her wrist.

"Other hand," said Ikaros.

Mardi's eyes widened. A dark flower bloomed on the back of her left hand — petals and stamens, a complex tattoo in black and purple. She bucked, trying to get off the bed, then sat very still as if she had changed her mind about reacting. A small smile crossed her face for a moment, then vanished. "What's happening to us?" she asked in a voice that sounded almost serene. "Why don't I know how to feel about this?"

Valeria leaned into Ikaros. Instinctively, he leaned back to stay out of stabbing range. "Yours is on your neck," she told him, inhaling as she got close. "Pretty."

He turned his head, but couldn't see his own flower tattoo. He glanced across to Dio for confirmation, and the boy nodded uncomfortably. Not Valeria playing a game. Except, of course, that Valeria was always playing games.

"What about you?" Ikaros demanded of his wife. Her scythe-knife was hidden; he knew it lay across her left hip. He could not see the fresh mark of a night-bloom anywhere on her pale skin.

Mardi kicked out at Valeria with one foot; her skirts jerked back. There it was, the dark flower picked out on Valeria's right ankle.

All three of them pulled their eyes to Dio, who shrank under their scrutiny. "I'm nobody, remember?"

"So you say," accused Ikaros.

"You're the one who said it!"

The door of the cabin opened.

All four of them stayed very still, except for Dio who had no sense of self-preservation and immediately sneezed.

The girl who entered was young, soft. Her scalp was covered by a tight linen cap. That and her odd-shaped gown were all in white, bleached brightly. This was an oddity that marked her out as foreign; white textiles were rare imports here in the Divine Kingdom. The girl carried a tray of water cups with the air of someone who had never done domestic tasks before, and was a bit excited about it. The scent of magic lingered on her, but only gently, as if she had been in its vicinity, and caught a little of the backwash.

"My mother will join us shortly," said the girl in white. She handed the cups to each of them, starting with Dio, who gave her a winning smile.

The ribbons that bound them to the bed had enough length to them that the prisoners could hold cups, raise them to their mouths. Dio was the only one who drank immediately, then stared around as if realising too late that he should have been more cautious.

As the person who had most recently drugged Dio, Ikaros was not sure if the young man's innocence was irritating or charming. No, it was definitely irritating. How had he survived so long?

Speaking of irritating: the pink ribbons were long enough to reach cups to mouths and that meant they were long enough to twist and manipulate. The girl stood near enough that Ikaros should be able to loop his ribbons around her throat and snap her neck.

The fact that he hadn't done it already was a weight on his chest; a premonition of doom. Something was wrong here, growing inside his head like a weed. Like a night-bloom in flower.

"You can trust what you eat and drink here," said the girl, glancing past Ikaros to the women on the other side of the bed. "We have no wish to harm you."

Valeria lifted her chin and glared; Mardi pressed a hand to her belly and looked skeptical.

"Why are we here?" broke in Ikaros. "Why have you marked us?"

"You're here because you tried to kill my mother," said the girl, more defiantly than before. Her sweetness fell away like a costume. "You're here because you're going to help us."

"I take it that isn't an offer," said Mardi, flexing the hand that had the dark night-bloom tattoo across it. "We don't get a choice. This mother of yours has taken our service by force."

Which would be — not fine, not acceptable, but something short of an abomination if not for the fact that all three of them were sworn in service already. The gods of the Divine Kingdom were notoriously jealous; theirs more than most. Priests who served two masters only existed in epic poetry: tales with messy and bloodthirsty endings.

Why had the Black Raven allowed this? Why was he not here already, enacting his vengeance on their abductor or, if he was particularly cruel, on his priests?

The door to the cabin opened again. The girl turned towards it with relief. "Mother."

Magic entered the cabin: a pulsing wave of brightness and colour and the scent of rose petals. Ikaros was dizzy with it. Eventually the power resolved itself into a woman, standing in the doorway, watching them all with a calm expression.

She was beautiful. Ikaros could not tell if it was the kind of refined beauty that artists painted on porcelain, or if it was merely that her power hovered around her eyes, lips, breasts, and every mote of his body wanted to please every mote of hers.

He wanted to be on his knees for this woman. He had not felt so overwhelmed with the need to be consumed by another person since he faced the Black Raven at fourteen years old.

Ikaros returned to himself, slowly. He was aware of the others, also recovering their senses.

"I am Calyx of the House of Flowers," said the stunning woman in the doorway. "All four of you attempted to end my life. And now you will serve me."

Her head was shaved bare. She wore layers of swishing silk in pinks and purples. A solid white column of linen fell directly from her throat to her ankles without any sign of how it was secured there; the clumsy garment would be uncomfortably hot in the sticky summer weather they were having. The linen displayed the image of a marble column, wrapped in ivy; it wasn't printed, but an illusion that wavered a little if you stared at it for too long. An excessive waste of magic, to use it as a personal adornment.

There was a calmness to this woman, reminiscent of an abbess or a mystic: the irritating kind of matriarch who was at peace with her life, probably because her god did not require her to kill people on a regular basis.

Laid beneath this woman's inappropriate wardrobe was her magic, in more layers than the silk.

Ikaros had made a terrible miscalculation. He had assumed this travelling royal was *pretending* to be a Petal of the House of Flowers because those women were considered untouchable; inviolable. He had done his research, damn it. Everything he read made it very clear that the imperial family's own magic was mostly ceremonial. Barely worth mentioning. Unimpressive.

Something must have been lost in translation between

her country, and his own, if a royal could also be a Petal — and one so very powerful.

His breath caught in his throat as Calyx approached the bed. Ikaros served this woman. He wanted to do anything she required. He burned to please her, and protect her, regardless of anything the Black Raven had to say about it.

This was going to be a problem.

3. Aboard the Silken Hare

Nothing had prepared Calyx for sailing on the River Divine. She had always been taught that other countries had no magic that equalled theirs. In the Imperium, magic was poured into books and vials and veins. Tightly controlled, carefully managed, discreetly distributed via higher education and secret societies.

In the House of Flowers, oldest and most prestigious of the colleges, Calyx had learned that the magic of the Imperium was supreme. Other countries, with their wild and unfettered scraps of magic dancing around in the grass and the dirt? Could not compare. Especially the arrogant Divine Kingdom, a land so backward that women were not allowed to train in magic at all, only to be used by their husbands or fathers as vessels of power.

If rumours were to be believed, the current royal family of the Divine Kingdom was so lacking in magic in their own bloodline that the Eternal King himself had arranged the deaths of twelve of his own sons for being 'too mortal'. That was the family she was sailing into.

The Divine Kingdom, such an antiquated culture that

Death and War were considered appropriate subjects of worship. And yet, they had a river like this. Wild, uncontrolled, available to all... brimming with chaos and power. There was magic everywhere, unconfined, taken for granted.

Even the most ordinary sailor wore tunics and pants made from an impossibly light, robust fabric that wore the footprint of magical construction. The stones that fuelled the ships carried the warmth of natural magic, freshly cut from mines.

Magic was everywhere in this country, accessible to everyone.

(And yet, somehow, women were to be deprived. Calyx wondered how many women actually took that lying down.)

Calyx stood on the prow of the *Silken Hare*, her hired river barge, gazing out at the water. The River Divine curled out before her, wider than any of the canals she was used to back home, teeming with life. The water was bright and layered with lights and colour, like the silks she wore.

The river was thick with magic. Heavy with magic. Alive with magic. Calyx wanted to drink every drop, swallow until she was bursting.

Beside her, the prisoner looked unimpressed. "This isn't going to work," he said in his deep, rasping voice. "You can't expect to get away with cheating the Black Raven of his priests."

"I don't intend to cheat your god of death," she replied, watching for the wince as she said the word 'death' aloud. Good. Some things should not stay unspoken. They gained too much power that way. "I intend to beat him, though. And the first step is you telling me how to break your contract."

Ikaros Swift, Hand of the Black Raven, gave her a distant smile. He was an attractive man. Rougher than the courtiers with whom she sported these days: he was solidly built like a bodyguard. His face was scarred and battered around the edges, but intensely compelling beneath that close-cropped beard. Far too many dents and scars for such a young face. Dangerous.

Once upon a time, she would have considered him exactly her type. But that was a lifetime ago, when she was a rebellious daughter of the Imperium, a neglected wife with time on her hands. Now, she was a matron. A widow. Mother of a girl old enough to sign a marriage contract herself (though she hoped to keep Nimue from that for a few years yet). Calyx had other things to worry about than whether a man would be good to her in bed.

"The payment was made," said Ikaros the Hand. His words came out sharply, swishing and vicious, like he was angry she was still alive to have this conversation. "Mark was accepted. There is no ending to my contract but the obvious one. It will be fulfilled when I kill you."

Calyx could feel the golden threads running from his veins to her own. Taut, alive with not only her power, but that of the river. She was connected by a similar thread to everyone on this boat (except her daughter), all sworn loyal to her service by the compulsion bond she had cast upon them. That final spell, the one she had exploded into the air out of sheer desperation as the assassins drew in around her… their threads shone bright instead of everyday dull. Like gold wire, everlasting.

Ikaros the Hand would never hurt her. He would not get a choice in the matter.

"We'll see about that," said Calyx calmly. "You and your friends serve me now. Your only mission is to get myself and my daughter to the city of Phoenix Burning, alive and well."

His eyes flitted to her, and then away, staring at the dancing, roiling colours of the River Divine. "We'll see about that," he echoed.

If anything, the thread between them grew brighter.

The other three priests of death were no more forthcoming. Calyx made sure to speak to each of them individually, but neither the Blade nor the Needle gave her anything more useful than the Hand.

The new bond compelled them to serve her, even to obey her. But it did not force devotion, or love, not at first. The magic would encourage that, in time. The longer they were compelled to serve, the harder it would be for them to separate their own feelings from the magic. For now, they could resent her all they wanted. They belonged to her, blood and flesh. Betrayal was unthinkable.

They could be more helpful in telling her what she needed to know: why on earth she had been made their target, and who was behind the plot.

"Surely someone broke a rule," Calyx said in frustration to Valeria the Blade. She could not get a read on the woman who had been in disguise as a laundress while Calyx drank tea with her hostess at the Blooming Cup, pretending she did not already know she was marked for death, four times over.

For a woman who was capable of getting her hands dirty

with servant's work, Valeria held herself like a queen. An angry, potentially violent queen, still garbed in the plainest of work gowns. (There was that fabric again, impossibly soft and breathable, perfect for this sticky, warm climate. Calyx rather envied the comfort — her own silks would be comfortable, but the formal stemma she wore over the top was thick and uncomfortable, tightly constraining her chest, providing unnecessary weight and warmth. Still, she could not be seen in public without it, even in a land of barbarians.

Valeria might be garbed like a laundress, but she reminded Calyx of one of her more intimidating magic professors, effortlessly judgemental and constantly on the verge of making a sharp remark.

She tried again to get through to the chilly woman. "I don't imagine this is how your usual contracts go. Aren't you angry about your failure?"

"I was," said Valeria the Blade, standing very still, her eyes on the river. A creature leaped out of the coloured waters; or a ghost of a creature. Part horse, trailing wings behind it, part... fish? Glistening with silver. Another leaped, its mouth tipped back as it tasted the air, and bright teeth gleamed. "Someone took away my freedom and gave me something more important to be angry about." Valeria kicked out her foot, revealing the black mark of the night-bloom on her ankle.

Calyx had not meant her spell to be quite this thorough. She had considered it her best option when the dreams began, warning her of the four assassins bearing down upon her. But as her skin prickled with awareness that the time was now, that danger was closing in, she had panicked rather. The charmed bond that she usually cast to compel service staff to basic loyalty, such as the geas laid upon every sailor on this river barge, was usually mild, allowing many personal freedoms to the bearer.

But her days in this country had changed her. The River Divine was stronger here than at the mouth of the mountains. When she cast the bond against the assassins, thinking only to stop them, Calyx's power had flamed wildly. As it turned out, her casting was so much stronger in proximity to this strange river.

The flower that marked those in Calyx's service was usually a pale violet shadow against the skin, not this deep, sharply defined tattoo of a flower she had never even seen before — not until her first night on the River Divine, between the mountain pass and the Blooming Teacup, when she had seen them at a distance, unfurling across the surface of the water.

The true service bond was a rare magic, something that even the highest-ranked of Imperium mages called upon sparingly. She did not know anyone living who had ever cast the bond on four people at once, let alone with this degree of intensity.

Hardly surprising that Valeria was unfriendly to her; she must feel like she was standing in chains.

"We have the same enemy," Calyx said, wanting this woman to understand her.

Valeria turned a chilly gaze in her direction. "I don't think you understand how enemies work." She winced for a moment, pressing a pained hand to her ribs. "But I'm sure I'll agree with you, sooner or later. That's what this magic of yours does, yes? It makes us your tools."

"How do I find out who hired you?" Calyx asked Mardi the Needle, when it was the other woman's turn to stand at the bow of the *Silken Hare*.

Beneath the deck there was the galley, storage space in the bulkhead, sleeping space for sailors and their hammocks, and so on. The two cabins were built on the deck level, back to back; when Calyx set out, there had been one cabin for her and one for her daughter but now they had their prisoners, she and Nimue would have to share.

In front of the cabins was the wheelhouse, a roofed enclosure from which the captain steered the ship. It was a big river barge, the largest she had been able to hire, though she had also selected the *Silken Hare* because it looked quite ordinary. Not the sort of vessel upon which one might expect to find two foreign royals on their way to the capital city, bound for the palace.

They were on their own, with no royal retinue or protection; it did not pay to stand out.

Calyx and Mardi stood on the deck immediately in front of the wheelhouse, facing the river ahead.

Mardi looked tired, but there was none of the strained energy that had radiated off her two colleagues. She was resigned, Calyx thought. Perhaps that was from being heavily pregnant: there was a point in that process when you had to learn to go with the flow of your body, stop fighting what you could not control.

Calyx had never felt more vulnerable in her life than during those months when she carried her daughter; it was worse, however, once the person she loved most in the world was separate from her, not always within reach to protect and guide. Nimue was everything. Did Mardi feel the same about her own unborn child?

"We don't know who paid for your contract," said Mardi flatly. "We never do. That's protocol. We serve at the will of the Black Raven. Everything else is... temple administration." She had been disguised as a guest of the tea house, before Calyx captured her. They had taken tea together. Mardi's clothes, though, weren't all that different to Valeria's — another dress in that strange, soft fabric. Dark blue instead of black, with a plum-coloured embroidered vest over the top to provide some shaping. It seemed like dark colours and comfort were preferred by most people in this kingdom, no matter their station in life. Calyx had not seen a single piece of white fabric since she arrived, and nothing to match the bright rose and lilac of the silk tunics and trousers she wore beneath her stemma.

"Don't you want to know who did this?" she pressed. "Who sent the four of you to kill me?"

"Oh," said Mardi the Needle, with an unexpected laugh in her throat. "The four of us. Yes, we're all terribly curious."

"Where's the nearest temple of the Black Raven?" If the priests could not give Calyx answers, she would have to seek them elsewhere. If one of the gods of this land was being used to sabotage her journey, she needed to know why. Even — *especially* if that god was Death.

Mardi shrugged. "There are twenty or so, spread around the kingdom, and they never divulge information about clients. You'd save time by working out who wants you eliminated, and working backwards."

"Where's the nearest temple on the river?" Calyx asked.

Mardi nodded ahead, to where the sparkling water curved out of sight before them. "There's a small shrine at the Hanging Market. You can't miss it, we'll be there before nightfall. I don't recommend you take any of us with you. We have a lot of friends in that market, and at some point Ikaros is going to figure out how to cut your night-bloom off his neck. When that happens, you'll be dead."

"Ikaros," repeated Calyx. Interesting that he was the one Mardi thought most likely to escape from her trap. "You have a lot of faith in his ability to rebel against my magic."

"I have more to lose from trying to escape," said Mardi distantly, her hand curving over her belly. "Valeria will watch and wait and bide her time because she hates failure more than she hates inaction. But Ikaros... he'll walk over broken glass to be free of you. I hate that I told you that. I hate that we serve you, that you forced us to this. But *I don't know how to fight you.*"

"I could have struck you all down dead, in the Blooming Cup," said Calyx quietly. Why was she feeling guilty about this? Why try to justify what she had done to her would-be murderer? "You planned to kill me, every one of you. Killing assassins would hardly cause an international incident, no matter how religious you are. I could have stepped over your dead bodies without a qualm of guilt and continued on my journey in safety."

Mardi turned towards Calyx, revealing a wild, pained expression on her face. "I know," she breathed. "And yet what you did to us is worse."

Calyx left her interrogation of the youngest of the assassins for last. Hopefully he would be more malleable.

It wasn't just his face that marked him out as young; all of the assassins looked like they were barely out of an academie. Dio seemed more nervous than the others, though, less poised. Was he an apprentice? New to his craft? That would explain the pointed expression that Ikaros the Hand exchanged with the younger man, as Calyx removed him from the cabin.

Like the others, Dio Taurus was compliant. He had a slightly glazed look about his eyes, less resentful than his companions.

His clothes were plainer than any of the others — rumpled black pants and a tunic not dissimilar to those worn by the sailors, dark colours, that same soft fabric. Bare feet — he hadn't even been wearing shoes when she took him. The bright purple and black night-bloom tattoo spread across his collarbone like a bruise against his light brown skin.

She did not know what it meant that her bond flower had changed in this country. Servants who took her bond back home wore the pale-petalled peony.

"How did you come to serve the god of death?" Calyx asked, as they stood together on the deck.

The young man didn't flinch like the others when she used the word 'death'. "That's a hard question," he slurred.

Calyx frowned. Answering her direct questions with

anything less than the absolute truth was unusual, under a bond as strong as this one. "What do you mean?"

"It's not — I just — huh." Dio's eyes fixed on a point up ahead. "We're here. The Hanging Market."

The *Silken Hare* had rounded a curve in the river. *You can't miss it*, Mardi Morency had said about the Hanging Market. That much was true.

The crew of the barge called to each other, slowing their glide through the water. Calyx felt the pulse of the workers through the threads that connected them lightly to her; they were doing their jobs, so the compulsion charm was barely needed.

There were fewer wild creatures in the water here; the living occupants of the River Divine must prefer to avoid the larger settlements.

It was daylight, and yet the Hanging Market blazed like a full moon in darkness. As they approached, Calyx could see canvas balloons the size of houses, coloured like wildflowers and bobbing high above the water. There were platforms covered in draped fabrics, like the most elegant treehouses and blanket forts and desert caravans. Staircases of wire and beads winding upwards, impossibly high, connecting what should be an unstable collection of surfaces. Gaslamps hung from bronze hooks at every level; it must be someone's job to light them all each evening, and she did not envy the task.

Calyx could see parasols and wings, some attached to people and some to tables. Even at a distance, the Hanging Market smelled of good food and magic.

So, this country is not such a culture-deprived backwater as we have heard.

On any other day, she might have enjoyed playing tourist. For a moment, Calyx was fascinated enough to all but forget the prisoner at her side. "Have you been there before?" she asked, when his awkward shuffling reminded her.

"I've been everywhere on the river," said Dio; a boy's boast.

"I see." She turned back towards the cabins. He scuttled after her, so completely under her thrall she didn't even have to tell him to follow. "I need a word with your colleagues," she said.

"I'm not actually," he blurted. "A priest of death. At all. I think I'm here by mistake. I should have told you before. Sorry."

Calyx stopped short. She whirled around, staring at him. There was no point in accusing him of a lie, not when the word 'death' came so easily to his tongue. The young man looked miserable, his whole face twisted up. "Why did it take you so long to tell me that?" she demanded.

What was wrong with her magic? He should have been tripping over himself to spill all his secrets. Even lying by omission was rare once the bond of obligation took hold. Then again, if he was not a servant of death, he should not have been caught up in this particular spell in the first place.

But no. Calyx could *feel* the strength of the spell, of the fierce golden threads that bound the four to her service. She had felt four of them closing, hadn't she? Or had she merely set her trap for four because that was the number she saw in her dream?

Four Black Ravens, trying to kill her. She had dreamed of that image for weeks, months before she even left the Imperium. There had to be four.

"I didn't like not telling you," Dio said, tripping over his tongue. "That's why I'm telling you now!"

Not one of them had told her. It had been *hours*. They

must have fought her bond every step of the way — which she should have expected from three powerful servants of a god who demanded their service elsewhere. Why had the bond not retaliated? They should have been coughing up flowers and leaves, the symbols of her magic. They should have been bleeding thorns from open veins by now.

If this young man was nothing from nowhere, how on earth had *he* fought the bond?

Calyx caught Dio by the wrist and dragged him along the deck. They met her daughter at the door of the cabin, holding a water tray.

"Nimue," Calyx said sharply.

Her daughter jolted. She was still wearing her formal white silks, a close-fitting gown over soft trousers. Her shaven head was hidden beneath a linen cap, while Calyx left hers bare. The girl's eyes went straight to Dio, and she blushed. "Mother," she said politely.

"What do you think you are doing?"

"Bringing the prisoners water," said the girl huffily. At sixteen years old, she had no true sense of her own mortality.

"Are you planning to drown them?" Calyx suggested with a sarcastic lilt.

"It's been a while since the last time. You said I could help. I want to help. It's *my* cabin."

Nimue wanted another peek at the prisoners, more like.

Calyx sighed. "This country might treat these people as if their acts are excused on religious grounds, but they are killers," she reminded her daughter. "Hardened, shameless murderers. You think I want you to spend a minute more in their company than is necessary, even with the bond protecting you from harm at their hands?"

"It's only water," Nimue protested.

"You will protect my daughter as if her body is mine," Calyx snapped to Dio, adding a pulse of compulsion to the thread binding them.

He nodded, looking eager to serve. "It would be my honour." Damn him, he sounded exactly like he meant it.

"This isn't a game," Calyx declared to her daughter before she entered the cabin. "This is our survival. Act accordingly."

When Calyx returned Dio to the cabin, all three of the assassins — the *real* assassins — were in urgent conversation with each other, crowded on the bed with the re-tied pink ribbons still holding them in place. Three pairs of wary eyes turned upon her and then softened, as if her presence reminded them how much they wanted to please her, serve her, protect her.

She had always hated the effect of obligation bonds when she was in training at the House of Flowers, and even later when she had her own household within the palace of the Imperium. The false smiles, the warm expressions, mixed with antipathy and strain. By the time she lost her first husband, Calyx had not only come to accept it, but embrace that connection with others. Life in a palace meant you could trust no one unless they were ensorcelled to serve your interests.

Once you'd seen a friend poisoned before your eyes, you learned the necessity of such precautions.

"The boy's not one of ours," Ikaros confessed, his deep voice filling the room.

"I'm not a boy," Dio said crossly. They all ignored him.

Ikaros was the spokesman. Did that mean he was the best diplomat of the bunch, or did it mean they thought he was the one of them that Calyx was most likely to respect?

(Did the two women defer to him because he was a man? It was so hard in an unfamiliar country to know what was culturally ingrained, and what was specific to personality.)

"I know that now," Calyx said, waving a hand at Dio, who obediently returned to the bed. "How did he come to be part of this little quartet?"

"You cursed us," said Valeria, raising her eyebrows. "Don't you know?"

"My vision told me there were four of you hired to kill me," Calyx told them all.

All three of the priests went still for a moment.

"Fuck," said Ikaros, shaking his head. "*Four*."

Mardi looked pained. "This is profane," she told Calyx. "An abomination. It should never have happened. There are systems in place. Once one of us takes the mark, there's no way for even one more priest to be..."

Ikaros placed a hand on her knee, to quiet her from spilling all their secrets. He met Calyx's eyes. "If there was a fourth expected at that teahouse, we don't know what happened to them," he told her. She felt the pulse of honesty through the threads that bound them.

"We can guess who it is," Valeria said sourly. "There aren't many candidates left alive."

Mardi let a small hiss out from between her teeth.

The threads tightened around them, and they all flinched at the tug of it.

"Stop dissembling," said Calyx. "Speak the truth and we will get through this as efficiently as possible."

"Servants of the Black Raven are solitary," said Ikaros. "That is our nature. We don't work in teams often except in training, and then no more than two at a time. But on the rare occasions I would need to work with a partner..." he hesitated, and spread his hands wide. "These are the people I would choose."

"Aww," said Mardi sarcastically. "He loves us."

Valeria pulled a face. "If they brought in all three of us, it's not a coincidence," she added. "We had a fourth that we trusted well, but he died, seven months ago."

Calyx noticed Mardi's face darken with sadness, and turn away.

"There's another," Ikaros volunteered. "But he's generally late to things. Not surprising he managed to miss out on this party."

"Who is he?" Calyx pressed.

Ikaros answered without hesitation, and promptly looked annoyed about it. "The Bow."

Calyx's eyes flicked to Dio.

"Really not me," he assured her. "I'm rubbish at archery."

"I wonder what can have happened to him," Calyx said. She eyed the four of them, then cast an untangling rune in the air.

If there was still one priest of death at large on the River Divine, contracted to kill her, then she would need to give the others as much freedom as possible so that they might protect her from the Bow and his arrows.

She knew she could trust them with her safety.

It was not as if they had a choice.

4. Beneath the Hanging Market

Dio had never felt so confused in his life. Everyone in the cabin except for himself and the girl in white looked like they wanted to kill each other. He was trapped on a boat with some of the most dangerous and startlingly attractive people he'd ever met, and constantly worried they were about to slit each other's throats in front of him.

At Calyx's command, the pale pink ribbons wriggled and shivered off the wrists of her prisoners, disappearing back into the bed. Valeria moved at once, testing whether she could leave the bed and walk as far as the wall of the cabin. Mardi made herself more comfortable on the pillows and glared.

Ikaros stood up, straightening his featherbrace, and addressing Calyx as if she were the only person in the room. "Let the boy go. He has no part in this. He is not a servant of the Black Raven. He isn't even a gladius."

As if Dio needed a further reminder that he was not supposed to be here; had no place anywhere. "Yet," he muttered.

Ikaros gave him an impatient look. "You're not helping."

Calyx faced off against Ikaros, beautiful and unrelenting. "I think you misunderstand the situation," she proclaimed. "My priority is to keep my daughter Nimue safe. That means travelling to the city Phoenix Burning without being murdered. If there is still one priest of the Black Raven out there trying to kill me, I expect all of you to defend me to the *death*. Even the boy."

Dio was sick and tired of being referred to as a child. Bad enough when the aunties did it, but these people didn't even know him! How much older than him could Ikaros be, anyway, five years? He barely had a crease at the corner of his eyes.

"Yes," Ikaros said slowly. "I understand. And because this is an extremely powerful magical bond, I appear to be invested in getting you safely to the far end of the river. Even if that means betraying my god."

Calyx gave him a thin smile. "My heart weeps for you."

"But the boy," he started again.

Dio groaned inwardly. *Twenty-two years old*, he wanted to say again, but he didn't want to inspire more of those impatient looks, like he was a burden to be shoved out of the way. To safety, of course, for everyone's convenience.

"What do you expect me to do?" demanded Calyx. "Drop him over the side? He stays."

Ikaros gave her a long, thoughtful look. "You'll need to register a complaint."

"Excuse me?" Calyx replied.

"At the next shrine of the Black Raven. I'll go with you. It's your best chance of finding out who took out the hit."

"You're going to help me?"

Ikaros' eyes darkened. "Does your magic not compel our service? We are bound to you."

Calyx glowed with power. Something golden pushed into Dio, into all of them. He could feel the magical bond threading him to his new mistress as tangibly as if there was a rope wrapped around his waist, keeping him tethered to her side.

"You will do everything you can to protect my daughter, and to keep us both alive until we reach the palace at Phoenix Burning," Calyx said. "I will release you once we are safe."

Ikaros gave the thinnest of smiles. "We in turn will have to trust that you will not misuse the power you hold over us."

As with everything else he said aloud, it sounded like a threat.

Dio had wanted adventure. Of course he had. Why else would he hurl so much time and effort at his applications for the gladii despite failing the exam over and over?

Service, yes, to his country. He wanted to serve. He'd always secretly thought that, given the right circumstances, he could be heroic. He had not imagined swearing that service to a foreign Petal of the Imperium, but if Calyx released him from the magical bond right this minute, it would not take much to convince him to stay regardless.

She and her daughter needed protection. Dio longed to help people. He had no money to pay for the next round of examinations, so it wasn't like he had anything better to do right now.

Once released from the cabin, the servants of the Black Raven prowled the deck, watching everything. They did not raise a hand against their new mistress, or make any attempt to escape. They were clearly biding their time, observing everything.

"Does your mother do this a lot?" Dio asked Nimue as they sat together, leaning against the barge railing. Calyx was keen to keep Ikaros, Mardi and Valeria away from her daughter, but she ignored Dio as if he was no danger.

He was unimportant in the grand scheme, of course. An accidental member of the new protection detail. He pushed away the annoying, whiny feeling of 'not good enough' that swept over him.

"Do what?" asked Nimue, whose eyes were constantly flitting this way and that, as if she needed to take in the view of both banks of the river at the same time.

"Compel people to serve her."

Nimue laughed shortly and then peered at him. "Oh, you're serious?"

"Is that kind of magic — normal? Where you come from?" He did not want to insult her, but it was hard to imagine...

"I mean," Nimue said, and waved her hand at the crew.

Dio looked again. There was a captain, a first mate, an engineer and an able seaman running the barge, plus another three sailors. Now he came to pay attention — there *was* a sheen about their eyes. A dutiful attention to detail that honestly, was not common for barge crews. No swearing. Not one of the crew eyed up young Nimue, or the more glamorous women currently prowling the deck.

Here and there, among the many tattoos you might

expect from barge workers or anyone else who sailed for a living, Dio saw the familiar curled petals of the night-bloom, in pale shades of grey and lavender. Not as vivid as his own mark, but unmistakably the sign of service to Calyx of the House of Flowers.

"All of them?" he blurted out, working to keep his immediate, horrified reaction off his face.

"Of course," said Nimue, her hands placed neatly in her lap as if she was accustomed to sitting still. Made sense if she had to wear white all the time — keeping robes like that clean must require an awful lot of doing nothing. She did not seem to have the faintest idea why this revelation might be a big deal to Dio, or anyone else. "We weren't allowed to bring our own people from the Imperium. Not a single bodyguard. Royalty don't usually hire outsiders. But my mother's future husband insisted we travel only with people from your country to protect us — and they didn't provide a retinue either. We had to hire them ourselves."

"So, you wouldn't do this at home, in the Imperium," Dio said, trying to understand. "At your palace or whatever. You wouldn't take people's free will from them before you allowed them to pour your tea or clean your floors, right?"

Nimue's round little face crinkled up slightly. "We don't need to," she said. "Serving the Imperium is an honour. Most of our staff have parents or grandparents in service. My first nursemaid was from a family line who had served the Imperium for seven generations."

"You don't need to put compulsion spells on them," Dio repeated. He could not help but think of his own army of aunties and cousins who worked in service jobs, one way or another. Earning a pittance, usually, even (especially) those who ran their own businesses.

"Well," said Nimue, blinking those pretty eyes of hers. "We don't *need* to. But it's palace protocol."

Imagine not having a choice but to serve your master... not only in the way that most people born to the lower orders had no choice. Compelled beyond your own reason.

The hand that Calyx had wrapped around Dio's heart no longer felt all that benign. Was he going along with this because it was his mistress' will that he accept the magical bond without a fuss? If he was not sworn to her service, would this new revelation spur him to action, to rebellion?

Dio had never rebelled against anything in his life, except the authorities who told him he wasn't good enough to be a gladius. Perhaps he was weak-willed. A coward.

Dio glanced up and saw Ikaros watching the two of them, a dark shadow against the cream cabin wall, all stubbled beard and blazing eyes.

Calyx's magic was strong, but Dio did not think that Ikaros had accepted their fate to serve her. Not yet.

"Wait," Dio said, after mulling this over. "Did Calyx use the bond magic to make the crew put shirts on?"

He had been low-key wondering why there were so few bare chests running around since he got here. Crew lived in loose, larkflax garments for the most part — the striped, baggy pants commonly called 'riverbags,' all in dark colours. But they rarely wore shoes unless going ashore, and in warm, sticky summer weather like they'd been having lately, they wore as little as possible. Even female-bodied crewmates would often strip down to nothing but a breastband and shorts in high summer.

But the sailors of the *Silken Hare* wore shirts. A few sleeveless vests here and there, but it was all suspiciously proper.

Nimue looked startled at his question. "Do they not normally wear shirts?"

The more important question was: had Calyx requested the crew to cover up, or had she merely *willed* them to do so?

Dio once spent one whole summer crewing a barge called the *Pearly Rat*, which was pretty much exactly like the *Silken Hare*. (There wasn't an odd job on the River Divine that he had not turned his hand to, one way or another.) Like most of his casual jobs he had been so far down the pecking order while aboard that he hadn't even rated a job title other than 'hey, lad.' He'd grown a few inches since then, but acquired no natural authority to go with them.

Dio always needed to scrape coins, in between his attempts at studying. Taking all those examinations was expensive — especially with all the extra cost of false identity papers, charmed disguises and the like. When he wasn't struggling to push facts into his head, he was hustling to pay for the next set of fake paperwork.

The summer he'd spent on the *Pearly*, he'd shovelled gleaming moon-jade chips to feed the engines. The jewels glowed with their soft magics as they disappeared into the chute. He'd scrubbed decks and unfurled night-sails and hit the occasional siren over the head with an oar to keep the crew from being lured overboard. (Obviously no one would have cared if young Dio himself toppled silently into the water, but he'd learned the trick with wax ear-plugs from the age of twelve.)

He had his river legs; he was unlikely to embarrass himself on that score. This particular journey had no surprises for him, except those created by his fellow passengers.

Today, the *Silken Hare* was working to a pre-arranged schedule: booked to dock underneath the Hanging Market for three hours, to refuel and take on supplies for the four day trip that would end at the city of Phoenix Burning, on the distant south-west coast of the Divine Kingdom.

Time enough for Calyx to visit the shrine of the Black Raven and register her complaint. She might fit in a little shopping and a visit to the baths, if she was anything like Dio's aunties.

She did not look like a lady of leisure about to enjoy an afternoon at the baths. Calyx appeared desperately uncomfortable as she waited on the deck, her shaved head bared to the sky. She had changed all her silken under-layers from pinks and purples to teals and greens, and the long, neck-to-ankle fall of linen she wore over it was covered in a pattern of hydrangeas.

Dio wasn't entirely sure if it was a different garment, or if she had used magic to change its appearance.

Calyx watched as the dock workers connected their equipment chute to transfer the bright green gems into the bowels of the barge. She stared as if she had never seen such a process before.

"Mithrix," said Ikaros, appearing at her shoulder. He gave off a combined vibe of grumpy but also helpful, as if he genuinely wished to be of service but also wanted to startle her so badly that she fell into the river. "Also known as moon-jade. Mined in our mountains."

"Your ships run on magic?" Calyx sounded bewildered

by the concept. "Ordinary people work with those rocks? Not educated mages, or royals?"

Ikaros gave her a thin smile. "The river is a thirsty wench. Makes the skin itch, doesn't it?"

"Speak for yourself," she said primly. "I find it all quite fascinating." It didn't sound like 'fascinating' was the word she meant, not to Dio. Frightening, maybe.

"I don't like magic," Ikaros growled.

"The only people who say that are those who don't have it," said Calyx, not meeting his gaze.

"Exactly my point."

The barge's captain crossed the deck towards them, in his purple and black riverbags and a tunic that was far too fancily trimmed for daily wear — he must have pulled it out from his festival chest. He doffed his tricorn hat to the Petal with more civility than Dio had ever seen a sailor give to a passenger onboard any ship on this river. "Ready to disembark, ma'am? They've sent a basket down for you."

"I am indeed," said Calyx. "Ikaros, Dio, you will accompany me up into the market. Captain, keep my daughter safe."

"As you will, ma'am," said the captain obediently.

Ugh. Travelling up into the market with Calyx and Ikaros meant Dio would have to stand between the two of them glaring at each other. Wonderful.

If anyone could overcome a powerful magical bond to strangle the sorceress who had cast the spell, it would be this man. Ikaros. When that inevitably happened, Dio didn't want to have to find out if the bond would force him to be all heroic about it.

Ikaros was staring after the captain now, mouthing the word 'ma'am' as if he couldn't quite believe it. Clearly, he was familiar with the rough and ready style of barge crews.

Calyx moved towards the large basket that brushed gently against the deck. A literal basket, sturdily woven of thick cane, and hung from a length of silk rope. It would bear the three of them easily, though they'd be at close quarters for a good ten minutes as they were winched into the upper levels of the market.

There was an awkward moment when the three of them faced the basket, but then Ikaros moved to unlatch the side to allow Calyx to step in. His face made it clear for a moment that he did not enjoy acting as a servant, then it flattened out to a smoother expression.

Dio had no idea what his own face was doing, but he suspected it was something like awkward terror.

"So, you're leaving your precious daughter on that barge with a bunch of sailors and my two colleagues," said Ikaros, his eyes blazing into those of Calyx. "No concerns about her safety?"

"None," said the Petal of the House of Flowers serenely.

Ikaros leaned in. "Where are your bodyguards, Calyx? Where is your retinue? Ladies in waiting, courtly knights to pass you sweetmeats and dainties. Is it normal to travel so light in a foreign land?"

"It was the wish of my betrothed," she replied, calm and polite. "A condition on our papers being approved to enter this country."

"Interesting," said Ikaros. "Your betrothed has little interest in your safety."

A small flinch marred Calyx's placid expression. "My betrothed knows how powerful I am," she replied.

Ikaros nodded, his eyes flashing. "So if we are to consider who might have paid good money to sacrifice you to the Black Raven, is your betrothed on the list?"

Calyx's calm facade cracked a little. "That is *quite* a suggestion."

"Isn't it?"

"It's because of the magic," Dio blurted. The tension between these two was unbearable. It felt like that time one of his cousins had been contracted to marry her least favourite of the neighbour's sons. The two of them spent the first two days of the wedding ceremony sniping so hard at each other that the groom got drunk, propositioned a surprisingly violent bridesmaid, and finally jumped a fence to flee in the middle of the night.

To this day, no one in Dio's family had ever heard what happened to the man after that. He was probably still running.

"What's because of the magic?" Ikaros demanded, looming over him.

"Everyone on this ship," Dio said miserably. "They're all bonded magically to the Petal."

"I hardly think that is of any importance," said Calyx dismissively.

Ikaros stared at her. "This is a hired barge. You turned it into a slave ship? Why?"

Calyx tilted her head in confusion. "Standard protocol," she said.

And there, that was what Ikaros the Hand looked like when he was speechless.

[illegible]

Calyx's calm facade cracked a little. [illegible]

[illegible]

[illegible]

It [illegible]. Dhi [illegible] between [illegible] the [illegible] [illegible] [illegible] the [illegible] [illegible] young [illegible] [illegible] finally [illegible] [illegible] [illegible] night.

[illegible] no one in Caro's family had ever learnt what happened to the man after that. He was probably still [illegible].

"What [illegible] of the magic?" Taron demanded.

[illegible]

"[illegible] on this ship," Dhi said miserably. "They're all [illegible] to the [illegible]."

"[illegible] think that is of any importance," said Calyx [illegible].

Taron stared at her. "That's a [illegible] large [illegible] to a slave ship? Why?"

Calyx [illegible] confusion. "[illegible]," he said.

And there, that was what [illegible] he'd [illegible] when he was speechless.

5. At the Shrine of Black Feathers

They passed the baths on the way to the temple of death. Calyx restrained herself from following the scented oils inside the silken curtains like a hound sniffing after bacon fat.

A bath. It seemed like an impossible dream.

The journey across the isthmus and the steep mountain ranges that had greeted Calyx on arrival into the Divine Kingdom had left a miasma of grime on her skin that could not merely be sponged away.

She had been mildly distressed to discover there were no proper bathing facilities on board the barge: that was why she had stopped to enquire about rooms at the Blooming Cup in the first place. Baths, it seemed, were plentiful and public in the Divine Kingdom, not restricted to personal bathing chambers. Even the nobles, Calyx was told by the gossipy women of the teahouse (including, she realised in retrospect, at least one of her assassins), often used the public facilities alongside their maids and peers.

For a country so intent on depriving women of power, it was oddly fascinating that they did not extend that to controlling their bodies, or banning them from public spaces.

Back in the Imperium, there were whole swathes of the city where no respectable woman could be seen, and many households where the mistress of the house was only able to leave with her husband's permission. Even graduates of the highest status colleges lost control over their bodies upon marriage if they happened to be female. It was hard to imagine that the bosomed brigand in a red kerchief she had just seen swaggering out of a Hanging Market wine den needed her husband's permission to do anything.

Here at the Hanging Market, with so many people of different types rubbing shoulders on the platforms between shops and stalls, Calyx noticed many different women. It was hard to miss how boldly they walked among men, the variety of clothes that they wore, how they spoke and conducted themselves as if no one expected them to be polite, or quiet.

Was it only *magical* women who were held back by this society?

In any case, Calyx did not have the leisure to indulge in a bath, not until she addressed the matter of the four assassins that had been sent to kill her.

(How much of her current resentment towards them was because they had distracted her from availing herself of the facilities back at the Blooming Cup?)

Dio and Ikaros fell in step beside Calyx, slightly further back, in the traditional manner of bodyguards, though she had no idea if either of them had ever worked in such a position. They looked reasonably subservient, so they knew how to play the part.

Ikaros had found the biggest loophole in the service bond: it had no power against sarcasm. He had taken to playing tour guide in order to exercise his rebellious spirit... or possibly just to make her afternoon as miserable as possible.

"You see that delightful mother-of-pearl tent, that's a spa run by a lass called Glynis. She hires three hairdressers, a masseuse and a manicurist, and because she pays fair wages for their work, and checked their references when she hired them, she doesn't feel the need to magically enforce their subservience."

"Your subtlety is noted," Calyx sighed.

"Are you sure? The Hanging Market is so full of examples of hardworking citizens who have not been casually bewitched to serve the whims of royalty."

"Please stop."

Ikaros was silent after that. Calyx did not know if it was the bond that stopped his tongue, or if he was biding his time. As long as he stopped talking long enough for her to get her impending headache under control, she did not much care.

Homicidal rage was a rare occurrence in the lives of the priests of the Black Raven. Ikaros had never thought of himself as an angry person.

Killing was a calming activity, not a way to settle petty emotions — it was a sacred act, and never personal.

They were trained to maim, not kill, if attacked outside their sacred work. Killing was only for the Raven, when the price had been paid and the mark named. It was a sacrifice and a sacrament, something one did as an act of service, not because you personally wanted a person to be dead.

Ikaros had never wanted to snap the neck of another person so much as he did right in this moment, walking half a step behind his new mistress. Calyx. Petal of the Imperium.

It wasn't even wrong, to want her dead. *He had her mark.*

Marked twice over — he had been hired to make her his target, but was well aware of the other tattoo, the delicate night-bloom that decorated his skin, warring with the scythe-knife of the god he served.

He had every right to end her life. He burned with wanting to push her into the arms of his god.

Right now, it was the one thing he could not do. Even thinking about how it might be done caused his hands to lock tightly at his sides, his breath to falter. The compulsion spell wanted him to serve her, not hurt her.

Ikaros had always hated magic in a casual everyday sort of way. Right now, he wanted to destroy the compulsion spell even more than he wanted to destroy Calyx.

Worst of all, if someone else burst out of these merry crowds right now and tried to hurt her, Ikaros would have to stop them. He had to protect this slave-making harridan.

If he did not stay calm, the curse upon him was going to blow his heart to pieces. He could already hear his pulse beating in his ears, too fast to be healthy.

Ikaros breathed. His chance would come. As long as Calyx did not make a direct order that counteracted his intentions, as long as he did not act on the rage that burned through every finger-width of his flesh, he had a chance. One chance, to be free of her.

She would never see it coming.

Most temples in the Hanging Market were small. Space was at a premium up in the airy higher levels. Like many of the shops and businesses around here, the Shrine of Black Feathers (smallest and least significant of all the temples devoted to the Black Raven) looked like a square yurt with a reception window, and a narrow doorway covered with soft layers of fabric. Black on black, with detailing of black. Gentle silver embroidery here and there hinted at a pattern of bird wings, but only upon close examination, and it really only served to emphasise the overall blackness of the decor.

It was as if someone had made a tiny storefront out of a discarded featherbrace, stretched thin on a narrow frame.

The stall next door belonged to a florist, garishly bright with a display of tulips and sunflowers. The juxtaposition of life and death in this particular spot never failed to amuse Ikaros, though a better example was the Shrine of Sharp Beak at Lake Lamia, a dark and looming structure sandwiched between a children's toy emporium and a sweetshop.

The ground beneath their feet was a structure of knotted rope woven in coarse patterns. It shifted with the breezes, only slightly more unstable than being on board a ship.

Ikaros failed to understand the popular allure of not having solid ground under your feet.

"You'll want to ring the bell," he advised Calyx.

A sensation washed over him, an uninvited pleasant

glow: a reward for being helpful to his mistress. The compulsion bond was the gift that kept giving. He hated it.

Calyx waved Dio forward, and the young man leaned into the window with a puppyish enthusiasm that made Ikaros respect him slightly less.

"There isn't a bell," said Dio, looking crestfallen.

Calyx glanced impatiently at Ikaros. He took that as permission to get closer to the shrine. He raised a hand to the soft door curtains, and a tinkling, jangling sound filled the air.

The handmaidens of the Shrine of the Black Feathers were his least favourite colleagues. Like many of the simpering dandies who lived and worked at the Hanging Market, the Shrine of the Black Feathers was so concerned with aesthetics and style that practicality went out of the window (and into the river, presumably).

There were three handmaidens who operated this particular shrine; Ikaros had made a point of never learning any of their names.

A young lady with dyed-black hair and matching eyeliner appeared at the window. She wore a tight-fitting gown that was a mockery of the formal featherbrace, using exactly twice as much black lace as might be appropriate in literally any other profession. "My name is Yeony, how may I help you?" she breathed.

Oh, Yeony. Yes, Ikaros did know this one. She was the niece of Mavadian, who ruled the Raven's Gate temple near Phoenix Burning with an administrative fist of iron, and had once taken Ikaros to her bed with the enthusiasm of a large mountain cat on the hunt for red meat.

"Always a pleasure, Yeony," he said, taking another step forward so that his hip brushed against the soft curtain of the shrine.

"Ikaros," said Yeony, her dark-rimmed eyes taking in his presence with an amusement that made him wonder whether she shared gossip with her aunt. "How can I help you this afternoon?"

He called out the formal words as quickly as he could, before Calyx realised there was anything going on. "Black Raven protect me, I claim sanctuary, the temple is under attack!"

As he spoke, Ikaros dived through the shimmering black curtains and into the blessed darkness of the shrine.

Feathers closed over the window, shutting out all light. The fabric curtains solidified into a mass of shadow. The shrine bumped and shook as the sacred sanctuary protocol took over.

"What the fuck?" snarled Yeony, grasping at his sleeve. "You can't do this every time you're pissed off at a client, Ikaros. The Black Raven doesn't like it, and the fines from the council of the Hanging Market are *astronomical.*"

Ikaros' stomach heaved. He had rebelled against his mistress. The bond did not like it, not at all. He might be protected here in the belly of the god he served, but his whole body was crying out to return to Calyx and beg her forgiveness.

Who would save him from himself?

"Going to need a bucket," he said with great dignity, and then threw up wet dandelions and clover all over the floor of the shrine, to the sound of Yeony the handmaiden screaming in protest.

Calyx stared in shock as the Shrine of the Black Feathers sealed itself up, becoming a tight black ball with no entrance or window. Large black feathered wings sprouted from the strange bundle of yurt. A moment later, the entire shrine dropped away from the florist stall, leaving a gaping hole in the Hanging Market.

"What was *that*?" Calyx demanded, whirling on an equally astonished Dio. "Is that normal?"

"Normal is not the word I'd use," he said, wide-eyed. "But um, shrines. They have a mind of their own, I've heard. My aunties say it's not wise to go up against, uh. Gods and their servants. Generally speaking." That was probably as much diplomacy as he could manage under the circumstances.

Calyx glared at the hole in the wall with a half-measure of fury. She couldn't even be angry at what Ikaros had done. She was just so tired.

"I'm done," she sighed, giving up on the day. "Time for a bath."

6. In the Baths of Acanthyos

"Welcome to the Baths of Acanthyos," said the attendant, who wore robes of white muslin and a head-dress of white feathers braided into silk ribbons. "Our baths were named after the noble knight of the Bright Owl who sacrificed her life in order that the White Lady might bathe in comfort."

"Yes," said Calyx, as calmly as she could possibly manage. "I can see the scene depicted on your walls in excruciating detail."

Marble friezes, to be exact, which were surely not the best choice of decor for a building suspended from a combination of silk ropes and magic, but then who would make the choice to build mid-air baths in the first place?

Calyx refused to be surprised at anything else this kingdom had to offer her. "I require a private bath."

"I'm afraid our private suites are booked for the next six hours," said the attendant with a smile that looked genuinely regretful.

"I won't bathe in the presence of men," Calyx said immediately.

"As you wish. That's the second request today for an all-female chamber, most unusual," said the attendant, making a note in her ledger. "You'll have to confine yourself to the pool of maidens and the salon next door. There are three ladies in there already."

"I'll survive."

If she could just get clean and have a few moments with her thoughts, surely, she could figure out what to do about her escaped assassin.

Calyx pushed her way past the whispering muslin curtains to the pool of maidens and stopped short on the cool tiled steps. (Tiles? How on earth could they have used tiles up here, wouldn't that be unbearably heavy?)

Two familiar faces gazed back at her, neither looking remotely surprised at her presence. Mardi the Needle, and Valeria the Blade.

Valeria lounged on the edge of the bath, only her feet dipping into the deep pool. She wore a gauzy green robe that had turned transparent against her skin, wet from a recent bathe, and her long hair was pinned up high to keep it dry. Mardi, waist-deep in the water of the delicious looking pool, was naked with all her prominent curves on display.

So many breasts pointed directly at her. Women of the Divine Kingdom were *shameless*.

"I told you two to stay on the barge," Calyx protested. First Ikaros' flight and now this. Was her magic losing its power?

The two assassins glanced at each other.

"I don't think you did," said Valeria.

"You told us to protect your daughter," said Mardi helpfully, one hand resting on her bare belly. "We can't do that from the deck of the barge. Not currently."

Calyx blinked with anger and confusion, just as her daughter came through the curtains on the other side, from a different pool. Nimue's shaven head was bare, and she had found a robe that was rather more modest than Valeria's, though that was not saying much. It was a dark, sheeny fabric that made Nimue look much older than she was.

"Oh," said Nimue, startled and embarrassed. "Mother."

"What do you think you are doing?"

"I wanted to bathe properly. It's been days."

Never had Calyx been more furious with herself for raising a child in a palace. What did she *think* was going to happen when the two of them ventured outside that world of privilege and safety? Nimue had no idea of what dangers there were for her, here in a foreign country.

"We protected her," said Mardi, sounding smug.

"She was pick-pocketed three times between the basket and the spice market," added Valeria. "At least, they tried. In the end, I took custody of her purse to save time." She indicated a small heap of their belongings, a little way from the water.

Calyx wanted to scream and shout at them all, but that was what Ikaros wanted. He wanted her unsettled and irrational so she would make a mistake, and then she would be dead and he would be free of her control.

Power often lay in not losing your temper even in the face of unbearable frustration. Vengeance was a dessert, not an impulse-eat.

Her thoughts were wild and furious... and she still wanted a bath.

They will see your scars, she thought for a moment, and that was even more infuriating. These were her servants. It did not matter what they thought of her. *Let them look*. It was not as if they did not have scars of their own. Calyx unfastened the stiff stemma and hung it carefully on a nearby peg so that it wouldn't crease. She removed the rest of her clothes quickly, the silken colourful layers, and hung them up as well, not wanting anything to get wet. Then, realising she had bared her back to them for too long, she turned and stepped naked into the warmth of the water, joining her two remaining assassins.

Valeria passed her a strigil and a bottle of scented oil, as if they were friendly colleagues who had merely happened across each other in the baths.

Nimue, clearly still expecting to be told off, perched on the edge of the pool. Her nails had been recently trimmed and reshaped, decorated with a bright purple polish.

Had Nimue seen Calyx's scars? Did she wonder about them? Calyx had worked so hard to conceal her secret from her daughter, and here she was, literally baring herself to them all. Ikaros and his behaviour had unsettled her more than she liked to admit.

"Where are our menfolk?" Mardi asked lightly.

"Dio is standing guard outside," Calyx muttered.

"I'm sure he'll be excellent at that," said Valeria in an encouraging sort of tone that was only about a quarter sarcastic.

There was an expectant pause.

"Ikaros claimed sanctuary at the Shrine of Black Feathers and disappeared on me," Calyx added grumpily.

The two assassins exchanged expressions that were more weary than delighted.

"Well, he would, wouldn't he," said Mardi. "What a melon-head."

"Don't worry about it," said Valeria with a shrug. "We'll pick him up after we're finished here."

"You can do that? You know how to...?" Well, of course they did. If she had learned anything from Ikaros' escapade, it was that Calyx did not know how anything worked in the Divine Kingdom, least of all the priests of the Black Raven. "Why?" she pleaded. "Why would you take my side?"

They were being so nice to her. Calyx was bone weary from feeling alone. This mild friendliness made her want to cry.

"Uh, because you forced our service," said Mardi. "Obviously. This is what our service looks like."

Calyx frowned. "You can't be happy about it."

"We're not. Valeria's livid."

"I am," Valeria said archly. "You can't tell, because I'm the mistress of my own emotions."

"We're going to help you, regardless," said Mardi, nudging Valeria with an elbow. "Aren't we, dear?"

"You've stopped fighting the bond," Calyx breathed. "Why?"

Valeria rolled her eyes. "You're a powerful magical woman who someone wants to kill quite desperately. That's unusual around here. Even for *us*. It's interesting. There's almost certainly going to be something in it for us, at some point."

"Besides," said Mardi. "I need to head back in the direction of Phoenix Burning sometime this month. I wish to retire from service before the baby is born, and the only place to do that through official channels is at Raven's Gate.

You're literally giving me free passage to the place I meant to go next."

"And if taking your side means thwarting Ikaros while attempting to curb his self-destructive nature," said Valeria. "Then that works for me. For now. Never assume I only have one reason for anything I do," she added sternly.

"You're so calm," wondered Calyx.

"I wouldn't worry about it," said Mardi. "Once we drag Ikaros back to the barge, Valeria will be horrendous company all over again."

"We bring out the worst in each other," Valeria agreed. "But right now, there is hot water to enjoy, and delicious bath oils. Why stress?"

Why indeed, stress?

"Nimue," Calyx sighed, ducking her head under water for a moment. "Please find the attendant who did your toenails. I want apricot."

An hour or so later, sweet-smelling and rather calmer than when she arrived, Calyx left the Baths of Acanthyos with her retinue after settling an exorbitant bill. (Public baths, it turned out, were not free for public use, when one demanded an all-female bathing chamber.)

Dio waited patiently for her on the rope platform outside the temple door, demonstrating skills that probably would make him a half decent gladius someday, if a gladius was anything like the guards back home. His eyes were constantly on the move, surveying his surroundings.

Ikaros stood at Dio's side. He looked dishevelled, and annoyed at the universe. Or possibly, just annoyed at her.

As Calyx approached, both men straightened to attention. Ikaros immediately looked like he wanted to throw himself off the platform for his own impulse.

"Easier than we expected," drawled Valeria. "How was sanctuary, dear heart?"

"Brief," replied Ikaros.

Mardi kissed Ikaros' cheek. "How long did you fight the bond before you came right back to find us?"

"About thirty minutes," he muttered.

"Sweet."

Mardi offered her arm to Dio, who took it with the chivalry that one might expect of a young man with many aunties. Valeria and Nimue walked together, which Calyx was not entirely happy about. Surely these women could be nothing but a bad influence on her daughter.

On the other hand, Nimue had probably never been safer from assassination than she was right now.

Calyx looked at Ikaros, unblinking. He sighed and offered her his arm as they made their way back through the market, heading for the basket that would return them to the *Silken Hare*.

"Did you find out anything about the person who hired the three of you to kill me?" she asked conversationally.

"No. The booking did not come from this particular shrine. And the spells that connect all of the Black Raven's temples across the kingdom have been down for two days."

"Is that usual?"

"Extremely not." He gave her a wary look. "Communication between temples is currently patchy, limited to couriers and river post. We don't exchange information on our clients by either method, to protect the privacy of our clients, and preserve the sanctity of our work."

"So," Calyx murmured, thinking it over. "A client could have paid for my death at multiple temples, and the system would allow it, while communications were down." A rather prosaic explanation, but it seemed plausible.

"This isn't a mere admin malfunction," said Ikaros, looking frustrated. "Normally the Black Raven would step in to ensure his servants did not break their vows in such a profane manner."

"And he has not."

"He has *not*."

"How often does your god speak to you directly?"

Ikaros gave her a fierce expression. "That is an extremely personal question."

"I expect you to answer it."

"Somewhere between often and never."

"And you personally?"

He gritted his teeth. "You demand to know?"

"I request," she said with a smile that made it clear she was not giving him a choice in the matter. Honestly, what a ridiculous man. She would not have to flex her power if he would submit, only a little.

Ikaros cleared his throat roughly. "I have been honoured as a humble servant of the Black Raven to hear his voice directly on six occasions. I have met him in person, so to speak, perhaps twice that. Over many decades of service, not counting the years before I was his priest."

"Indeed," said Calyx, not sure whether to be impressed or not. She was certainly adding items to the list of reasons for Ikaros to want her dead once he was free of her spell. *Decades*. How could he have served for decades when he looked younger than she did? Was he exaggerating? The bond should not allow him to dissemble, but perhaps there was enough truth there to compensate. “How does it feel, to have such a close connection to your god?”

“Sacred,” Ikaros snarled.

She did not press further.

7. At the Night Lock

"So," said Valeria in a low, teasing drawl. "Your escape plan came to naught."

"Fuck you," said Ikaros. "Enjoy your bath?"

"Swimmingly."

They were back on the *Silken Hare*, the two of them lounging on the deck as the evening grew dark around them.

A few hours south of the Hanging Market, the crew had brought the *Silken Hare* in to anchor at the Night Lock, along with a line of other river boats. They'd made good time considering the delays.

Night-sailing was rare, as the wild magics of the river were particularly feisty at night, and it was unusual to find a crew willing to overlook their superstitions. (Reasonable caution, Ikaros might correct, if anyone was so rude as to refer to 'superstition.' It was hardly paranoia if you knew the river was full of creatures that could do all manner of damage to a boat and its crew.)

Calyx, of course, had bent the crew of the *Silken Hare* to her will, and they would probably have sailed on without complaint if she pressed the matter. Still, she would have needed a crew twice the size to justify sailing through all shifts.

In any case, if you did not make it past the Night Lock by sunset, there was no budging until dawn the next day, when each boat would take turns being dropped (or lifted, if travelling north) to the next level of the river. Lockhands knocked off early, and knew how to make themselves scarce so they couldn't be bribed or bullied into opening up ahead of schedule.

The banks here were high and grassy on both sides, so it felt rather like being moored in a tunnel surrounded by lapping water.

Ikaros and the others could easily climb from the deck of the *Silken Hare* on to a concrete walkway and from there, to freedom. It wouldn't be difficult except for the magic that roiled in his head.

Calyx had not bothered to cuff them for the night or even tell them to stay put. Clearly Ikaros' failed attempt to use the sanctuary of the shrine against his new mistress had left her confident in her control. Sadly, not over-confident. Even the thought of walking away right now made his stomach cramp, and his tongue taste of dandelions.

The Black Raven had been no help whatsoever. What was the point of a god who did not defend his priests when their service was commandeered by another?

The communication breakdown between the temples went some way to explaining how three (or four) of them had been hired for the same mark, but Ikaros knew there must be more to it than that. Such a thing could not happen by accident.

Someone deep in the service of the Black Raven had betrayed them all.

"One of these days, dear heart," said his wife — former wife — often estranged but currently surprisingly congenial wife, idly combing her fingers through his hair. "You will learn to go with the flow. Why not simply protect this stray foreign woman and her daughter, and figure the rest out when we get to Phoenix Burning? Not everything has to mean you at war with yourself, or the world."

Ikaros gave her an irritated look. "Why aren't you angrier about this? Normally you'd be the first to set fire to a client who decided they had purchased more of you than you were willing to allow."

Valeria had literally set fire to more than one client over the years. Their god never punished her for defending herself; purchasing a mark was sacred, and non-temple killings were discouraged, but the body and minds of his priests were their own.

Until now, damn it.

"Perhaps I've been craving the serenity of a river holiday," said Valeria.

Ikaros peered at her, wondering if she was drugged up. But no, her pupils were normal. She looked relaxed. It was disturbing.

"Don't examine me like you're a knight of the Bright Owl," she said, sounding irritated. "I'm fine. I have a plan, that's all."

"What kind of plan?"

"To go along with everything our dear mistress Calyx wants of us, until she releases us from her service at Phoenix Burning," said Valeria happily.

He eyed her skeptically. "And then?"

"And then," she said in the soft tones of someone greatly looking forward to a treat. "The second she drops her compulsion, I'm going to murder the bitch before the rest of you get near her."

Ikaros was watching Valeria closely, as was his habit: she was generally the most compelling and most dangerous person in the vicinity. So he saw the moment that pain overwhelmed her, the second that she declared her true intentions for Calyx. Her face twisted in a silent gasp. Something bright and blue emerged from her tear ducts, streaming wetly down her cheeks.

Forget-me-not buds, clearly painful. At least they didn't have thorns, though they still made her bleed at the corner of her eyes as they squeezed out from that impossibly tiny space.

"You bastard," Valeria moaned, staring at the blood-streaked flowers for a moment before crumpling them in one hand and casting them to the deck. "I was working so hard not to imagine it too clearly. Now I have to start all over again. Good pet. Complacent servant."

She forced herself to calm down, her shoulders rolling and her eyes losing their usual stormy gleam. "There we are," she finally slurred. "Nothing to see here but service and compliance. I recommend you try it, dear. It's good for the soul."

Ikaros walked away from Valeria in disgust, but there wasn't anywhere to go. Around and around the deck.

They were surrounded by night-blooms opening, on the surface of the river. The flowers drew in clusters around each boat in the lock, like a halo of bruises. Their complex petals were a dark, dusky purple and black. They would be invisible as the water darkened into night except for the eerie brightness of their stamens, like tiny wavering lanterns made of moonlight.

Ikaros had seen the phenomenon before, many times.

He had never paid more attention to them than any other kind of flower — though now, of course, knowing that this particular flower was marked on his skin as deeply as the scythe-knife of the Black Raven, they took on an extra significance.

He noticed Mardi sitting at the bow, her eyes fixed on the glowing patterns of night-blooms against the darkening waters of the river. Before Ikaros could approach her, he smelled that familiar floral perfume and drew back moments before Calyx drifted across the deck to stand beside Mardi.

He intended to eavesdrop, but Mardi barely spoke a few words before Calyx was whirling around, disappearing into her cabin, face grim.

"What did you say to her?" Ikaros asked, joining Mardi at the bow. There were no flowers bleeding from her eyes or ears, so whatever she had said to offend their mistress, it did not trigger a poor reaction from the spell that bound them.

"I asked about her taste in poetry," his friend murmured.

"Seems fake."

She turned to him, her eyes laughing. His breath caught for a moment, unused to seeing Mardi happy after her months of misery. "Why don't you ask her yourself?" she suggested.

"Perhaps I will." Right now, shoulder brushing comfortably against hers, Ikaros did not particularly wish to move. "How long to Phoenix Burning?" he asked idly.

"Six days, the captain says, if we stay on schedule."

Ikaros sighed heavily. "Could be worse, I suppose."

The ship was sleeping.

Dio remained awake.

It was Ikaros who had determined that each of the four of them would keep a watch on the ship… in fact, he intended for the night shift to be divided between himself, Mardi and Valeria, but Dio pushed himself forward to be included.

"I suppose you have been training to be a gladius," said Ikaros grudgingly. "You must retain some useful skills."

"It's watching a river," Dio shot back. "It's not complex."

For that, Ikaros had given him the graveyard shift, right in the middle of the long night.

Dio did not like to examine too closely the warm glow it gave him, to be allowed even this small amount of trust. He half expected Ikaros to be haunting the shadows like a beady-eyed crow, to check on his work, but no — in fact, when Ikaros had come in to wake him, he took Dio's place on the bed in the death priests' cabin and fell asleep beside Valeria almost instantly.

Dio had stared for a few moments at the three of them, side by side. He had thought it strange enough that Mardi and Valeria did not seem bothered to share a bed with him — a stranger, but somehow it was Ikaros' trust that felt more hard-won.

It required trust, surely, for them all to be willing to fall asleep in each other's presence?

In any case, Dio could not linger to stare at the sleeping

assassins for long, not if he was going to do the job they expected of him.

So, two hours on deck with nothing to see but the occasional lantern from the watchmen patrolling the night lock. Nothing to hear but the snoring of sailors on deck, and the lapping of water against solid objects.

Shortly before it was time to wake Mardi for her turn (marvellous how Ikaros's distribution of shifts gave Dio the job of waking a pregnant woman), he spotted a figure dart along the top of the cabins.

Lightly, Dio ran along the deck and climbed the side of the cabin that Calyx shared with Nimue.

He saw him again: a man with long dark hair, caught in a braid. The man wore black, though his skin shone out bright in the moonlight like he had been carved out of marble. He crouched on top of the other cabin, the one containing the priests of the Black Raven.

The intruder did not seem especially bothered about having been seen; on the contrary, he smiled at Dio's approach, and placed one finger to his lips. His eyes were a startling shade of violet that Dio had never seen on a man before.

"Are you the Bow?" Dio hissed. Who else was it likely to be? "You can't free them. Not yet." Even this much disloyalty made his throat close over, and a sticky-sweet taste of pollen fill his mouth. "Are you here to kill Calyx?"

If this was the Bow, then he likely had received the same order as the others, to assassinate the Petal of the Imperium. Unlike Ikaros, Mardi and Valeria, there was no magical compulsion to stop this man making his kill.

There was something otherworldly about the intruder; he didn't have the same rough edges as the priests of death. No scars, no callouses on his soft fingers. No weapons, come to that. He was *lovely*. Perhaps the most beautiful person Dio had seen in his life, and this was a week that had brought him into the orbit of Ikaros, Valeria and Mardi.

Did the Black Raven only choose servants who were aesthetically pleasing?

"Don't worry about it," whispered the stranger. "I'll try again later."

"Wait," Dio protested, but the intruder leaped off the cabin roof, and ran lightly across the deck, climbing the frame of the night lock to make his escape.

Dio should raise the crew with a cry, he knew that. Some night watchman, if he let someone wander around their boat without stopping him. Some gladius he would make.

Somehow, the thought of making a sound did not occur to Dio until after the intruder was long-gone into the night.

8. Before and After the Temple of Many Knives

Calyx had slept badly; she was not yet accustomed to the light sway of a riverboat, even one tethered to a night lock. Her own troubled thoughts had not helped matters. It was nearly dawn when she finally sank into proper sleep, and then a few hours later she startled awake to find her daughter's side of the bed not only empty, but cold.

"She's fine," said a deep voice.

Calyx froze, her eyes sliding to the door. It was closed, with Ikaros leaning against it. He was still and calm, as if he had been standing there for some time, observing her in her sleep.

Not creepy at all.

"Where is Nimue?" she asked, gathering her royal dignity around her as she sat up. The embroidered night-robe that her maid had packed for the journey was a thoroughly matronly garment; she might as well have been wearing a padded dressing gown or a suit of armour. It had been fine for the first night as they made their way across the mountain pass, but was far too much for the sticky summer nights on the river.

(Presumably there were a few lighter sleeping garments packed in the trunks with the trousseau intended to be used after her wedding, but that didn't help Calyx now, with the warm night air of the River Divine making the night-robe clammy and too heavy under blankets.)

Ikaros shrugged. "Flirting with Dio. Walking around in circles. Learning knife skills from Valeria. Your daughter's had a busy morning."

Calyx narrowed her eyes at him. "I expect you to take better care of her."

"I'm not her nursemaid. My job is to get you both to Phoenix Burning safe and sound. If you want someone to protect her from pretty faces and the dangerous influence of assassins, you picked the wrong team."

"Your job is to serve me," Calyx said fiercely, tugging at the magical threads that bound them.

Ikaros winced, though he pretended to be unmoved by the pressure of the threads. "I'm aware," he said.

Awake only a minute and she was already losing control; she had to do better than this. Be better.

First, she had to find out what was written on her back.

Calyx had been rattled last night when Mardi casually mentioned what she had seen in the baths. She fled instead of asking for help. And Ikaros, Ikaros was the one whose loyalty she needed to test.

"I need you to do something for me," she told him now, sliding out of bed. She bunched the night-robe in her hands and pulled it off in one swift movement. She was naked underneath.

"I think you've wildly underestimated my intentions here," said the priest calmly.

Calyx turned her back to him.

She had never stood naked before any man except her husband; in the Imperium there were so many women trained as chirurgeons, healers and mages that there was no need for such impropriety. But this was the Divine Kingdom, and while Calyx had no wish to indulge some of their customs (such as the criminal restrictions on magic imposed on so many women), if she had learned anything at the Hanging Market it was that bodily modesty was not common in this country.

"What do you see?" she asked Ikaros, her own voice trembling a little. "What do you see on my back?"

"Scars," he replied, his tone softer than she had imagined possible. "Quite a few scars."

"The words, priest," she snapped. "Are there words on my skin? Tell me."

She heard him step closer. "There are."

"How many?"

"Thirteen words. Two lines."

She gasped out a breath of relief. "*Gods be thankful.*"

Poetry on your back, was all Mardi had said with a curious smile as if inviting Calyx to explain it an amusing quirk. Calyx, shocked into silence, had imagined there might be whole stanzas on there already. She had not been careful enough, had not been checking. This was one of the hazards of travelling without a maid.

Two lines of poetry was manageable. It was not too late to cut it out before the malady took hold.

(Unless it was a particularly short poem, but such things did not exist in the Imperium where less was never more.)

"You sound surprised," said Ikaros, inviting her to explain further.

Calyx remembered who he was, who she was, and that

she was naked. "That is none of your concern," she said sharply, moving to the travel trunk and pulling out a set of silk day-robes. Pink, turquoise, purple. She dressed herself slowly, not wanting him to see how much this moment of necessary intimacy had bothered her.

Hopefully her new husband would not require her to stand about naked in the presence of other men; this experiment had demonstrated that it was not to her taste.

"Do you want me to write down the words?" Ikaros asked abruptly.

"That would be appreciated." She would not show her relief at him asking the question; she was glad he thought of it so she did not have to beg him.

By the time Calyx had arranged her robes to her satisfaction, Ikaros had written out the two lines of poetry on a sheet of paper in bright, wet black ink.

At last, to the city of petals rising
She rode on honeyed cloud

She knew those lines. One of the epic poets: Janudel, perhaps. Or Bathor. Not a sonnet, then, or a quintain. She could breathe; she had time.

Ikaros regarded her thoughtfully, blotting the black ink from his fingers. "I have questions."

"Do not ask them," Calyx said immediately. An order, not a request.

He tilted his head at her, and for a moment she saw a flare of rage in his eyes as he realised the questions would no longer rise to his tongue.

It was almost comforting, to be reminded that he hated her.

"Apparently," Ikaros said a moment later. "I have nothing further to say."

"I need a surgeon," she informed him. "As soon as possible. Before we reach the city. Can we find one on the river or will we need to divert inland?"

He blinked slowly, as if considering all the questions he was no longer permitted to ask. "The knights of the Bright Owl do rather cluster along the River Divine. Almost as if this is the most dangerous part of the country."

"The knights of the Bright Owl," Calyx repeated. "Is that what you call healers here?"

Ikaros gave her a swift, sharp grin with no humour in it. "The knights are to the Bright Owl what I and my colleagues are to the Dark Raven."

Calyx huffed impatiently at him for talking around the question instead of merely answering it.

"Yes," said Ikaros after a moment. "They are healers. There's a temple harbour coming up soon, and I think there's a Temple of Many Knives among them. Their clientele are rather select but I get the impression you're a rather important person. I'm sure they will make room for you."

"Thank you." She frowned at him. "That information came rather readily to hand."

Ikaros spread his hands wide. "I am apparently here to serve."

"Are you very familiar with all the temples up and down the River Divine?"

"I may have asked our captain which we can expect to pass over the course of our journey."

"Why?"

He did not answer at first; a small rebellion. Calyx waited. After a moment or two of awkward silence, during which she did not repeat the question, Ikaros twisted his face in discomfort and spat what appeared to be half a geranium into his palm. "I thought it might be interesting to investigate whether the magical communication setbacks of the Black Raven's temples are a more widespread phenomenon."

"It would indeed," Calyx agreed. "That was a good thought."

Ikaros capped the ink bottle and got to his feet. "As I am no longer able to ask questions, I imagine my detective skills will be rather lacking from now on."

Calyx almost laughed. "You may ask questions of other people," she allowed.

Once more, that flare of fury in his eyes, which he smoothed out entirely before he allowed himself to speak. "Such a benevolent mistress you are," said Ikaros.

Dio had always found that food aboard riverboats was much the same, whether you were crew or passenger. Rice or noodles in bulk, dressed with eggs or eel or shellfish and vegetables, the sauces sweet and salty. Soup — there was always a pot of soup boiling away in the galley. One of the benefits of boat travel was that the cooking fire never went out. Dio imagined that the soup they ate today had been endlessly cycling with fresh water and ingredients tipped in every day for months or even years.

It tasted good and filled you up; best not to think too closely about how it had happened.

Tonight, berthed in a small harbour servicing a cluster of temples, the crew and the assassins and Dio all ate on the deck together, waiting for Calyx to return. She had only taken Ikaros with her, and had not told anyone on board anything else, including which of the temples she so urgently needed to visit.

No temple of death this time, at least, as there was not one here. There was one for the knights of the Bright Owl of healing, one for the clerics of the Silver Hawk (god of war) and one for the mystics of the Grey Lark (goddess of the hearth, fertility and protection).

Perhaps Calyx was keen to get pregnant, or to prevent a pregnancy. None of Dio's business.

As he ate his soup and rice, he watched a small cohort of gladii patrol the harbour in their blue and gold uniforms — the livery was different for every city and province, but the river patrols had their own. As always, Dio tried not to hate them for having the job he had been struggling to qualify for in so long; as always, he mostly failed in this, but who would know one way or the other?

Nimue had gone to bed before supper, agitated at her mother's odd behaviour.

"Bedding in," Dio heard one of the sailors say to the captain in passing. "No word from the mistress yet?"

"She said it might take awhile," said the captain in a gruff, disapproving voice.

Dio leaned back against the side of the boat; it was odd for him, having nothing to do. He'd been staying with aunty after aunty all year, which allowed him to save up some coin but meant a plethora of chores and tasks. When he wasn't working for his roof, he was cramming his head with the words that all kept falling out before the next examination came along.

Nearby, he heard Mardi and Valeria conversing quietly over their own bowls of rice and soup; they must assume no one could hear them, as they sat quite a distance from the crew.

But this was the River Divine at nightfall. Words always travelled further than the speaker intended. Useful for sailors shouting urgent instructions back and forth; more useful still for the quiet eavesdropper.

"What do you know?" Valeria asked, stabbing a piece of roast eel from her own bowl and adding it to Mardi's; taking in return three pieces of mushroom.

"There's a curse of sorts," murmured Mardi. "I've heard of it before. Not here, but abroad."

"You and Bors and your travels," said Valeria, rolling her eyes dramatically. "Never letting us forget how worldly you are."

"You're not as funny as you think, dear heart," replied Mardi, sounding long-suffering.

"Funny, that's what the last man who kept secrets from me said, just before I stabbed him three times. Tell me about the curse."

"I could be wrong," said Mardi, and then she did mutter a line or two that was too quiet even for Dio to hear. "But it was poetry. At least, it looked like it. Didn't you notice in the baths?"

"I saw the scars."

"The woman I heard about had a whole sonnet on her calf. A classical piece by Adelius. It appeared, line by line, over years."

"By magic?" Valeria said skeptically.

"We just sailed past a winged dolphin, don't tell me you don't believe in magic. Here, on the River Divine?"

"I believe in magic," Valeria said. "I don't believe in poetry. You think our High and Mighty Petal is cursed?"

"That woman with the sonnet. She was found dead, hours after the last couplet appeared on her skin."

"Oh," said Valeria, clapping her hands. "So, this is a ghost story."

"What I'm saying," Mardi hissed. "Is that I was right all along. No need to fight the bond. Our mistress will be dead soon enough, and we will be free."

A moment later, Dio heard an urgent rustling sound. When glanced over, he saw Mardi throwing up bright purple blossoms over the side of the boat.

"Better that than through your tear ducts," said Valeria. "Believe me."

Calyx left the Temple of Many Knives with a new scar on her back, tightly bandaged, and three vials of a pain-relieving draught that smelled of violets and mercury.

The knight-surgeon had wanted to keep her longer, but she could not afford too much of a delay. According to the captain, they would have reached the Eye of the Basilisk today if not for her stop, which meant they were now at least half a day behind the original schedule.

Calyx was tempted to slow their voyage even further. She was not looking forward to what awaited her at the end of this river.

She had bought herself more time, at least. Thank goodness for Mardi Morency's sharp eyes, or she might not have known about the new poem quite so soon.

The *Silken Hare* was quiet as Calyx crossed the harbour

with Ikaros at her side. He had stayed with her through all of it — the surgery, the recovery. Always eagle-eyed in case that fourth assassin turned up to finish her off once and for all.

"Thank you for your assistance today," she said as he handed her up onto the quiet, dark deck of the river boat.

"Don't mistake it for kindness," said Ikaros. "I don't have a lot of choice in my actions these days."

The air was warm, but Calyx was feeling shaky and aware of the creeping pain beginning to descend as the first wave of anaesthesia wore off. She shivered. "Why do you despise me so much?"

"You mean, other than you stealing my freedom?"

She gaped at him. "You were literally trying to kill me at the time. I hardly think a *death merchant* can claim moral high ground."

His eyes were bright as they passed a string of lanterns outside Calyx's own cabin. "My god does not accept contracts on the innocent. If he accepted you as a sacrifice, you earned it."

"I forgot I was talking with a man of faith," Calyx snapped. "Given that your god does not usually accept four contracts for the same mark, how are you to know that the choice of victim was not also an administrative error?"

"Errors like that don't happen," said Ikaros flatly. He waved her towards the door of the cabin. Valeria was on the roof, watching them both with unblinking eyes, playing sentry.

"I see," said Calyx. The pain was making her irritable; she would have to take a vial of that potion soon. "It upsets you, does it, to consider the possibility? I wonder how many other lives you took over the years that may have been subject to similar administrative errors? Even condemned criminals are allowed time for an appeal between sentencing and execution."

Ikaros' mouth twitched a little, as if he found her amusing. "Not in this country."

"Ohhhh, this country!" Calyx moaned in frustration. And she was trapped here. Forever, in a best case scenario. "How can you stand it?"

Ikaros glanced up, briefly meeting Valeria's gaze as if they were taking part in a silent, shared conversation. "Practice," he said.

9. In the Eye of the Basilisk

Dio had run the Basilisk dozens of times in his life. When you spent your childhood going from pillar to post, from auntie to auntie, and the River Divine was the most common highway in your country, well. It stood to reason. Add to that all the hours he'd spent working riverboats, and he had long since lost track of how many times he had crossed this particular part of the river.

It was no surprise to him, then, in the late morning of the third day of their voyage, when the water surrounding the *Silken Hare* went dark green all of a sudden, as if they had passed into a patch of particularly virulent algae.

He didn't think anything of it until Nimue, trudging around the deck as usual, cried out and stepped back from the rail in alarm.

"Oh," said Valeria, not looking up from the complex card game she was playing with Ikaros a little way from them. "Are we at the Basilisk?"

"Sacred flame," gasped Nimue. "What is happening to the water?"

"It's just what the river does," said Dio. "Don't you come from a palace full of magic?"

"Not this kind of magic," she said, deeply unsettled. "Why is the water so very green?"

"Basilisk venom," said Valeria without hesitation. "More importantly, does 'sacred flame' count as swearing where you come from? You've been around sailors for three days, surely you can do better than that."

Dio knew that the priests of death were dangerous people, but over the last few days he had come to know them as de-clawed versions of themselves; he wasn't as afraid of them as he probably should be. Right now, he rolled his eyes at Valeria and beckoned Nimue to join him at the bow of the ship.

"See that tall column of basalt up ahead?" he pointed out. "That's the Eye of the Basilisk."

The green waters around them swirled and churned as if the gods themselves were boiling broth. The waters ahead grew angrier and wilder the closer you got to the imposing column.

Is the water really — venom?" Nimue asked nervously.

"No, that's just Valeria being a bitch. The Basilisk is a sacred remainder from one of the ancient nameless gods, so magic gets a bit frenetic around it. But the captain's an old hand, he'll sail us through safely."

Nimue turned large eyes up to him. "When you say frenetic... what does it do to people who have magic?"

Dio considered. "Nimue, do you have magic? Like your mother?"

"Not like my mother," she said immediately. "Her magic is... beyond what most can reach for."

Interesting.

"But you have some?" Dio wasn't really sure how magic

worked. He'd had a friend, Mateo, when he was young. Mateo had shown 'promise' and was eventually apprenticed off to a fire mage out near Chalcedony. Other than that, Dio's main experience with magicians were the hushed conversations between his aunties that he was not supposed to overhear, about smuggling this or that woman across borders because her husband or brother had discovered she could work magic, and was likely to report her to the authorities.

The gladii had to know enough about magic to enforce the laws, but they only concerned themselves with what was forbidden. Dio had done his best to memorise the various legislations on the topic but they were only available in library tomes, printed small, and he'd never made much headway.

"A little," Nimue confessed, in a very small voice. "I can make things float sometimes. Minor air magic. If I was trained, I might be able to fly eventually."

"That's not small," Dio said, impressed. "That's at least... medium. Isn't it?"

"I haven't been trained, though." She sounded disappointed

"Because you're... a princess?" He wasn't entirely sure of her royal status, and whether that meant a title or not.

Nimue looked sombre. "The Empress has many nephews, nieces, grandchildren. Royal educations get spread out among the various academies, so we represent a range of different skills. It gives her more options when selecting our marriages and vocations. Too many cousins of my generation have strong magic, and had already been sent off for training with the House of Flowers or the House of Platinum by the time my turn came to be chosen. They thought I'd be better off with languages and diplomacy."

"That wasn't what you wanted?" Dio could understand that, at least — the disappointment of not getting to do what you most hoped for.

Nimue sighed, her gaze fixed on the roiling, deep emerald water as the river barge made its slow and steady way forward. "I asked to go to the House of Steel and become a knight like my father. Of all the academies, that was the one I longed to join. But I was too short at twelve when they pick the pages. Then I thought, maybe something else physical. In the House of Madrigal I could have learned the bardic arts, dance... I love to be outside, and the House of Pegasus would at least let me ride more often, perhaps learn to specialise in a sport. But neither of them wanted me either. I was never able to prove I was particularly good at anything I liked. The House of Velvet is where they put all the imperial children who don't show a particular excellence at *anything*."

"Seems the wrong way around," said Dio. "Wouldn't they want to pick the best for that sort of thing?" Diplomacy and languages... for someone like him, who had been obsessing for so long about joining the gladii, that sounded a lot like spycraft. Specialised work.

"I suppose it's the default skill required for a royal," said Nimue wistfully. "Helps us to survive a dull marriage in a foreign court, which is where most of us are destined to be sent."

Something suddenly occurred to Dio. "Is that why you're going to Phoenix Burning? To be married off?" She seemed awfully young for that — he had several younger cousins, and the aunties would have words to say if any of them came home with a spouse before the age of twenty, let alone got themselves or someone else pregnant.

Nimue laughed a little. At least he'd cheered her up.

The talentless and mediocre had to stick together. "It's not my wedding," she said. "Mother's the one on the trading block. She was my age when she had me — I suppose they think she's good for another round of heirs in a new country."

Oh, of course. Dio had forgotten what Calyx said, at the Hanging Market — that she had a betrothed who had determined how she would travel down the river, without any official guards. Strange there had been no gossip at the Blooming Cup about an impending marriage in the Divine King's household. Royal deaths and royal weddings were the most popular topics of gossip among Dio's aunties, when they weren't passing secrets about female magic. At least he'd have something good to share with them all when this was over.

"Does the Divine King know your mother is magical?" Dio asked thoughtfully.

Perhaps his majesty was looking to add a new round of heirs of his own. There hadn't been a queen in Phoenix Burning for many years. Surely all of the mysterious deaths would scare off most royal houses looking to make a good alliance.

"I think that's her main selling point," said Nimue. She leaned over the bow, hand outstretched to the water. "*Why* is it so green?"

"I told you, magic," said Dio. "Wait, don't touch the water!"

She was too high up, of course, to be able to reach it... but this was the River Divine.

Nimue flexed her hand thoughtfully, and the water beneath the bow jumped up to meet her. Green fingers interlocked with hers...

"Oh," said the girl, breathing faster, but not looking distressed. "That's more than I..."

Pain hit Dio in the gut. He bent over, gasping. Across the deck, he saw everyone reacting — Valeria and Ikaros, holding on to each other to stay upright. The sailors, the captain... they all looked to be in terrible pain.

For a moment, Dio saw bright threads connecting them all, glowing with golden magic, tangled together. Every thread led to the cabin, of course. To Calyx. This was the binding spell.

Only Nimue was free of it, and she had her own magical business going on. A ball of green water engulfed her hand, and she was smiling, laughing, playing with it as if she had no idea of the danger...

The door of the cabin slammed open. Calyx stepped out, looking pale and shaky. Her skin was greyish beneath her bright silk robes. Had she slept at all since her mysterious visit to that temple?

"What is this?" she screamed. Every thread connecting her to nearly everyone on the barge turned emerald green instead of gold.

Dio blinked, and then he could not see the threads at all. But Calyx herself, *Calyx* was green.

She staggered a step or two, practically into Ikaros' arms. Of course he was there to catch her. For someone who claimed to resent the bond so much, he was quick to set himself up as Calyx's most personal bodyguard.

Calyx opened her mouth and something dark and green convulsed up out of her, long strands like seaweed. Ikaros stepped aside as she coughed it all up on the deck.

"Look," cried Nimue with a squeal. She, at least, was having a marvellous time.

Dio looked. The green water was no longer a ball

surrounding her hand. It engulfed her entirely, a thin shimmer of emerald covering every inch of her skin, her clothes, her head. Behind her it spun out, creating the shape of bones and tendons and feathers...

Nimue had bright green wings, formed from the water of the river.

Flying after all, Dio thought wildly.

The captain leaned out from the glass-walled wheelhouse, shouting something about the Eye of the Basilisk. When Dio turned back, he saw the huge column of basalt bearing down on them, closer and closer. The barge was heading directly for it.

Nimue spread her wings wide, and leaped overboard. Dio threw himself at her, reaching... but as his hands brushed the glowing feathers, he was overwhelmed by a searing sensation of bright, bright pain.

It was dark when Dio awoke. He lay on the deck, feeling the gentle lap-lap of the water nearby. The decking was damp underneath him. It was dark, too dark to see anything properly. His head felt fuzzy. "What happened?"

"You got a little close to the river," said a low, male voice. Familiar, but Dio wasn't sure why. His whole body felt on high alert. "Don't worry. Once they steer past the Basilisk, all will be well."

"Have they not done that yet?" Dio tried to push himself up on his elbows, but a firm hand shoved him on the chest, pressing him back to the deck.

"Hush," said the voice.

"Ikaros?"

"No." The voice sounded amused, now. "My name is Aodhan."

"Have we met?"

"Briefly."

Dio thought now of the man with long braids and pale skin, the one he met briefly at the night lock. "You're the Bow," he breathed. *The fourth assassin*. "Why is it so dark?"

Something soft brushed his forehead, like a kiss. The sensation went straight to his cock. Embarrassing to get hard from such brief physical contact but considering that Dio had spent the last several days figuring out that his type was 'hot assassin,' it was perhaps understandable.

"Sleep it off, Dio," said the voice, still sounding amused. "You're not in any danger."

He lowered himself to the deck again, feeling the reassuring sensation of planks beneath him. "Don't assassinate Calyx," he mumbled. "She's not hurting anyone. Got a wedding to go to."

"I know all about that," said the other man, his voice dangerously close to Dio's ear. "Ssh. Here we go. Nearly through the troubled waters."

The barge bucked a little, rocked beneath them.

Dio reached out. Tor a moment, in the darkness, he found a hand to hold on to. "Aodhan," he begged. "Don't kill anyone."

There was a laugh, a deep and attractive sound. "No promises," said the man in the darkness.

10. Through the Whispers

There were many reasons to hate travelling on the River Divine, as far as Ikaros was concerned. The Eye of the Basilisk was high on his list. He'd never run the Basilisk with powerful mages on board before... and it did not improve the experience.

Calyx was still recovering from the magical surges, which had screwed with the pain potion she was still taking, after her visit to the Temple of Many Knives. For a few moments, there, when the raw magic of the Basilisk overwhelmed her, it had felt to Ikaros as if those threads tying the crew and priests to her service might shake the whole ship apart. She'd calmed it down in the end, settled the ship without too much damage, but it took a lot out of her.

As for the daughter...

Nimue was quiet, the little imp, shaken after her antics almost killed them all. She hadn't gone over the side, at least, despite the river's best attempts to take her. Dio got the credit for that.

Dio, who was still unconscious, hours after the drama at the Eye of the Basilisk. The young man was laid out in the bed that the four prisoners still shared, though rarely all at the same time.

Nimue, frightened and guilty and simultaneously avoiding her mother, sat at Dio's bedside, waiting for him to wake up. One of the sailors must have brought her in the wicker chair from wherever it was in this crate they stored furniture for fancy ladies.

Ikaros was not hovering at Dio's bedside, but he had spent most of the day in this bloody cabin regardless, idly keeping an eye on matters. In case anyone grew wings again, or anything similarly absurd.

Sometime before the light of the day faded outside, the captain of the vessel came to speak to him. Ikaros was damned if he knew why he was being treated as the leader of this expedition while Calyx was asleep in her own cabin, but somehow this had been decided over his head and behind his back.

"If we keep going, we'll be at the Whispers by dusk," reported the captain.

Ikaros gave him a pained expression. He had lived more than fifty years in this god-touched country without bothering to learn most of the secrets of this river. He didn't remember anything in particular about the Whispers. Forest on both sides, he knew that much. Weeping willows all the way. Quiet enough, last time he'd come through.

"And that means?" he asked, rather than guessing what the problem might be.

"No night lock on this side," said the captain. "Sailing through the Whispers overnight is not unusual. The marsh grass is so thin that no one gets through this section at speed —"

"So we might as well be sleeping while we go," Ikaros completed.

"Exactly, sir. But it's your decision. We can anchor and wait until morning if you don't mind further delays."

It should be Calyx's decision, but Ikaros was not going to wake her up now. Apart from anything else, he was still unable to ask her a direct question.

No, he was going to make the call on her behalf. Worst of all, the magic compulsion was sunk so deep in him now that he actually wanted to do a good job.

"What aren't you telling me?" he asked. The last thing they needed tonight was more surprises.

"The Whispers can be busy," the captain said reluctantly.

"With ships?"

A long pause. No, he didn't mean ships.

Ikaros dredged up what memories of river tales he had reluctantly picked up over the years. There were ballads about the Whispers, weren't there? Sappy ones, by the handful. "Nereids? Naiads?" He never could remember the difference between them.

"Both, sir," said the captain. "The Whispers is where the fresh water meets sea water. Things can get a bit interesting."

"Brilliant," Ikaros groaned. "Go on, then. Best we do this when most of your men are asleep in their hammocks."

"My thoughts exactly," agreed the captain, and made his way out.

"He didn't ask my opinion," Nimue said in a small voice, from where she was tucked into the only chair in the cabin.

"Did you want to make the decision?" Ikaros asked her. He refrained from calling her 'child,' but thought it very loudly.

"Not especially," she muttered.

"Well, then."

The two of them both looked at Dio. By all appearance, he was sleeping peacefully. Ikaros had tried all manner of methods to wake him, including some he was not proud of... and still, the young man slept.

"Do you think he'll die?" Nimue asked.

"Not of this," said Ikaros. He wasn't trying to be kind; he felt certain. "Believe me, Dio Taurus is capable of surviving far more risky scrapes than accidentally grabbing hold of a river-infused baby mage with more power than she knows how to handle."

Nimue huffed quietly.

Ikaros could only hope he had offended her enough to shut her up for a while.

"He's marked by death," she said, a few moments later.

The word *death* reverberated through his skin; most people knew better than to say it aloud in the presence of a priest of the Black Raven. It wasn't that they were in denial about what they did, or what their god represented. It was more that the concept was too large, too sacred and significant to be contained in such a weak and unimportant thing as a word.

(Calyx said it deliberately, all the time, trying to get under his skin. He didn't like to think about that too closely.)

"Dio doesn't have a mark," Ikaros said shortly. "Except the one your mother put on him. Some people are born unmarked." He had done his research on the young man, as much as he could, before securing that room at the teahouse. As the good-looking nephew of the proprietor, Dio had been subject to much speculation and gossip among the kitchen-hands, maids and even some of the regular customers. A casual bed partner or two had offered surprisingly enthusiastic testimony.

"Not Dio," said Nimue. "The captain. His sleeves were rolled up, and I saw the scythe-knife on his forearm. It's lighter than the one on your hand."

Ikaros hadn't even noticed. No wonder the man treated him and the others with such deference. "He's not one of us. Not a priest."

"I didn't imagine so. What does it mean?"

He sighed. Had her mother given her no preparation for moving to a new country with its customs and traditions? "What do you know of our gods?"

"You have five of the sky," Nimue recited as if she had learned this, at least, from a book that knew what it was talking about. "The Divine King is sixth. The others are long lost, no longer worshipped. Priests are marked from birth..."

"No," Ikaros interrupted. "Nine-tenths of our population are marked from birth. The gods choose their favourites early. Most people go about their lives, knowing which god liked them best, and no more than that. When it comes to priests and mystics and knights... we *choose* to offer a higher service to the god that chose us. A knowing choice."

"So, the captain was chosen by the Black Raven," Nimue said quietly. "But he did not choose to become a priest?"

"Few receive the sacred calling. Our captain would pay the tithes to the Raven, as well as the Divine King. If he felt the need to wish for healing, or creativity, or martial skill, or fertility, he might leave offerings at another god's temple, too. We are all free to choose."

Choice in service was a sacred tenet. It meant everything to Ikaros.

Nimue tilted her head. "That's why you're so angry at my mother," she said softly. "She took your service without giving you a choice."

"One of the reasons," he said gruffly.

Dio moaned gently. "Don't kill anyone," he murmured.

Ikaros was not willing to let anyone, even this strange wide-eyed child, know how relieved he was that the lad was waking up. "No promises," he said abruptly, leaning over the bed.

Nimue laughed, and then looked horrified at herself. "That's not funny."

Ikaros raised his eyebrows. "It's a bit funny."

Calyx awoke to a darkened cabin. Once again, her daughter was nowhere to be seen, though it was clearly night. Where on earth had she gone now?

She had to do better about protecting Nimue. When she thought of what might have happened when those green waters at the Basilisk rose up and awoke her daughter's magic...

It had been a shock. Calyx had never considered that Nimue's latent magic was anything to be concerned about. If it was significant, then Nimue would have been whisked away from her at a young age to train as a Petal, or headhunted by the House of Platinum to become one of their Sages.

It had been a relief when Nimue was designated

diplomat and scholar for her education; now, Calyx wondered if she should have been paying closer attention. The power she felt emanating from the edifice named the Basilisk had recognised something in Nimue, even as it tore through all of Calyx's magical defences.

(In that moment it had been all she could do to hold on to her bonds; for a moment she had truly thought all those threads about to snap, and it would be a disaster now to lose the compulsion that held this whole crew and her prisoners in her service.)

She was paying for all of her recent magic — the last of the pain relief potion had dissolved into dust when they passed through the Eye of the Basilisk, leaving the recent attentions of the knight-surgeons to ache without remedy.

This river and its secrets. It was astonishing that every Petal of the Imperium had not left their land in droves to sail up and down these waters, drinking every drop of unique and unusual magic.

Calyx pulled a light teal robe around her, and stepped out of her cabin. She could hear what sounded like gentle music nearby...

The boat was bobbing gently on the water, untethered, edging forward at a glacial pace. The darkened shapes of trees crowded in from all sides, susurrating with an eerie whisper that slithered inside the ears. Calyx could see that now-familiar purple glow in the water of night-blooms, bright and flowering against the darkness.

As she rounded the deck, she found her people.

Nimue stood at the bow, leaning casually against the railing. It was all Calyx could do not to run after her, snatch her to safety. But her daughter was smiling.

(Nimue had been smiling, too, when she drew that

magic from the water and played with it. Calyx could not recall seeing her so delighted since this voyage began.)

Valeria sat balanced on the railing itself, with Mardi standing by to make sure she didn't fall forward into the river. Dio was there too, looking exhausted but very much awake. A few of the younger sailors were clustered in a group, pointing and staring into the water. Ikaros stood guard over them all.

There was laughter from the river around them, beneath them. Tinkling otherworldly voices. As Calyx reached the edge of the barge, she saw spindly limbs, silvery hair. Creatures of the River Divine gambolled together in what was either a mock-battle or the first act of an operatic orgy.

They wore no clothes, of course, these figures of marsh mud and greenery, these living souls of clear and grey waters. Breasts bounced everywhere; impossibly rippling muscles glowed and flexed. Even their feet were perfectly shaped.

The magic of these nymphs tasted happy, and rich. When Calyx breathed in, she could feel how powerful they were, and how little they cared about power.

Mardi was singing, her voice rich and deep. A song of salt-water meeting fresh, of creatures called naiads and nereids. Of hair and hands and water play. It was a pretty song. Nimue looked entranced by it; by them all.

I'm losing her to this river, Calyx thought, and wondered where that thought came from.

Ikaros saw Calyx first and made a few stiff steps in her direction. "You can sleep more, if you wish," he informed her gravely. "I've got this."

Calyx was not going to fool herself that this man had fully accepted the bond she laid upon him. But it was stronger in him now than when she first sent out her terrified, emergency burst of magic to capture them all. Ikaros felt like hers.

The compulsion had taken him deeper, over the last day or so. When she looked at him, all she saw — all she *felt* from the golden threads of magic tangling them together — was a capable pair of hands. A man to whom she could entrust her daughter's safety. Despite his occasional furious glances, and his relentless sarcasm.

"I'll stay up a little longer," Calyx said, though she did feel shaky on her feet. "I might never see a sight like this again."

Ikaros nodded abruptly, turning back to the others.

The *Silken Hare* swept on, slowly through the night. The trees around them continued to whisper, and the naked nereids and naiads hurled salt and fresh water at each other with gentle screeches of delight.

Truly, the River Divine was full of wonders. Calyx was beginning to wish this journey would go on forever. There was nothing nearly so marvellous waiting for her when they reached their destination.

She did not want to trouble her thoughts with plans for Phoenix Burning. For now, there was only the river.

11. At the Reticent Wombat

"A tavern," repeated Calyx. She was seated in her cabin — which did have chairs, at least, unlike the one shared by the assassins where the only furniture was the bed.

She had Nimue on one side of her and Mardi Morency — who had been giving an impromptu embroidery lesson — on the other.

Ikaros stood before her, waiting for a response to his request, far more deferential than usual. Calyx felt a flutter of memory of herself standing before her Mistress of the Academie, asking for a day pass.

Nimue clapped. "I've never been to a tavern."

"You're not going," Ikaros snapped, in unison with Calyx, as if they were parents who finally agreed on something. Mardi snorted with laughter at them both.

Nimue pouted. "I want to drink ale and eat onion dumplings," she muttered.

"What have you been reading?" Calyx asked. "No, never mind." She turned back to Ikaros. "Any particular reason for this sudden interest in taverns?"

He twitched a little, so she knew there was something he wasn't telling her. "I want to sift for rumours. We still don't know who marked you, and whether they have more attacks planned. Obviously, you can stay on the boat in safety..."

"So kind," Calyx murmured.

His eyes flashed darker. "Unless there's more you should have told us already. I cannot protect you if I'm not prepared." It was not a question; could not be a question. Calyx had used her magic to prevent him from doing that. Somehow, with that deadpan delivery of his, he had managed to let her know exactly what he wanted to ask, and could not.

Calyx had no intention of indulging his curiosity. She was the one who asked the questions around here. "How do I know you won't try to flee like you did at the Hanging Market?" she inquired.

"I won't," Ikaros said. "I know better now. Let me protect you."

There was no gleam of rebellion about him; no spark of resistance. He was as sullen as ever, but entirely brought to heel.

Calyx pressed down any guilt she felt about that. "I will come with you."

Ikaros looked irritated. "Then one of the others will have to join us. A pair of eyes to watch out for crossbow bolts while I'm asking questions."

"I quite fancy an onion dumpling," Mardi spoke up.

"It's decided," said Calyx, smiling sweetly.

Ikaros did not smile back.

Dio felt entirely recovered from what happened at the Eye of the Basilisk. Everyone else still treated him like a sickly child, only allowing him light duties. In this case: keeping Nimue company while she sulked about not being allowed to go ashore to the Reticent Wombat, a tavern at Cask and Barrels, a small township built out directly on to the water. In other words: babysitting.

The buildings of Cask and Barrels were all made of wood, oiled to be waterproof, curved and rounded everywhere that most buildings would have corners. The overall effect was that the entire township was a cluster of barrels perched on stilts - hence the name.

Naturally, the place was well known for its alehouses.

Valeria disappeared the moment they docked, claiming there was a haberdashery with hair ribbons that had to be seen to be believed, though literally everyone saw her command use of a small skiff and head directly to the rounded doorway of the local weapon-smith.

"She'll be less irritable after a few hours playing with Chalcedonian steel," said Ikaros with a shrug. Clearly his experience at the Hanging Market had taught him — and Calyx — that true escape was not possible.

After Ikaros, Calyx and Mardi headed to the Reticent Wombat by way of another skiff, Dio found himself lost in idle thought. He wondered if his own passive acceptance of Calyx's compulsion charm would make it easier for him to break it. To test his theory, he put some time into imagining how he might sneak away from the *Silken Hare*. No matter how hard he thought it, he couldn't make himself throw up flowers or even feel the magic twitch in reproach.

Which was all well and good, but he also couldn't actually bring himself to put his escape plan into practice. Apparently, the magic knew him better than he did.

It began to rain, an especially slow and droopy rain that didn't seem worth the effort it would take to take shelter. If anything, the air grew warmer for the added wetness

"I could disguise myself," grumbled Nimue, flopping down on the deck beside him. "All I want to do is get a look at a real tavern. See a few locals. Taste something that wasn't boiled in the same pot as all our other meals."

Dio eyed her linen cap and soft, expensive robes. "What kind of disguise? Sew on ears and a tail? Some sort of giant red nose?"

She rolled her eyes at him. "I could borrow clothes from one of the crew."

"You know they only wash their gear every few months," he warned.

Nimue looked briefly disgusted, and then annoyed, and then nodded slowly as if this explained quite a few things about living conditions on board ship.

"DIO TAURUS!" The voice rang out across the damp decking, loud and female and carrying a familiar air of 'you are in so much trouble, young man,' which instantly flung Dio back to his childhood.

"Hello, Auntie Shanith," he mumbled, scrambling to his feet and tidying his shirt as a short woman in a flowery headscarf came marching over the oily dock, a small and sticky child towed in her wake.

"What are you doing down there?" demanded his aunt.

"I'm working," he protested. Which was true, actually,

not a convenient excuse, though there had been little discussion of recompense with his new employer.

Auntie Shanith's golden-brown face broke into a wide smile. "Good to know. You couldn't pop in to see me?"

"I didn't know you were here," Dio protested. Last he had heard, Shanith and her three daughters (the sticky imp had to belong to one of his cousins but Dio couldn't dredge up a name for the life of him) were living in Lark's Glebe in the mountains to the West.

"I wrote to Dapheen last month! We had to move to town for Alun's work — he's a tailor, you know."

Dio had no idea who Alun was. One of Shanith's sons-in-law, he had to assume. "I haven't been staying with Dapheen for a while now. I've been up at the teahouse with Auntie Beto."

"Oh, send Beto my love!" Auntie Shanith squawked. "And who's this lovely young lady?" She gazed thoughtfully at Nimue with what could only be described as 'niece-in-law eyes.' The aunties disapproved of early marriages, especially when the youngsters were not yet set up in a proper profession, but they liked to plan ahead. And besides, Dio was starting to edge out of the age group of 'don't you get yourself tied down too young, fellow-me-lad" and into "Isn't it about time you settled down, boy?" territory.

"Dio's my bodyguard," piped up Nimue.

"Is he now?" squealed Auntie Shanith. "Aren't you coming up in the world, duck?"

The rain was getting more determined. Dio used his hand to keep it from dripping into his eyes. He saw Nimue shiver a little beside him, though he couldn't see how she could possibly be cold. "I'm working on it," he promised her. "You should get on out of the rain, Auntie Shanith. I'll write soon, now I know where to direct it."

"You do that," she said, pointing at him. "We have so much to catch up on. Lessie's having twins!"

Dio could swear he had never met a Lessie in his life.

Ikaros hated having a retinue. He had hoped to check in with Janna, ask a few useful questions and get out again. He had a certain way he liked to do these things: hovering at the edges of other people's lives, one eye on the door.

Every other business in Cask and Barrels was a purveyor of beer, whiskey, wine, or fried fish on sticks. They also had, ironically, the second best barrel-maker in the country.

The Reticent Wombat was the most respected tavern hereabouts, and not only because it stuck out so far across the river that it was often the first port of call by default. The food was made of actual food, the beer came from decent breweries, and the prices were fair. If it wasn't built on stilts over the River Divine, Ikaros might well have made this place his local. Instead, it was one more location he could never entirely trust.

He hadn't been here in years, so he didn't recognise the muscle lurking at the door, and only recalled a few of the regulars. It made his skin itch, that lack of familiarity.

With Mardi and Calyx in tow, there would be no hovering in the shadows for him. They had to sit at a table, food and drink had to be ordered, and... well, it was more of a production than he usually preferred.

Janna wasn't at the bar, but Ikaros caught Emberley's eye easily enough, and waited for her to serve him.

(She took her time, which served him right.)

Emberley was a solid girl, with good shoulders for shifting barrels. Her hair was lighter than her mother's, braided back in a queue like she was a soldier going to war. She was taller, of course. Everyone was taller than Janna.

"Look at you, old man," Emberley drawled as she pulled him a pint. "Slumming it on the river with the rest of us. Is everywhere else on fire?"

"Charming as ever, Emb," Ikaros said, putting in an order for drinks for Mardi and Calyx too. As an afterthought, he requested onion dumplings, just so Calyx could tell her daughter she'd had the full tavern experience. "You're not old enough to be serving drinks."

Emberley's eyebrows went up. "Bet you half a sparrow?"

He let that slide; he had no actual idea how old she was. If pushed to guess he would have said fourteen at most.

"Where's your mother?" he tried.

"Ladies' luncheon at the Bell."

"She's cheating on you with another tavern?"

Emb rolled her eyes. "Half-price fruity drinks and a handsome bard plucking all the right strings. We can't compete with that around here." She waved a hand, indicating the sparse crowd. There were no female customers except the ones Ikaros had brought in with him.

Ikaros frowned for a moment, wondering if he had time to nip across town to the Blue and Bell, which had the benefit of being on land, at least. This visit was a bust if he couldn't speak to Janna.

Emb sighed at him, levering onion dumplings off her griddle and filling a basketware platter with more dents in it than the others. "Or you could ask me what you want?"

"Gossip," he admitted.

"Fresh out." She shoved the basket at him. "Hey, speaking of gossip..."

"No."

"Is it true you and Valeria finally called it quits?"

"Will you win money?"

"If you tell me it's true, I'll throw a fucking party."

"Behave," he said sternly.

"I'll start when you do, old man."

Emberley certainly *sounded* old enough to sling drinks, and her movements behind the bar made it clear she'd been doing this job a long time. He'd lost track again. It was so easy to do.

Calyx observed Ikaros with interest as he bantered with the girl at the bar. There was something about his body language she couldn't quite make sense of.

Mardi, meanwhile, was knitting a mass of soft purple yarn into an object that couldn't possibly be expected to end up a wearable garment, least of all for a baby. For someone whose embroidery was worthy of a palace harem, she did not have the talent for these thicker, wooden needles.

The priest they called the Needle took her duty seriously. Mardi might have a lap full of lopsided knitting, but her eyes took in every vulnerable spot, lingering on windows and doorways in turn, looking over each of the customers, then back to the escape routes. Her gaze never dropped to her lap at all — which might go something towards explaining how she had created such a tangle.

"People like to see pregnant women knitting," Mardi explained, though Calyx had not asked. "It makes us appear less homicidal, which is interesting because it definitely has the opposite effect on our inner thoughts."

"And the needles can be a weapon in a pinch?"

Mardi gave her an extremely dry look. "Anything can be a weapon in a pinch."

Ikaros returned to them with drinks and a basket of pale, glossy crescents with crusted grill marks.

"You and the bartender had a great deal to say to each other," Calyx observed.

Ikaros paused deliberately, as if checking how many seconds he could resist what she wanted of him; she hadn't asked him a deliberate question, after all, but her intent was clear. "She's my granddaughter," he admitted.

"Oh, is that Emberley?" exclaimed Mardi, and waved across the tavern. "She looks so grown up."

"Tell me about it," muttered Ikaros.

"*Granddaughter*," said Calyx, staring at him. She had assumed he younger than her — despite his haunted eyes and the old-fashioned close-cropped beard, she would never have taken him for older than thirty at most.

"I started young," said Ikaros.

"*I* started young," Calyx said sharply. She'd been fifteen when she married, sixteen when she gave birth; too young for it all. "How can you have a *granddaughter* Nimue's age?"

Ikaros gave her a wolfish smile, and managed not to provide a clear answer for that. "Emb's not as useful for the more shadowy sources of gossip as her mother, but we don't have time to hang around and wait for Janna to get back. Unless you're willing to let me run across town." Not a question.

"No," Calyx said immediately. "We shouldn't move too far from the barge."

"I agree."

"So this was a waste of time?"

Ikaros shrugged and bit into one of the dumplings. The pungent smell of sweet onions hit the air. "Not if you're hungry."

"Ikaros," she pressed. "Exactly how old are you?"

He looked bored with the topic, then paused and thought about it, not answering.

"You've forgotten again," accused Mardi.

"I haven't." He frowned. "I was going to say fifty-ish."

"Ha!" Mardi mocked. "You left the 'ish' in the dust nearly a decade ago. You were past forty when *that* one was born." She indicated the girl behind the bar. "See, this is why I have to retire. I don't want to glance up one day and find I misplaced a few decades, and my child's whole life-span with it."

That, for some reason that Calyx could not guess at, inspired a particularly flat stare from Ikaros, and an instantly apologetic glance in response from Mardi.

"Go on, then," he challenged her. "How old am I?"

One moment Ikaros was bantering with Mardi, and the next... the smell of shadows overwhelmed the sticky onion dumplings and other tavern scents.

The Black Raven's priests always knew when their god and his works were near. A shivery sense of *presence* that someone was about to meet their end, of natural causes or otherwise.

Time slowed. Ikaros tried to look everywhere at once, scraping back his chair.

He saw Mardi moving in his periphery, tense and professional. They spun around at the same time, back to back while still balanced on their rickety stools.

Calyx had barely begun to notice their reaction. She sat like a daisy in the centre of what was about to be a thunderstorm.

There were three mystics by the fire, grey-clad and daubed in fertility charms. Wispy beards and barely a pectoral muscle between them; Ikaros had already written them off as no threat.

A cluster of sailors gathered by the bar, joking and drinking.

An old man at another table, rolling dice between finger and thumb.

At the high window, a shadow...

Ikaros reached out and closed his hand around the shaft of an arrow shot from above. He caught it; snatched it out of the air before it could hit its mark. Splinters and fletching grazed his skin in a burst of burning pain.

Someone screamed — not Mardi or Calyx, not Emb. One of the mystics, perhaps.

The shadow was gone.

"You've got this?" Ikaros demanded of Mardi, already on his feet.

She had a knife in her hand, and moved behind Calyx, as close as she could be. "Of course. Go!"

Ikaros ran.

12. Across Cask and Barrels

The boardwalks of the township were greasy and uneven, slick with warm rain, a bad combination all around for running. Ikaros felt his boots skid against the boards as he pursued the attacker — *assassin*. Too many twists and turns around these rounded, barrel-shaped buildings, too many gaps between them, rope bridges and sagging, missing planks.

He kept upright, kept running. Here and there he saw his target ahead of him — an inch of black cloak whipping around one building or another.

"Kaldoran!" he yelled at one point, because there was no denying he knew exactly who had shot that arrow at Calyx. "For fuck's sake."

The Bow ran; the Hand pursued him. One priest of the Black Raven against another. (But the Black Raven wasn't here, was he? Their god had remained distinctly quiet over the last few days.)

The paths ahead straightened; Ikaros saw the black cloaked figure clearly now, covering a long line of rope bridge between this half of town and the buildings on land.

A gaggle of laughing women, all loose-limbed and drunk in the middle of the day, were crossing the bridge the other way.

One of the women was less than half the height of the others, stocky in her miniature proportions, her hair a dark tangle pinned on top of her head. Ikaros' eyes met hers for a moment, just as the assassin pushed past the women…

"Oi!" the shortest woman yelled, and took the Bow out at the knees with a slamming sideways punch.

The Bow fell on the slippery rope bridge, shaking it wildly. The women cackled, hanging on to the sides like the locals they were, unbothered by the drama or the immediate peril.

By the time Ikaros reached them, the tiny woman had a boot on the throat of the assassin, who was staring wild-eyed up at her. (He could have killed her, of course, in twelve different ways, but their god looked askance at the random deaths of civilians.)

"Hello, Ikaros," giggled one of the taller women, elbowing her friends. The others cat-called him cheerfully, with whistles and applause.

"Ladies," he greeted them in return.

Janna, her boot still clamped on the throat of the Bow, rolled her eyes. "Don't flirt with my friends, Da."

"Right back at you, my heart." Ikaros stood over his fallen colleague, and motioned Janna to step back out of the way. "Reynard. It's been a while."

Reynard Kaldoran, Bow of the Black Raven, snarled at him. He was a good-looking man — the Raven liked his servants attractive for no reason Ikaros could fathom — with shoulder-length black hair and a flowing moustache that he thought made him look dashing. "Working for a mark," Reynard said between gritted teeth. "Always knew you were a disloyal prick, Swift."

That was wounding. "Extenuating circumstances," Ikaros replied. "I don't recommend you try for her again."

"I serve the Raven."

"We all serve the Raven," Ikaros said defensively. A wave of sensation washed over him — not quite revulsion, but a shudder of something. Calyx's bond making its feelings known? His god finally deciding he had something to say? In either case, it came to nothing.

"Really," said Reynard. There was blood at the corner of his mouth — he must have bitten his tongue when Janna took him down. He sneered up at Ikaros. "Looks like something else to me."

"Chuck him off the bridge," advised one of Janna's friends.

"Waste of a hot man," whined another. "Let me have him."

Ikaros wrinkled his nose. "Have you been on the eucalyptus rum, Teanne?"

"Boo, hiss," said Peraya, one of the ladies. Ikaros had known her since she was twelve; she'd since had three kids and countless husbands. "Don't shame us, Ikaros. I'm getting married!"

"Again?" said Ikaros mildly.

"We could," said Janna as if she had been giving the matter a great deal of thought. "Chuck him off the bridge. Not my Da, though I can't say he doesn't deserve it sometimes. This bloke."

Inside Ikaros' chest, Calyx's bond flared with heat, approving the suggestion. The smaller, older bond that tied him to his god shivered at a distance.

The Black Raven disapproved, did he? Nice to know he still had skin in the game.

"Nah," Ikaros said finally. "Let's just rob him."

"Don't you fucking dare!" roared the Bow, struggling again.

The ladies closed in, delighted.

"I volunteer to pat him down for weapons," said Paraya.

"Not until you've had about three cups of coffee," said Ikaros, fending her off.

"Coffee back at Janna's!" hooted one of the others.

"Coffee with rum, ladies," added another.

They all tottered off across the bridge. Janna remained, watching with an impassive expression as Ikaros stripped Reynard Kaldoran of all weapons and coin, including the devilishly lightweight bow that fitted neatly to his back.

After a moment's thought, Ikaros tied the man's wrists to the rope bridge, which should slow him down long enough for them to get back to the *Silken Hare* unscathed.

"Do you know who hired you to take out the Petal?" he asked, almost conversationally.

"Don't you?" snapped Reynard.

Ikaros leaned in. "If you haven't started asking questions yet, my dear, you really should. I wouldn't be surprised if you'd deliberately missed our appointment at the Blooming Cup because you knew something was wrong about this job. You always love sneaking around like that. Setting traps. Knowing more than you should."

"I'm not going to tell you anything," said the other man.

"Of course not. That would be breaking the rules, just as knowing who hired us is breaking the rules. But think about how it happened that four of us were given the same mark. Is that normal temple business? Or something questionable?"

"You're lying," the Bow snapped.

"Am I? Does that sound like me?"

"The Black Raven would not do that to us," said the Bow sourly.

"Yes," agreed Ikaros. "I've been wondering about that for days. Haven't you?"

Reynard Kaldoran did not speak again. His glare said it all.

"Sorry for interrupting your girls' day out," Ikaros said lightly as he strolled back towards the Reticent Wombat. This was the longest he had spent time in Janna's company in years. Five or six years, perhaps, judging by how Emberley had grown.

They made an odd sort of pairing, he assumed, if anyone saw them at a distance — his daughter 's head only came up to his hip, though she never struggled to match his stride.

If anyone noticed them walking across Cask and Barrels on this grey, drizzly afternoon, they'd probably be more concerned with all the weapons hanging off Ikaros; Reynard had not travelled light.

"Don't worry about it," said Janna. "It's Paraya. There will be another wedding along in a minute. How are you doing?" she asked, nudging him as they walked

"Me? I'm fine?"

"Hmm," she said, an annoying habit she had picked up

from her Ma — saying nothing and everything at the same time.

"How are things with the tavern? And Emb."

"You don't care about all that," Janna said dismissively.

"I don't not care about it," Ikaros said, a little wounded.

She tipped her head back with a scornful expression. Oh, yes. That was like her Ma, too. Days like this, he wished Layla was still around to defend him against his daughter's wrath. Then again, they'd always been a dab hand at ganging up on him.

Valeria stood waiting outside the tavern, casually holding a battle-axe that came up to her shoulder. As well as her new toy, she'd acquired a fresh featherbrace from somewhere local, so she looked like a priest again: her body sheathed in the fitted, embroidered black coat like it was a second skin. Swishy larkflax trousers and shirt underneath the sharp tailoring. Pointed boots that would make a man cry when she (inevitably) walked all over him. Her hair had been rebraided too, by a professional. She'd poured quite a bit of money into this small town on this show of businesslike glamour.

"Oh, look, it's the evil stepmother," said Janna. "And here I'd heard you two were on the outs. Emb owes me a pair of crows."

"Behave," Ikaros sighed.

Valeria nodded as they approached. "Mardi took Calyx back to the barge," she informed Ikaros. Then she glanced down her nose and said: "Janna," in a begrudging sort of greeting.

"I'd hug you, Val," said Janna. "But I wouldn't want a hint of affection to make you disappear in a puff of smoke." She tilted her head back to look at Ikaros. "Take care of yourself, Da."

"You too," he said, tossing Reynard's purse into her hands. "Buy some coffee for your ladies. All the coffee."

"Cheers to that."

They pressed their knuckles together for a moment, his against hers, and then Janna returned to the tavern, and her life.

Valeria gazed steadily at Ikaros for a moment, then looked away. "Did you finish him?"

"No," Ikaros muttered.

"I don't know how I feel about that."

Neither did Ikaros. Conflict roiled inside him, his loyalties at war with each other. The bond to Calyx would have been deeply satisfied if he'd put a knife between Reynard Kaldoran's ribs. But he liked the man, damn it. They were friendly enough. They'd worked together for years — or rather, side by side, in the same profession.

Bors had loved Reynard almost as much as he loved Mardi. More, some days.

Still, Ikaros wasn't spitting up daisies, so he couldn't have fucked this up too badly. Calyx would have to be satisfied.

"Let's get back to the barge," he said to Valeria. "The sooner this voyage is over, the better."

13. Past the Muses, Near Lake Lamia

"We need to talk about your husband," said Ikaros.

Calyx raised her eyebrows. "Which one?"

"Whichever husband you think most likely to want you dead." He could not ask questions of her, still. This continued to enrage him, in a background sort of way. More enraging still was that he had almost got used to it.

Don't get complacent, Swift, he reminded himself several times a day. *Or you'll end up playing her servant until the end of time.* Surely there had to be some way to be free of it.

Meanwhile, he was stuck playing word games to learn anything useful from her.

They were passing the Muses, a series of tall, stately standing stones overlooking the river, beyond the lip of a low cliff. In his youth, Ikaros had attended festivals at the Muses: gatherings of bards, dancers and artists, not to mention a dizzying array of god-fearing young people ready to experiment with mind-altering substances.

A music festival was a good place to find your mark. No one expected to be assassinated while swaying their hips to an experimental harp trio.

There was no festival happening today, though it was tipping towards the sultrier depths of summer. Soon there would be garlands strung around the stones every other week. For now, the Muses looked grim and lonely, standing guard over the river as the barge moved smoothly past.

"One of my husbands is dead already," said Calyx, who clearly had no appreciation for the significance of the scenery. "And the other is yet to plight his troth in any official capacity. Surely it's traditional to wait for the wedding night before you try to murder your bride."

She had a sense of humour about this. How annoying.

"It would be useful," said Ikaros, his voice about as clipped as he felt. "If you put some thought into who might want you dead before you make your vows. Unless you already..." No, that edged too close to a question. His throat tightened up, not allowing him to proceed.

Her eyes were warm on his. Annoying. Like this was some cute little game. "I signed no proxy marriage contract, if that's what you're asking," said Calyx. "A betrothal contract, yes, but..."

What are the implications of that contract if you die before you reach Phoenix Burning? The question hovered in his head, unable to escape. Frustration scorched across the inside of his mouth.

Her eyes were amused. She was not taking this seriously. It made him want to slap her. To shout at her. To pin her against the wall of the nearest cabin, and...

Calyx leaned into him. Even her breath smelled like flowers, this maddening woman. "Ask your question," she said, and the command settled over him like a gentle cloak.

Permission to speak should be one more humiliation, but instead it came with a rush of relief as Ikaros was released from the magical compulsion to ask no questions of her.

Coming hard and fast behind was the realisation that he wanted to bed her. Desire washed over him, hot and fierce, and he tamped it down. No good would come of that particular impulse.

"Does the Divine Kingdom benefit from you dying *before* the wedding?" he asked in a raspy voice.

Calyx turned away from him, though she was already standing so close that he could reach out, stroke her cheek, pull her into his arms...

No. For all Ikaros knew his attraction to her was another mortifying side effect of the bond she had forced upon them all. No way of knowing that without asking Mardi and Valeria some extremely intimate questions. He would rather wait until the River Divine froze over.

"There's no marriage," Calyx said softly. "If I or my prospective bridegroom die before we make our vows, the dowry is to be returned. The alliances and agreements and trade contracts all melt away. It's as nothing without the wedding taking place."

"But the royal family bid you make your own way to the palace, with no royal guard to keep you safe." Suspicious. Dangerous.

"Yes, I've been thinking about that," she admitted. "I can see why you'd wonder if they were deliberately exposing me to danger. That makes no sense, though. After all those negotiations with the Imperium, they'd have to start from scratch. Why bother?"

Why indeed. What would they have to gain from bringing Calyx here and letting her die halfway down the River Divine?

Nothing was not the answer. Someone had done it. Someone must benefit.

"So," he murmured. "Either the Divine King changed his mind after making the betrothal arrangements… or someone *else* wants to stop him marrying you."

Calyx turned back, tilting her head towards his. "I'm not marrying the Divine King. Did you think I was?"

"Who, then?" Ikaros' throat was dry, and not from finally being able to ask her as many questions as he liked. He refused to believe it was because he had an opinion about this woman's intended.

"The Thirteenth Treasure," said Calyx. "Heir to the kingdom."

The first twelve Treasures, sons to the Divine King, had all died over the last two decades, under circumstances ranging from slightly suspicious through to downright scandalous — though Ikaros knew for a fact that none had been called as sacrifice to the Black Raven.

Natural causes, every single one of them, according to official rulings. And that was far more suspicious than a crossbow in the night, or a blade in the throat.

"Isn't he a child?" Ikaros asked abruptly. Surely, the youngest of the Divine King's children had been born ten minutes ago. A week, at most. He never paid that much attention to royal politics. The last time he'd heard anything about a royal birth was… oh, no, that was actually before Emberley was born. Never mind.

"Older than I was when I was first married," said Calyx, sounding rather put upon. "I'm sure he can't be delighted to be wedded off to an old matron like me, but it's hardly something to hire four assassins over."

"You're not old," said Ikaros absently, trying to work out if her perfume was jasmine, rose, or some other flower he couldn't identify. Whatever it was, he needed to get away from it. His skin was prickling all over with wanting to touch her.

Calyx laughed gently — a horrendously alluring sound — and patted him on the arm like he was some faithful retainer. "So charming," she said with a fond sort of sarcasm. "You'll get on marvellously at the palace, with courtier skills like that. Naturally, you don't think I'm old. You're an antique."

"I think the Thirteenth Treasure hired us to kill Calyx," Ikaros remarked to Mardi and Valeria, later in the day as the *Silken Hare* drew near Lake Lamia.

"Obviously," said Valeria, her voice dripping with scorn.

"Keep up," said Mardi. "We worked that out ages ago. Prince doesn't want to marry a bride old enough to be his mother, can't rebel openly against his father."

"If you weren't so busy making calf-eyes at our new mistress, we would have explained it to you earlier," added Valeria with a smirk.

Ikaros briefly considered murdering them both with his bare hands; decided against it. "Do we tell her?"

"We've spent the last day or so not telling her, and neither of us has bled buttercups out of our ears," said Mardi. "I think we're all right. As long as we plan to kill him at some point. The bond really wants us to do that."

"I may want to kill him independently of the bond," mused Ikaros.

"Oh you do have a crush," said Valeria. "Thought so. Sweet."

"This one has a plan," added Mardi.

"Wonderful," muttered Ikaros. Nothing chilled his bones more than his wife with a plan. "Let me know when you need me to be involved. Wait until the absolutely last minute, if you can. Keep me on my toes."

Both women gave him identically nasty smiles.

"*Way* ahead of you," said Valeria. "As always, my love."

14. Under Sparrowbridge, Round the Sapphire

The crew and passengers of the *Silken Hare* spent an uneventful night moored at a night lock known as 'the Nightingale' which sounded utterly charming if you didn't know that it had once been the Divine Kingdom's most notorious brothel, and the decorative spiked cages hanging from hooks had been used for humans, not birds.

Dio had not been visited in the night, or in his dreams, by his mysterious man in black who might or might not be the Bow. He was trying not to be put out about it.

Nimue fidgeted up and down the barge, getting more nervous as the river drew them inexorably towards their destination.

Dio had heard the assassins speaking about Calyx, and husbands, and general plotting. He tried to stay out of it.

This whole trip had been like a strange dream. When it was over, and they reached Phoenix Burning, he was going to have to put some thought into what came next.

Was he really going to spend his whole life trying and failing to pass the exams to become a gladius? He'd been so sure that it was his future. His destiny. But now...

It was having all this time to think. That was the problem.

"Hold your breath as we go under Sparrowbridge," said Valeria to Calyx, as the *Silken Hare* approached an extraordinary bridge, white and carved with intricate wings and beaks. "There's a legend that this is where mortals can travel deep down to the Otherwater to rescue their lost loves. If you breathe in as you pass under the bridge, one of their souls might latch on to you for the rest of eternity."

"Really?" said Calyx. The superstition did not surprise her, though she was a little startled that Valeria had bothered to warn her.

"No," said Valeria, sounding bored. "Not really."

Ikaros held his breath as the barge floated under Sparrowbridge. He was not a superstitious man. No one could consider themselves superstitious after meeting their god face to face, and pledging to his service.

He hated this river, hated its wild and unpredictable magics.

But he'd been nine years old the first time he was told that you should hold your breath under Sparrowbridge, and it was hard to fight that kind of conditioning.

He caught Mardi's eye as he did so, and noted that she was also, quite discreetly, holding her breath.

They both sputtered with laughter at each other, once they were safely through.

"What is that building?" whispered Nimue, huddling at Dio's side as they rounded the curve in the river where the Sapphire stood resplendent. "It hums with magic," she added.

Dio understood her caution after the business with the Basilisk. "It's a theatre sacred to the gods," he told her.

"But it's huge."

The giant domed palais had a faceted pattern to its blue glass roof, so that it did indeed resemble a giant cut sapphire. It was famed as one of the Wonders of the Divine Kingdom, and had hosted spectacles, festivals and opera for centuries.

"The Divine King tried to have the Sapphire moved to Phoenix Burning for his coronation," Dio told her, playing tourist guide. "He said it was a waste having it all the way out here when it could stand a celebration of his glorious rule."

Nimue looked confused. "But it's sacred to the gods. Is the Divine King so very jealous of them?"

Ikaros, a little way from them both, let out a snort. "In a word," he said dryly. "Yes."

The Empress of the Imperium, Calyx's elder sister Niniane, toured the Divine Kingdom when she was young. At the time, Niniane was one of three heirs — cousins about the same age, expected to prove their worth before the ultimate heir was selected. Niniane had lorded it over her younger siblings for years, that she got to travel to such exotic lands as Morgaunel, and the Orions, and the near-mythical Divine Kingdom.

She had never mentioned the River Divine. Not a single word, which now seemed like an extraordinary omission.

Niniane had, however, talked about the Sapphire: a grand opera house that looked like a sparkling gem the size of a small mountain. She went on and on about the beautiful sculpted trees that surrounded it, the acres of blue and purple flowers that spiralled out from its magnificence. The play of the light against the jewel-like facets.

Here I am, then, Calyx thought as the barge moved slowly past the architectural marvel. *I made it. I'm here. Look at me, Niniane, following in your footsteps.*

If only she could turn around and go straight back home.

Ikaros had often wondered in an idle sort of way what kind of damage could be wrought upon the exquisite beauty of the Sapphire, in all its angled glass facets, with a single crossbow bolt.

Today was not the day to find out.

15. Going Back to Pandemonium

The further south they went, the busier the River Divine became. River traffic was so thick that the *Silken Hare* had to slow to a crawl, barely faster than walking pace.

It was already getting dark, and they had yet to reach the Frisky Foxglove, the tavern that was their intended berth for the night.

Dio found a corner far back on the deck so he could eat his spiced cabbage rice and sweet fried eel in relative peace. There was a wild, jangling tension between his fellow passengers, and he wanted nothing to do with it.

Let Calyx and Ikaros glower resentfully at each other, while Valeria and Mardi sniped under their breath. Let Nimue sulk and sigh.

He wanted no part of their drama.

He was ready for all this to be over so his real life could begin.

He wanted...

(*He wanted the pretty man with dark eyes who apparently had lost all interest in stalking their boat.*)

He wanted some idea of what his future held.

Dio was used to not getting what he wanted. Right now, all he wanted was to eat this tasty eel and rice without being dragged into someone else's shit.

As he lifted a particularly delicious-looking morsel to his mouth, a shadow fell over him.

"Dio Taurus," said Valeria, looming over him like the extraordinarily beautiful edged weapon that she was. "You're coming with me."

Dio chewed, swallowed. Barely tasted. "Where?" He asked. "Also why, and how?"

Why me came to mind, but he didn't voice that particular lament.

She flashed her teeth at him in a vicious smile. "Don't you want adventure in your life?"

"No!" Maybe.

How was answered for Dio before where or why. Valeria had no compunction about stealing a skiff, and even less compunction about making Dio do the rowing.

"How are we able to do this?" he asked her. "Without, you know..." And he mimicked throwing up daffodils.

"I'm doing this for Calyx," Valeria said serenely. "To serve and to protect. She doesn't need to know everything I do as long as it is entirely in her interest."

Dio pulled on the oars. "And that works, does it?"

Valeria's smile looked rather fixed; behind it, her teeth were gritted. "So far. You should try the same."

Dio considered it briefly, then shrugged. "Everything I do is in her interest. I don't need to fake it."

"I'm *not* faking it." She sagged, and took a few deep breaths. "I'm fine. We're fine. This is all about keeping Calyx safe."

"Must be," he agreed cheerfully. "Otherwise we wouldn't have got this far."

There were a few other tiny boats like theirs on the river, more so now that night was falling, mostly loaded with merrymakers moving between larger barges and river-yachts, or heading for better amusements on dry land.

Even if Valeria had her best interests at heart, Calyx would probably be displeased about this. It gave Dio a scratchy feeling in the back of his head, like an orchestra playing ominous music from a long way away.

Dio still didn't know *why*, but he was starting to get a sense for *where*. Nearly all of the small boats, and some of the large, were heading in the same direction, and it wasn't towards the Frisky Foxglove. "Are we heading back to Pandemonium?" he asked.

"Look at you," said Valeria with a smile that might have appeared warm, if she were a stranger. "I keep forgetting you're a local."

Somewhere along the way she had traded in the plain dress she had used to pretend she was a laundress, at the Blooming Cup. She now wore a long, detailed featherbrace, with soft blacks underneath. A line of silver embroidery that looked like Mardi's work called attention to the fact that Valeria's décolletage was what his aunties would call 'barely decent.'

(It was fancier than Ikaros' jacket. No surprise at all that Valeria had more expensive taste.)

As they got closer to the better lit side of the river, with lanterns and hissing gaslamps hung along the dock, Dio noticed that Valeria had lined her eyes and lips too, with something that made her look extra glamorous, extra dangerous.

"I've left my club gear at home," he said quickly. "You'll want me to stay in the boat?" He could play the servant happily enough, but he really didn't want to go inside.

"Oh, no," said Valeria with another smile, this one hungry. "I have plans for this evening, stowaway. One is to watch you dance."

"I didn't stowaway anywhere," Dio protested. "Technically, I'm a kidnap victim."

He was still wearing the shirt and pants he had been sleeping in, when that first kidnap occurred. Several days on board a boat with very basic washing facilities had not improved them any. He'd traded a pair of sandals from one of the sailors a day or two ago, but they were a little too large.

"Yes," Valeria mused. "You should play the victim when the Divine King's men finally catch up with us. Good idea."

"Wait," said Dio. "What do the King's men want with us?"

Dio's aunties, without exception, disapproved of Pandemonium even harder than they disapproved of low-cut gowns, shirtless men, teen marriages, and the growing trend of buying your meats and fishes from the markets already marinaded and spiced.

Dio had visited the club a few times back in the day, despite the high cover charge. This was the sort of thing you did when you were a student and you had mates with adventurous tastes. He'd allowed himself to make friends when he was first training up for the gladius exam, before those same friends all qualified and left him behind. (It hadn't occurred to Dio to save his money, back then — it never occurred to him that he would fail the first time, and second, and third.)

The first time he'd ever kissed another man was in a back room of this particular establishment, as the thumping music and perfumed scents overwhelmed his senses.

Later, Dio had briefly worked for a merchant's wife who had a side hustle of hiring out male escorts to her friends for fancy parties and other outings... late nights at Pandemonium had, for a month or two, been an intrinsic part of Dio's life.

Stepping back into the darkened, glamorous club at Valeria's side, he recalled the night he was chased out of here by a husband who disapproved of how his wife was spending her pin money... and that was the third time in his short life that Dio had almost drowned in the River Divine.

"You seem tense, dear," murmured Valeria. "Act like you own the place."

"I don't think that would make me relax," Dio shot back. "The financial margins on a business like this are surprisingly small."

Valeria gave him a scornful look over her shoulder. "Follow me, look pretty, say nothing."

That he could do.

Dio was not even surprised when Valeria went directly to Lanyet, the glamorous hostess of Pandemonium. She was a slender woman with very dark skin, garbed in a tailored suit designed for a man. Thin pin-stripes pricked at the satin sleeves all the way to the cuffs, and down her long legs. Lanyet's hair was cut short, which wasn't all that startling after spending so much time around the shaven heads of Calyx and Nimue.

"Valeria," purred Lanyet. She lounged in a booth lined with velvet cushions. It had a good view of the cabaret floor show, and the ten-piece band playing sultry music. From this booth Lanyet could see every corner of the club, despite the flickering lanterns. "Lovely to see you. I was sorry to hear about Bors."

"It's been forever," agreed Valeria. "You've seen Reynard lately?"

"Not for months, my dear. I've been feeling quite abandoned!"

The two women kissed on the mouth, and then Valeria settled into the booth as if they were old friends.

Lanyet glanced only briefly at Dio, who had slipped into his practiced gladius stance. "Not bad," she said, looking him up and down. "Not like you to travel with protection, Val. Where's that deadly husband of yours?"

"Poisoned him," said Valeria brightly. "Not entirely; he'll survive."

"You're losing your touch."

The women laughed as they shared the joke.

"Aren't you one of Kalista's boys?" asked Lanyet, glancing back at Dio.

He stood even more to attention at the name of his former employer, but shook his head. "Must have one of those faces, ma'm."

"Kalista's not here tonight," said Lanyet, clearly amused by him. Even more amused when Dio let a little of his relief show on his face. "Oh dear. I hope she didn't do you any lasting damage."

"Lanyet," said Valeria, sipping from a glass that had been handed to her by some silent servant hovering nearby. "I need some information."

"Coming out and asking for it right away?" Lanyet pouted. "That's no fun. I'd expect at least an hour of flirting around the topic first."

"No time, my dear. I'm on a job."

"No one I know?"

"No one you care about. But I'm a touch concerned." Valeria scootched around the booth so her body folded against Lanyet, half buried in the cushions. She leaned in, and whispered intimately in the other woman's ear.

After a moment, Lanyet's mouth broke into a long, thoughtful smile, and she started whispering back.

"Are we done?" Dio asked as they moved back through the spiralling, colourful club. Valeria leaned on his arm, draping herself across him. They were the most chaste couple in here.

Bodies writhed and danced and touched and slithered around them. Lamps in all colours swung from all angles, sending a kaleidoscope of shadows, colours and rainbows against the silhouetted customers all finding excuses to touch each other.

Dio almost took a wrong turn into a giant silk wig on the head of an opera singer with two semi-naked men cradled to her bosom.

"This way," Valeria hissed, and tugged on his arm.

"Back to the boat? I thought you wanted to make me dance."

"Under normal circumstances, dear heart, I'd be delighted to watch you dance for my amusement," Valeria assured him. "But we'd better not waste time."

He didn't ask if she had what she needed; Valeria would only tell him what she wanted him to know, in her own time. "You want to get back before Calyx realises we sneaked out?"

"No," said Valeria with a throaty laugh. "I want to get out of here fast because Lanyet drugged me. If you don't get me into that dinky little rowboat soon, I might start killing people."

She tipped back her head, still smiling, and he saw that her pupils were violently enlarged - and a brilliant, unnatural shade of blue.

"It's not a drug," Dio breathed. "You must have been dosed with some kind of magic."

"Oh," said Valeria, her smile widening along with her sapphire eyes. "That's so much worse."

16. At the Frisky Foxglove

Nimue got her onion dumplings. Mardi, who apparently had a softer spot for the girl than Ikaros had realised, went into the Frisky Foxglove to collect them personally, along with a cask of cider as a gift for the crew of the *Silken Hare*.

"Buttering them up?" Ikaros observed.

Mardi, looking more cheerful than she had in days, tipped him a wink. "Perhaps I'll be a tavern keeper as my next career. The first rule of business is to keep your staff content so they'll work harder for you."

"If you say so," said Ikaros dubiously. "That's the future you want for your young one, is it? Running a riverside bar, at the beck and call for scoundrels and sailors?"

Mardi settled down on the deck, making herself comfortable on cushions she had brought out from the cabin. "Why not?" she said lightly, opening her own basket of dumplings, and smacking Ikaros' hand when he reached for one. "It worked out fine for yours."

"That's different."

"Is it?"

"Janna's family have owned that tavern for generations, on her mother's side."

"Well?" Mardi patted the curve beneath her dress. "This little one's mother could be doing anything by the time she's born. I certainly don't intend to induct her into the current family business."

"I thought — sewing and such?" Mardi wasn't *just* called the Needle because of the time she'd gutted three men with the same rapier.

"Maybe," Mardi sighed. "I always thought I'd end up a seamstress. But it's hard on the hands. And the eyesight. I'll be ageing again, once the Raven releases me. I have to think about the future. Far ahead, not just where my next meal is coming from."

Ikaros didn't like to think about it. Mardi had been a constant for him, for the last twenty years. Soon she would slip away from them, into a life of constant change while he and Valeria continued, untouched by time.

Losing Bors had been a fast, sharp pain. Losing Mardi would be a slower, more drawn out kind of ache. Most of it would happen when they weren't paying attention.

"What if the gods want her?" he asked, eyes drawn back to her belly.

"They'll have to kill me first," Mardi said with a ferocity that took Ikaros aback.

He hadn't realised she was still angry at the Black Raven. It shouldn't have slipped his notice. He'd been spending too much time distracted by Calyx and her concerns, not paying enough attention to the people who mattered.

"Where's Valeria?" he asked, to change the subject.

Mardi took her time finishing a mouthful of dumpling. "Sleeping, I think."

"So early?"

"She'll take first watch, she said."

For a calm, competent killing machine, Mardi was a terrible liar. Ikaros watched as she ate two more dumplings, one after another: an excuse to not say anything else.

"I don't see Dio on deck," he said after a moment's thought. "Did he skive off to the tavern?"

Mardi said something around a mouthful of dumpling and tried to look innocent.

What was Valeria up to? Wait. "Are they fucking?" he asked.

Mardi coughed, half-choked on a dumpling, and spat it on the deck at his feet. "Oh, you *arsehole*," she said when she could breathe again.

"They are?"

"Of course they're not."

"Good, he's a child."

Mardi rolled her eyes and wiped her mouth on a napkin. "I know you find it difficult to tell the difference because we're all mayflies in the wind to you, but he's a grown man, and it's none of your business who Valeria takes to her bed anyway."

"I know that. The second part. Dio is *twelve years old*."

"Twenty-two."

"Same difference."

Something hit the barge. It was brief vibration of something small bumping against the side, but Ikaros and Mardi both tensed.

Then, low voices arguing, and a splash.

"That way," said Ikaros, and took off without waiting for Mardi. Competent killer she might be, but she moved a lot slower these days.

Ikaros leaped on to the rail on the starboard side of the barge, looking down — and saw Valeria and Dio, tussling wildly in a skiff. Two oars had already gone overboard, floating off out of reach.

The little rowboat was strangely illuminated in purple light, surrounded by a halo of night-blooms. It was as if the glowing flowers had been drawn to the fight, clustering in because they'd smelled blood in the air.

"What," Ikaros said.

Dio glanced up, and Valeria took the opportunity to shove him overboard. Her head tipped up, and for a moment Ikaros saw her pupils burning blue, unnaturally bright. She turned away and leaped into the water herself, on the other side of the rowboat, making for the dock.

"Monster," said Mardi breathlessly, at Ikaros' side. "She's on *monster*."

Dio, dripping wet, hung on to the side of the rowboat. "Someone dosed her at Pandemonium," he called up.

"Shit," said Ikaros. No need to ask why Valeria had hared off to Pandemonium; some actions were inevitable. They needed to know more about Calyx and the political situation they were crashing into at Phoenix Burning. They might still be days away from the city, but the Queen of Pandemonium always knew more about what was going on than the King's own spies.

Someone else guessed what Valeria might do. Someone had got to Lanyet before her.

Monster, though. That was a nasty trick. It was a war

drug, dispensed only by clerics of the Silver Hawk. In a human soldier, it sparked a berserker rage known as the killing fever. Strategic use of that particular outcome was the reason that the Divine Kingdom hadn't lost a naval battle in the last hundred years. The reason that no one had ever successfully invaded their wealthy country via the mountain passes in the North.

A kingdom so wealthy in resources would be considered rich pickings for all passing empires, but the gods and their servants had always managed to protect its borders. The Silver Hawk's methods were a little more brutal than the rest of them...

No one sane would hand out monster out as party favours, unless they wanted to create pure chaos. An ordinary human on the drug would likely become infused with a violent rage, fighting all who stood in their way until there was blood on the deck. For Valeria, a trained assassin carrying more knives than your average weapon-smith's forge, that kind of homicidal fire could carve a bloody line through the entire country.

Someone had been angling to do some damage... or to cause one hell of a distraction.

One thing was for certain, Ikaros couldn't let Valeria anywhere near a crowd of people. He had to shut this down, fast.

"Protect Calyx," Ikaros ordered Mardi, and ran lightly along the rail, leaping for the ladder leading up to the dock. A soaking wet Valeria did the same, on another ladder further down, climbing so fast it looked like her fingers and toes barely touched the rungs.

A few heartbeats ahead of him, she ran for the tavern. A tavern full of people. Ikaros did not classify them as innocents — no one was truly innocent. But they were noncombatants. Even professional soldiers inside those walls were off-duty. None of them deserved Valeria on a rampage.

Valeria's clothes, heavy with water, did not slow her down. She was as dangerous as Ikaros on a good day — it was a long time since they'd truly tested which of them could beat the other in a real fight. With monster running through her system, Ikaros was not sure he could stop her without killing her.

Valeria turned on the threshold of the Frisky Foxglove and gave her husband a brief, toothsome smile before she ran inside, bright curved blades gleaming in each hand.

Ikaros ran after her, murmuring a prayer beneath his breath.

Blessed Raven, save your servant.

He wasn't talking about himself.

By the time Dio made it up over the railing on to the deck of the *Silken Hare*, Mardi had taken charge. Calyx, who emerged from the cabin to find out what all the fuss was about, was now refusing to go back inside.

"Ikaros has it under control," Mardi insisted. "You need to stay undercover."

"You don't give me orders," Calyx replied stiffly.

"See me spitting cherry blossoms? Keeping you safe is easier when you do what I say. If your damned bond can tell the difference, try giving me the benefit of the doubt."

Calyx frowned, and her eyes flashed. "Tell me what is happening with Valeria."

"Someone took her out of the game," said Mardi,

crowding Calyx back towards the cabin door. "Ikaros is trying to mitigate the damage, and if I was going to make an attempt on your life, *this is the moment I would choose.*"

There was a sound like an exhaled breath, and then a dull punch. Dio didn't realise what it was, at first, until he heard Calyx's scream cut through the night air.

Mardi had shoved her to the deck. She staggered for a moment, still shielding Calyx with her body. As Dio reached Mardi's side he saw an arrow, a whole god-cursed arrow sticking out of her, just beneath her ribs. She reached for him as she fell, and he managed to grab her hand.

"Trap," Mardi said, as she hit the deck. "Protect the —"

Petals erupted from her mouth.

Note down the Frisky Foxglove as one more tavern where Ikaros could likely never drink again.

The place was packed with customers, though the bard had already stopped playing by the time Ikaros made it inside, and there was blood on the floor. A big man with tattooed hands lay at Valeria's feet, and the rest of the crowd had pressed back to give her space.

She held her scythe-knives, both bloody, and stood with her teeth bared, choosing her next victim.

"There's another one!" someone yelled as Ikaros entered, dressed in the same fine blacks as his wife. Clearly there was no hiding that they were both priests of the Black Raven.

"I'll handle her," Ikaros announced to the tavern at large. "No one else needs to get hurt."

Some knuckle-head smashed a chair over his head from behind.

Ikaros used the momentum to carry him forward, taking Valeria out at the ankles. She screamed in fury, and Ikaros only just swept his hands up in time to block her from stabbing him in the neck.

As quickly as he disarmed her, she found more knives on her person. He twisted her wrist to take a particularly wicked scythe-knife, and she stuck him in the meat of his arm with a fruit-parer.

Frustrated, Ikaros forced her flat on the floor with the weight of his own body. He pressed his forearm hard across her throat. Perhaps if she lost consciousness, he could drag her back to the barge to sleep it off...

Valeria's pupils flashed blue and black, then blue again.

"Stay down," Ikaros growled.

Her hands moved faster than he could see, and he had to flinch back to avoid being stabbed in the face by yet another knife. (This was one he'd never even seen before; twenty-five years since the first time they married each other and she could still surprise him.)

Ikaros rolled back out of range, and Valeria rolled with him. Her other hand flicked out to pull the fruit-parer lodged in his arm; now she had two knives again.

The tavern hadn't exactly emptied out; a bar brawl like this was not to be missed. But those of the crowd who were brave or curious enough to remain were pressed up against walls and the bar itself, staying out of the way now it was clear that the true battle was between the two priests.

Ikaros leaped to his feet, as did Valeria. They circled each other. Her eyes still flashed with the unnatural blue of the magical killing fever; sweat rolled down her forehead. Ikaros did not know much about the side effects of monster. What happened to those soldiers who survived their battles?

As long as her eyes were on him, she was not killing anyone else.

Valeria let out a scream and leapt at him, knives flashing in the low lantern light of the tavern.

Ikaros swerved, ducked and avoided every blow. Each time her knife did not hit home, fury and frustration flashed in her uncanny eyes.

"Punch her in the face!" called one sailor, waving his tankard enthusiastically.

"Stab her in the gut!" yelled another.

It was rare for Ikaros to have such warm support from a crowd. Valeria's first victim must have had friends at the Frisky Foxglove.

He narrowly avoided one feint by Valeria and felt a table at his back. Running out of space here.

Valeria screamed like a banshee and ran at him. Ikaros swerved once more and caught her arm, smashing her head-first into the table that had been behind him.

His mouth and throat closed over, and he bent over the crumpled figure of his wife, expelling dandelions and clover from his lungs. Not from hurting Valeria, surely.

Calyx.

Valeria rolled, bleeding from the nose and mouth. Bright red buds and petals flew from her lips.

Somewhere, their mistress needed them and they had failed her.

"We have to go," Ikaros told her. Pain burst through the side of his thigh. He didn't have to look down to see what she had done. "Stop fucking stabbing me. Calyx is in trouble."

Valeria laughed, her eyes still bright from the drug. "Priorities," she slurred, and slid off the table to the floor.

There was blood on the deck, and Mardi lay horribly still. No, wait — she was still breathing in little, quick huffs. A rose petal clinging to her lower lip fluttered. Not dead yet.

Dio didn't know enough about the human body to know how bad it was. In all his studies for the gladius examinations, he'd never come up against 'which parts of the torso can you shoot without instantly killing a person?'

Blood on the deck had to be a bad sign.

Calyx stared at him, then at Mardi. She crouched frozen by the doorway, where Mardi had shoved her.

"You heard her," Dio said desperately. "Get into the cabin. You have to stay out of sight."

There was a knife near Mardi's limp hand, a dagger that she must have drawn when all this started happening. Dio scooped it up by the hilt.

"Where's Nimue?" Calyx asked, still wavering on the threshold. She looked around wildly. "Where's my daughter?"

"This is clearly a trap," Dio shouted. "And you are *all out of assassins.*" Thorns stabbed his throat for his insolence, and he tasted blood in his mouth, but it was hard to feel bad about it.

Footsteps sounded hollowly across the deck. A priest in black strode towards them. He had a pointed beard and long moustache, but half his face was covered by a black, beaked mask that made him look entirely sinister. Shoulder-length black hair. He wore a heavily decorated featherbrace, which featured the same kind of embroidery Dio had seen Mardi adding to Valeria's garments in the quiet moments on deck. Black feathers tufted at his collar and cuffs. The rest of the priest's clothes were made of soft larkflax, so you wouldn't hear rustles in the night — though his heeled boots weren't exactly discreet.

This wasn't Aodhan, Dio's mysterious man of the night. This man looked far more confident, elegant and dangerous. A fashionable city priest out on the town for a night of elegant murder.

A wooden longbow was slung on the assassin's back, and he had swords hanging from his belt. He had clearly managed to stock up since his encounter with Ikaros back at the Cask and Barrels.

The Bow. This had to be the Bow.

(And that meant, presumably, that Aodhan was not?)

The Bow held Nimue, one hand pressed to her mouth, dragging the girl along beside him as if she weighed nothing. Calyx's daughter looked terrified, but she was complying with her abductor. No sudden movements, no fighting back. Good. She might survive this.

Her linen cap had fallen off somewhere, baring her scalp to the night sky. It made her look even younger than she was.

The crew of the *Silken Hare,* every one of them compelled to serve and protect Calyx as well as her daughter, all ran at Nimue's abductor in twos and threes.

None of them had the fighting skills to match a servant of the Black Raven. The Bow beat them off easily, with fluid motion of his other hand and the knife he held in it, without letting go of Nimue.

"Stop," said Calyx abruptly. She wasn't talking to him.

The sailors fell back, released from her magical bond. Without a blind need to protect her from this stranger, their natural response was to watch the scene warily.

"Let my daughter go," said Calyx, staring down the assassin. "I'll give you whatever you want." She was glowing a little, her skin brightening.

Raising her magic, Dio suspected. Trying that trick of hers again, to pull the Bow into her service as she had the others? She'd had worse ideas.

The Bow gave Calyx a courtly smile beneath his mask, while tightening his hold on Nimue's throat. "That was the general idea," he said politely.

Dio was the only one left. The only person on this barge (still conscious) whose job it was to keep Calyx alive. He had put in hours on training over the years. Disarming, duelling, all the basics for a gladius. He might not have a god on his side, but he had Mardi's dagger, and he was sure he could slow the Bow down long enough to...

The Bow threw Nimue directly at Dio. She stumbled, crying out, and Dio caught her before she could trip over Mardi's body. Before he could steady her, before he could do *anything*, the Bow made his move.

He seized Calyx's wrist as if pulling her into a dance. The air was full of a sudden flurry of black birds, all feathers and wings, fluttering in a dark cloud around the Bow and Calyx.

Dio pushed Nimue aside and ran into the wild, flapping mass of black ravens. They vanished as quickly as they had appeared, leaving empty air behind. Air and black feathers, drifting down around them all.

The Bow and Calyx had vanished.

17. Past Parliament in Ruins

The Bow's ship was a black feather, floating. The sail, catching impossible winds, was a shadow against the night sky. This was magic, Calyx knew, but not a magic that felt at all familiar.

She leaned against the mast and shivered, watching the shapes of the banks and trees and docks shift past them, impossibly fast, illuminated by the moon and the purple glow of night-blooms in the water.

The Bow did not speak. He still wore the mask, which made him look more like a statue than a person.

He had raised no hand against her. He had not killed her, though she was certain he must be the fourth priest who had been hired to take her life. *Four ravens, in the dream that had alerted her to the danger.*

Above them, the black sail fluttered, and the ship darted forwards through the water.

Light as a feather.

Ikaros carried Valeria back to the barge: she was bound in ropes provided by the landlord of the Frisky Foxglove, and dosed up to the eyeballs on Ikaros' last supplies of shaderoot and honey.

It was enough to knock a regular human unconscious for a day, but Valeria's eyelids still fluttered, fighting it. Her heartbeat was too fast, a thready and erratic pulse. Whatever thrice-damned alchemist had come up with the monster formula hadn't cared whether their wild fury-fighters were still breathing after the battle was over. As long as their job was done.

Something was wrong with Calyx, he knew, even if it was just that Ikaros and Valeria had been gone from her side too long, dealing with their own shit. Ikaros had a dandelion stem caught in his teeth when he returned to the *Silken Hare*.

"We need the knights of the Bright Owl," he barked as he leaped back on to the barge, Valeria limp against his shoulders. "Where's the nearest temple?"

No one looked at him. The crew were clustered around their captain, all eyes on Calyx's cabin.

A shaky Nimue stepped aside, so Ikaros could see that Mardi was lying on the deck, Dio leaning over her body.

"Bors is dead," she screamed at him, the forbidden word like poison on her tongue. "Why won't you let me die too?" A memory — more recent than he cared to admit.

"No," said Ikaros. Just that. A rejection of the whole

idea that Mardi, of all of them, could be dead. Mardi was getting out.

She had survived *that*. She could survive this.

Dio looked desperate. "There's a lot of blood," he said, packing linen tightly around the arrow, careful not to disturb the shaft. "But if there's a temple we can get to in time?"

Not dead, then. Not yet.

Ikaros looked to the captain, who cleared his throat. "South from here," he informed them gruffly. "Past Parliament-in-Ruins. Six or seven hours at legal night speed."

"And if we break some laws?" Ikaros suggested.

The captain nodded. "I'll see what I can do." He spoke quickly to a couple of his men, and the crew moved around them, getting ready to undock the barge.

It shouldn't be Ikaros making these negotiations. He looked around. "Where is Calyx?"

Calyx was not a damsel waiting to be rescued. She was not a pawn. The last time assassins had tried to take her down, she took them off the board.

She could feel them out there, somewhere. Ikaros, Valeria, Mardi. Even Dio. The bond still held. They were hers. But she didn't need them to ride to the rescue. She had her own power.

Calyx reached out with her magic, feeling the extra flush of bright clarity. She had been feeding energy from the River Divine for days; she was mightier than she had ever been.

She summoned her strength, to throw it all at this man, this priest who thought he could kidnap her, of all the indignities. She was a Petal of the Imperium. No man could resist her.

The Bow turned, his eyes shining in the moonlight. "Try it," he invited her in a low, dangerous voice.

Calyx threw it at him. Every petal. Every mote of magic. She blasted him with it all, with stems and leaves and petals, petals, petals. Colours streamed out of her, pink and yellow, blue and scarlet, green, green, green...

By the time they reached him, they were nothing but black feathers, dancing on the wind. Then dust. Then the breeze itself.

"What are you?" she asked.

The Bow smiled a white-toothed smile. A dark shadow darted around him, resting on his shoulder. A large raven with unblinking yellow eyes.

The air shivered, and there were more ravens. Crows. Black birds of all sizes and shapes, clustered around the ship, perching on every surface, all the way up the mast, and on every railing and edge. All staring at Calyx.

"I'm the chosen one," said the Bow, stroking the wing of the bird on his shoulder. "Save your flowers, Petal. You can't touch me."

Ikaros did not dare remove the arrow from Mardi's body. It hadn't killed her yet, and as far as he knew it was all that was stopping the rest of her blood from pouring out of her. The linens packed in tight by Dio's shaking hands were wet with her blood, but they had slowed the flow of it.

Mardi breathed, not quite conscious, shaking with something that might have been pain, or shock. Nimue brought blankets to tuck around her, but the shivering had nothing to do with cold, not on a thick summer night like this.

It was enough to make Ikaros wish he hadn't used the last of his shaderoot and honey on Valeria, though that had been the right call at the time.

Valeria was past the fighting fury of the monster she had consumed, but her body was not reacting well in the wake of it. Her skin too hot, and she had fallen into a shallow sleep, disturbed by quick, erratic breaths.

Nimue brought blankets for her, too, creating a makeshift bed on the other side of Ikaros, who would not leave either of them.

Occasionally, he choked on a blade of grass or chewed leaf as it rose up in his mouth to remind him of his own failure.

As long as that kept happening, Calyx and her bond were still alive. He hadn't failed them yet.

Ikaros sat on the deck, a woman he loved on either side of him, willing the barge to go faster. The captain was a good man, committed to the rescue despite the fact that the crew, apparently, were now free of Calyx's service compulsion. Ikaros had no doubt that a bill would be presented, all in good time. For… they sailed south, faster than they should in the darkness of night.

"Feathers, you say," Ikaros said, when he could trust himself to speak.

Dio, pacing the deck, stopped to nod sharply. "I haven't seen magic like that before. At least…" He stopped. "It reminded me. Of what you did to the Shrine of the Black Raven, at the Hanging Market."

"That wasn't me," Ikaros muttered. "It's not *people magic.*" He could use it a little of his god's power — such as the feather spell he sent ahead to the nearest Temple of the Bright Owl, in the hopes they could send a knight to meet the barge. Small things, flutters of dark shadow and feathers. Brief, glancing touches of the Black Raven and his grace.

Sometimes a prayer really could make all the difference.

Ikaros had seen more dramatic miracles, performed in temples and shrines. Created by some of the older, more long-serving priests, so in touch with their god's love that they could reach out and use his feathers for their own worship. Valeria had been a master of miracles back in the day, though she rarely bothered now. Sometimes it was a performance. Sometimes, as with the Shrine at the Hanging Market, it was a built-in form of self defence. Ikaros himself had never been blessed by a miracle as powerful the one described. The miracle that the Bow used to take Calyx.

"The Raven?" Dio asked quietly.

Ikaros nodded. "Our god has picked a champion."

He had known that the bond Calyx threw at him compromised his service to the Black Raven. It was impossible to think otherwise. But it was a deep humiliation, to have your god working against you.

"Then," said Dio, worrying at his lower lip with his teeth. "Why didn't he kill her? That's the job, isn't it? You and Mardi and Valeria were all supposed to... why did he take her alive?"

"I don't know," Ikaros said. He didn't want to discuss it with Dio. The boy wouldn't understand. Ikaros needed Valeria and Mardi alert and alive, so they could be properly angry about this together. So they could save Calyx and... and...

And finish things with the Bow, one way or another.

Let them both survive this night. A few more hours, and he'd have them in the hands of the Owls.

"Parliament-in-Ruins," said the Bow. It was the first thing he had said in hours.

Calyx, half-asleep against the feathered mast of the swift black ship, jolted awake and glared at him, then at all the ravens and crows that were glaring at *her*. "What?"

He nodded to the port side of the black feather ship. "Wouldn't want you to miss the view."

Grey silhouettes rose up, bone pale against the dark trees behind. The ghosts of domed buildings and spires. It looked like a city that had been asleep for centuries, rotting away.

"What happened here?" Calyx asked, but the black feather ship was pulling ahead, away. Around the curve of the river, which looped back sharply so they could see the Parliament-in-Ruins again, from the other side.

"They say the Black Raven sucked the souls out of a hundred members of Parliament," said the Bow softly. "Centuries ago. They were voting for war, and the Black Raven put an end to it by stopping a hundred hearts in a single breath. The Hawk of War rose up against him in protest... and the River Divine ran red with blood."

Calyx shivered. "Not much of a bedtime story."

"Then the Divine King came along to save the kingdom

from our warring gods, huzzah," added the Bow. He was staring back behind the speeding yacht, as if his thoughts were still tangled in the past, in those strange, lost buildings.

"You said centuries ago," Calyx said, frowning. That couldn't be right.

"He's not a *young* king."

"But I've read — they sent genealogical charts with the betrothal contract. There have been ten Divine Kings in the last three hundred years." What had she got into with this royal family? Or had this priest of death merely chosen to torment her instead of murdering her?

The Bow gave her a biting grin. "All had the same name, though, didn't they? Check out the portrait gallery when you reach Phoenix Burning. It's a sight and a half. You're marrying into a family that doesn't like to let go of things."

"Wings," said Dio suddenly, as the *Silken Hare* approached the creepy domes and spires of Parliament-in-Ruins. "I hear wings."

Ikaros, checking Mardi's pulse for the fourteenth time that hour, could hear it too. A distant fluttering, the low whistle of wind against feathers. "Arm yourselves," he warned.

Dio crouched near him. "Where exactly are we supposed to find a stash of weapons?"

"Strip Valeria," Ikaros said dryly. "She's good for it."

"Try it and I'll gut you," his wife murmured through chapped lips.

"You're awake," said Ikaros, pleased with this development.

"More or less," she said with a grunt. "Wings, you say?"

The crew were gathered around on deck, muttering to themselves. Over the silhouetted domes of Parliament-in-Ruins, other shapes appeared out of the cloudy night. Winged creatures, circling.

"God comes for us," said Valeria, letting her eyes fall closed again. "Knew he'd be a gentleman about it."

"You always were the dramatic one," Ikaros said. He dropped his knife to the deck and stood up, facing the circling birds. "They're not ravens."

Owls poured down from the sky upon them, screeching and flapping. Several crashed together, and a tall woman in white emerged from their collision of feathers.

"Two miracles in one night," said Ikaros, striding to greet their visitor. "Aren't we lucky."

The knight of the Bright Owl ignored him and made straight for Valeria. "What have you been up to, dark eyes?" she asked.

Valeria huffed a soft laugh. "Slightly poisoned. Don't mind me. My friend has an arrow in her ribs and a baby on the way."

"It's not on the way right now," said Ikaros, suddenly finding a new thing to worry about. "Is it?"

The Knight gave him a skeptical look over one shoulder. "I'm going to designate you to boil some water, regardless," she said, in a voice more sarcastic than him on a good day. "Should keep you out of my hair."

"Where are we going?" Calyx asked as the sky began to lighten. The black feather ship seemed less tangible as night ended. Less real. A nightmare with a mast and rudder...

The ravens and crows had all drifted away, taking to the air. She could still see them sometimes, swooping and calling to each other in the lighter sky above the mast.

"To meet a friend of mine," said the Bow.

Calyx turned away from him, stretching out a cramp in her leg from sitting too long on a hard wooden bench "I was expecting death," she said in a sour voice.

"Yes," said the Bow. "That's who I mean."

Death did not come for Mardi or Valeria in the night. The Knight of the Bright Owl, who went by Ulwen to her friends (and apparently counted Valeria among those friends, wonders would never cease!) worked tirelessly for hours. She brewed ugly potions to flush Valeria's system, drew the arrow out of Mardi's side and closed the wound with neat stitches, and left them both groggy and healing in the cabin together, tucked side by side into the bed like sisters waiting for a nursery story.

"How did you find us?" Ikaros asked, as the Knight sluiced blood from her hands on the deck. "Did the temple get my message?"

Ulwen gave him a bright, sideways sort of smile. "I owed Val a favour," she said. "This is how that works. Doesn't your god send you where you're needed?"

Ikaros thought of that morning in the tea house, a lifetime ago, his crossbow bolt trained on the Petal of the Imperium, ready to strike. "Sometimes," he said. "Mostly he leaves us to our own devices."

"There's your trouble, then," said Ulwen. She removed the blood-stained apron she wore over her white robes, and shook it once. The blood vanished, leaving the apron spotless. She tucked it away in a satchel that hung over one shoulder. "You chose the wrong god."

Not much to say in response to that. "How's the baby?" Ikaros asked, since he was fairly sure he hadn't missed Mardi going into labour. He'd expected more screaming.

Ulwen looked amused now. "Who's asking?"

He rolled his eyes at her.

"The baby is exactly where she should be, for six months," said Ulwen, taking pity on him. "But a wound like that is hard work to mend, even with my intervention. Mardi shouldn't be on her feet, let alone getting shot at."

"She's retiring," said Ikaros.

The Knight of the Bright Owl looked unimpressed. "Not soon enough."

Something fell, from above. Ikaros reached out and caught it; a tiny sliver of shadow as the sky brightened into day. A message; a warning.

"Oh," said Ulwen in an understanding tone, as Ikaros turned the black feather over in his hand. "My god does that too. Enraging, isn't it?"

Ikaros sat on the end of the bed, watching the women wake up. Valeria stared at the ceiling for a moment, then met his gaze. "How many did I kill?"

"Only one. A few light maimings. Could have been worse."

"I'll have to do penance," she winced. "Can't even say it was self-defence."

"You definitely started it. Who dosed you?"

"That bitch Lanyet."

"Figures."

That was the Bow's method of old. He wouldn't just go straight for the kill, oh no. He sowed chaos on his way. Setting traps for his victims here and there, knowing most of them might never be sprung.

Easier to shoot someone when they were distracted. And of course, he knew them all too well.

This was why it was a bad idea for priests to have friends.

"Are you well enough to work?" Ikaros asked.

Valeria blinked. Her pupils were back to the normal size, at least, and no longer had that alarming, unnatural bright blue hue. She seemed calm. "Well enough. What do you have in mind?"

He lifted the black feather that had fallen from the sky. "We have an invitation."

She rolled her eyes. "That cock. Why does he always have to play with his food?"

"Might be the only way to get Calyx back."

"And that's necessary, is it? Oh." Valeria bent double, grunting with pain. "Yes, all right," she snapped, spitting out what looked like elderflowers. Small, foul, gritty in the mouth. "Work, then. Which of us is going to tell Mardi she can't come?"

Dio dozed off a little. He hadn't slept much through the night, too worried that if Mardi or Valeria stopped breathing, Ikaros was going to drown himself in the river.

But it was daylight now, and they were heading in the right direction for Calyx (he could feel that, the pulse of the bond thrumming in his veins), and Ikaros looked a hell of a lot less haunted.

Dio didn't want to disturb Valeria or Mardi, who currently had the bed in the cabin that the four of them had been sharing with varying degrees of awkwardness (and, to his great surprise, lack of awkwardness).

He borrowed a blanket instead, and curled up on deck, in an out of the way spot near some crates. He was only going to sleep for a few minutes. Enough to get him through what was promising to be a long day.

When he opened his eyes again, it was dark, and the ground was covered in feathers. Black feathers, soft to the touch.

His mysterious stranger, Aodhan, sat nearby, arms around his knees, staring into the distance. Dio blinked at him, wondering in his sleepy haze if those long braids would be as soft as the feathers if he touched them.

"You're not the Bow," he said.

Aodhan looked at him, a quick dart of a look, then away again. "I never said I was."

"Sorry I assumed. You're one of them, though," Dio added, stroking the black feathers that carpeted the... no, they were not on the boat any more. There was grey grass beneath the feathers, and broken walls rose up around them in curves and tattered, crumbling stone. This was Parliament-in-Ruins. "You serve the Black Raven. It's kind of obvious."

Aodhan sighed, looking pensive. He was ethereally pretty in the moonlight — or whatever kind of dreamlight it was, as there was no moon overhead. "Dio Taurus," he said. "What do you know about the Thirteenth Treasure?"

Dio shrugged, wrinkling his nose. "Not much to know from my end of things. Royalty. They don't exactly mix with my sort."

He had so many questions to ask, but somehow none of them rose to his tongue right now. His mouth felt like it was full of feathers, too.

"Can you keep a secret?" asked Aodhan.

"What kind of secret?" Dio blurted immediately. "I mean, yes, but only if it won't hurt Calyx. Or my friends."

Were they his friends? This strange bunch of killers he had been tied to for days and days, by magical vines and stems and whatever else made up Calyx's foreign magic.

Eh, didn't help to fret about it. Dio was loyal regardless. He was just built that way.

"Do no harm," said Aodhan in a soft voice. He turned, and crawled his way up Dio's body as if he was a cat. Hands pressed on either side of Dio's hips. Knees pinning his legs to the ground.

Either Dio was about to be murdered, or kissed. It was a dream, so he didn't have a lot of say in it either way. But he tipped back his head a little, because kissing seemed like a much more appealing idea.

Above them, he saw the domes of the long-abandoned Halls of Parliament, hollow and skeletal; left to the wild animals. Starlings nested in the high windows. Creeping, crawling creatures burrowed amongst the broken mosaic tile.

The wind drifted through broken windows, abandoned doorways, making spooky sounds.

Aodhan's mouth tasted like salt, and feathers. They kissed for a long time.

"Is that the secret?" Dio asked as they broke apart.

Aodhan nuzzled at his jaw, finding the rough skin where Dio had failed to shave two days in a row. "It will all make sense when you wake up," he promised.

It did not, in fact, all make sense when Dio woke up.

18. At the Cauldron...

Calyx had never been so cut off from her magic in her life. Not since before she was old enough for the House of Petal, when her guardians dosed her up with magic suppressants for public appearances, out of fear that one of the royal children might accidentally cause an affray.

Every time she reached for her power, she felt herself blanketed by darkness. Nothingness. A void she did not want to prod at too closely. At one point, she spat out a mouthful of black feathers.

Her back itched. She knew it was the skin healing after her recent surgery, but without the ability to get to a mirror, her old anxieties rose up around her. How many lines of poetry this time? How close was she to the end of the verse?

Were these the words that would kill her?

The black feather ship had berthed on a tiny island, if one could even call it an island, directly at the place where the River Divine divided in three directions. It was called the Cauldron, according to her abductor. There was nothing here: no tavern, no temple. Just a cluster of rocks, sticking up in the most inconvenient place imaginable.

There was traffic everywhere: all manner of skiffs and ships and barges. They were close to the city now. The river was lined with buildings and roads and industry.

Calyx stood at the stern of the black ship, gazing at the busy movement of boats on the water. No one looked her way. No one seemed to even notice that a high-masted black ship dripping with black feathers up and down the sails was moored here, a single still point rebelling against the flow of the water.

The ravens were back, clustered along the thin lines of the mast and sails, their beady golden eyes darting every which way.

"He'll come for you," said the Bow. His own eyes looked haunted, and his cheeks were a little too hollow beneath that beaked mask of his.

The mother in Calyx wondered when he had last eaten; the man was a wreck. Clearly not a natural kidnapper.

"Ikaros," she said softly. "Oh, yes. He'll come for me."

She could feel the threads of the bond that now only connected her to four servants: Mardi, Valeria, Ikaros, Dio. All strong. Mardi must have survived the arrow, and Valeria had survived whatever strange magic was thrown at her.

They would come for her. Ikaros would save her. She had no doubt.

He hated her too much to let someone else kill her.

"Who hired you?" she asked. "Who has the arrogance and the resources to pay four servants of the Black Raven to kill a Petal of the Imperium?"

"I don't need to know," said the Bow. "*I* haven't turned my back on everything I believe in."

"Clearly not," said Calyx, with a glance up at the feathered sail.

She had thought releasing the barge's crew from her

bond might have freed up some of her magic, given her more to work with. But here, surrounded by the Black Raven and his feathers, she only felt dull and exhausted.

I want to go home.

Dio kept darting looks at Valeria. She seemed fine — more than fine. In the light of day, she was standing tall, her fancy black featherbrace buttoned neatly, and her soft larkflax trousers tucked into those shining boots.

Last night, he had seen his death in her eyes, when the drug overwhelmed her restraint. *Monster*. He was lucky to have got off with a dunking, especially considering the bloodshed she caused at the Frisky Foxglove.

Valeria's eyes were back to their normal colour now, no dangerous gleam of unnatural blue to warn him she was dangerous. Merely the ordinary amount of dangerous.

The *Silken Hare* continued to sail south. They were now nearly at the Cauldron and Three Crows, named because of how the river forked there, becoming three separate river branches named Coronis, Corby and Corax. Corby led east to the coast. Corax wound its way south to Delpha. And Coronis twisted and turned south-west-south, curling towards Phoenix Burning. The capital city of the Divine Kingdom. Their final destination.

Ikaros was certain they would find the Bow and Calyx at the Cauldron. Dio knew it must be true, because the magical bond that infused his bones and skin was likewise tugging him in that direction. (If the barge turned around to sail upriver, he believed it would tear him to pieces.)

Mardi slept through the day, while the healing charms and potions of the scary owl lady did their work.

Ikaros hovered near Valeria, as if he did not entirely trust her not to start murdering people all over again.

Nimue was quiet, as she had been since her mother first disappeared in a cloud of feathers.

Dio knew he should tell Ikaros or Valeria about Aodhan.

(They had to know him, surely. There couldn't be an endless supply of beautiful men with a taste for black feathers floating around the River Divine. He had to be a priest. Another one of them. But Aodhan had asked him to keep a secret, and besides it was a dream, wasn't it?)

Dio *should* tell them about his night-time visitor, but he already knew that he wouldn't. Instead, he concentrated on keeping Nimue company while she fretted about her mother.

"It will be all right," Dio told her. "Ikaros won't let anything bad happen to Calyx."

Nimue was miserable. "What if she's already..."

"Believe me, I'd *know*." He rubbed his stomach, which was where he most often felt the tug of the bond. Or perhaps he was hungry.

At the reminder of the bond's existence, Nimue looked even more distressed. "What my mother did to all of you. It's not right, is it?"

Dio quirked an eyebrow at her. "Coming around to the Divine Kingdom way of thinking?"

Nimue shrugged. "She released the crew, to stop them getting themselves killed when the Bow appeared. And look at them. They're working just the same as they were. We sailed through the night so much faster than we should have done. No one has betrayed us, or hurt us. It's not very trusting, is it, to enforce a work contract with compulsion?"

Dio was all for encouraging her to accept that it was a bad thing to perform magic on people without their permission, but the timing was unfortunate. "I'm not sure the lesson to take away here is to trust everyone unconditionally. The Kingdom can be a dangerous place, Nimue."

She scoffed. "I've been trained in diplomacy. What's the point in having those skills if my mother clenches her fist around the heart of everyone she meets?"

"If she hadn't done it," he reminded her. "Ikaros and Valeria and Mardi... at least one of them would have literally killed her." He wasn't sure why he was defending Calyx... unless the bond, of course, had its own opinions.

"I know," Nimue said sourly. "I know she *had* to do it. But I'm starting to hate it. Would Ikaros be working so hard to save her life if she hadn't compelled him into service?"

"I would," Dio said immediately.

"I know," she said, patting him on the arm. "And that's terribly nice of you. But I'm not sure you're typical."

Ikaros and Valeria held a final meeting in the cabin, so that Mardi could make use of her fleeting moments of wakefulness between the doses of healing potion that Ulwen had insisted upon, to speed her recovery.

"You can't kill him," Valeria said.

Ikaros knew he couldn't. That was the worst of it. He should have put an end to Reynard bloody Kaldoran back at Cask and Barrels. He was going soft. He couldn't even blame it on Calyx's influence — her magic wanted him to kill the Bow.

But Reynard was one of *them*. He belonged to the Black Raven. Ikaros had known him since he was a lad — or at least, a swaggering teenager who thought he knew it all. Reynard wasn't doing anything wrong here. He was the one following the correct procedures. It was Ikaros, Mardi and Valeria who had done all the betraying.

"Why can't I?" Ikaros said, regardless. "He shot Mardi."

"I don't think he meant to do more than get me out of the way," said Mardi softly. "Calyx was his target. She's the mark."

"If that arrow had been over by a few inches... or lower, damn it." Ikaros had spent his life surrounded by dangerous and capable women; he'd ditched chivalry as an unnecessary virtue a long time ago. Even he would hesitate before shooting an arrow into a pregnant woman.

"Let's not pretend he isn't the best archer we've ever known," Mardi reminded him.

"I'm aware you think he's wonderful."

"Normally he is wonderful," she snipped back. "This has been an unusual week."

"He sent Ulwen," Valeria said unexpectedly.

Something white-hot went through Ikaros — resentment? Wounded pride? "He what? Why did no one tell me?"

"I didn't know," said Mardi, blinking. "She's your friend, I thought she sensed you were in danger," she added to Valeria. "Owls are mysterious like that."

"I sent a message," Ikaros snapped.

Valeria shook her head, her mouth a tight line. "Ulwen tried to hide it — knew I might mistrust her. But it wasn't her god who sent her to save us last night. Her temple didn't get the message from Ikaros until later — you know the featherspells are slow right now."

Ikaros wanted to tear down the walls of the cabin with his bare hands. "Mardi's been drinking her potions all day, and you're only telling me now that Ulwen is in league with the Bow?"

"Mardi is going to be fine," Mardi snapped. "I don't love what Reynard did to me, Ikaros. I don't love what he did to Valeria, either. But I think it's worth noting that he went to some trouble to *not kill me*."

"He knows us too well," Ikaros said in frustration. "That's not good in an enemy."

"I don't care. Bors would hate this so much. Killing Reynard is not an option... ugh." Mardi winced and coughed, finding violets on her tongue. "This fucking bond. I don't even care. There are three of us, we can save Calyx without killing the Bow. It would end everything, Ikaros. The Black Raven would not forgive us taking the life of one of our own, even in self-defence. And I would not forgive us either."

"We have to assume there is some hope of a future beyond Calyx and her bond," agreed Valeria, spitting out a few violets of her own and pulling a face at the taste. "We only kill the Bow if there is no other option."

"It can't be either of you," Mardi added. "If the Bow must be taken out, the only one who should risk the Black Raven's wrath is the priest about to retire. Me."

"No," Ikaros said immediately. "You can't risk that. What if he takes the baby to punish you?"

"Well, then. None of us should kill him." Mardi turned her head to Valeria, wincing a little as she shifted position on the bed, despite having every cushion in the known universe piled behind her. "What did you learn from Pandemonium before Lanyet spiked your drink?"

"Nothing good." Valeria perched on the end of the bed. Both she and Ikaros were still treating Mardi like she was fragile. No wonder she was so grumpy. "Everyone's talking about the Petal and her royal marriage contract, and how she has the Black Raven's protection. We're the gossip of the river."

"Marvellous," groaned Ikaros. "Too much to hope that her intel was false, as the Bow clearly got to her before we did?"

"Oh no," said Valeria immediately. "She was all smirky about it. Nothing Lanyet loves better than sharing information. I know when she's lying."

"Just not when she's spiking your drink."

Valeria ignored that dig with an aloof expression. "I asked if she thought the palace was in favour of the match. All the high aristos end up at Pandemonium sooner or later. I thought she might have heard something useful."

"And?"

"The Thirteenth Treasure is the last of the Divine King's sons. His last chance to add magic to the royal bloodline — which is ironic given how the king's own policies have sent magical women into hiding for generations. Officially, the palace are all for the match with Calyx. And our presence in her retinue has kept anyone from wondering why she was left to travel south without protection."

"It has to have been some kind of test," Ikaros muttered. "Perhaps the king didn't believe she had strong enough magic?"

"Someone wants her dead," said Mardi, yawning again.

She should be dead, Ikaros thought furiously. The Bow

had taken Calyx instead of killing her there and then. Why would he do that?

Why would the Black Raven let him?

"They're coming," said the Bow, his gaze upriver.

"I know," said Calyx, not bothering to look. She could feel them on their way, the threads of the bond tugging them closer. Her priests. Servants. Knights.

She had half-expected to be tied to a mast like a heroine from an old epic poem, but the Bow seemed to think he could trust her. He also seemed to think that whatever magic he had borrowed from his god was enough to keep Calyx buried under it.

He had reckoned against how good it would feel, to have Ikaros and the others approaching. Never mind the River Divine with its wild magics; her strength was coming straight back to her.

Calyx leaned against the mast.

Green stems burst from the rough grain of the wood, small but fierce licks of colour. Up in the sail ropes, too high for her abductor to see them, daisies began to bloom.

Calyx smiled.

"So dramatic," groaned Valeria, when she saw the ragged, black-feathered ship, tied up to the rocky island. "Someone's been listening to old folk ballads."

"Why this place?" asked Nimue. "It's so exposed."

"Tradition," said Ikaros. "The Cauldron and the Three Crows. It's where priests used to duel, to prove their love and loyalty to our god."

"Sounds barbaric," said Nimue.

"Sounds hot," said Dio, and gave an unrepentant grin when she smacked him on the arm. "Oh, come on. You wouldn't swoon if two pretty people were fighting over you?"

Nimue looked unimpressed. "How do you know he's pretty? He was masked."

Dio flapped a hand in the direction of Ikaros, Valeria and Mardi, all armed and dangerous. "Look at the rest of them. You have to assume."

"Nice to be appreciated," said Valeria dryly.

"Pull up close enough for us to board," Ikaros called to the captain, who gave him a confused look.

"Board what, sir?"

"Oh, damn it." Ikaros went over to give directions, as it seemed that none of the crew could actually see the black-feathered ship.

Dio shivered a little, wondering why he and Nimue *could*.

"Change of plan," Ikaros said a few minutes later, returning to the group. "The *Silken Hare* is going to keep going down the Coronis. Mardi, Valeria and I will catch you up, when we have Calyx safe."

"Wait, no," Dio protested. "What about me?"

"You have no place in a duel between priests," said Ikaros.

Dio felt his face go hot with embarrassment. Once again, he wasn't good enough. "I'm bonded to Calyx as much as you are," he argued.

"And the bond will, I am sure, be delighted at how well you protect her daughter."

Dio groaned with frustration as the three assassins, all glamorous and stabby, marched off in the direction of the skiffs.

"Welcome to the children's table," said Nimue with a sour expression.

19. ...and the Three Crows

Despite what the ballads said, it was rare for priests of the Black Raven to do battle with each other.

The clerics of the Silver Hawk, that was another matter. Even the knights of the Bright Owl had been known to have a skirmish or two, usually over healing theories or the theft of potion ingredients. The friars of the Blazing Phoenix had regular duels, but as they mostly involved lutes, oil paint or ritualised dance, no one had ever worried too much about them.

There was, of course, the tragic romance of Taliskar and Marchamp, centuries ago: two priests of the Black Raven whose violent love-death triangle with a foreign queen had inspired a wealth of poetry and art. But they were the exception, not the rule.

For the most part, the priests of the Black Raven experienced little conflict between themselves, if you didn't count the colossal chaos-theatre of Ikaros and Valeria's on again, off again marriage.

"I'm here," said Ikaros. "Let's do this."

The *Silken Hare* swept on its way down the Coronis, with no priests on board. The captain had been charged with taking Nimue in the direction of the relative safety of the temple gates leading to Phoenix Burning. Dio had been convinced (with great reluctance) to stay on the barge also, on the grounds that *someone* had to keep Nimue safe.

Mardi and Valeria were... elsewhere, making their own choices. Ikaros knew they had a plan. At least one of them would be hiding nearby, within crossbow range, though there was literally nowhere to hide. He didn't need to know what their plan was.

He had always expected to rescue Calyx alone.

It did not take long for Ikaros to walk across the Cauldron; this tiny heap of grey pock-marked rocks was only marginally larger than the barge he had been living on all week.

From here you had a perfect view of the tines of the River Divine where they forked into the Three Crows: Coronis, Corby, Corax. Ikaros was not looking at the view.

Reynard Kaldoran stood near a tethered ship that shouldn't exist — an ethereal yacht-shaped silhouette of feathers and shadows. Ikaros had heard legends about the

Raven's ship. Songs. He had never expected to see it with his own eyes.

The Bow was not visibly armed, which meant little when it came to their kind. He wore a formal featherbrace jacket, tailored and ornamented, over soft black larkflax trousers, the standard working outfit for them all. Black feathers at the collar. A wing print stamped into the leather of his boots. And still that damned dramatic mask. He could poke someone's eye out with that thing.

A light trail of silver embroidery traced around Reynard's buttons. The coat met at the base of his throat, secured by a brooch that Ikaros recognised. Silver and blue enamel, depicting a decorated stave. It belonged to Bors, their fallen comrade. A nice touch.

Calyx was there too, standing a little way off, in her bright pink, white and lilac garments that were always so jarring to Ikaros' eye. She didn't have a coat, not even a hood or scarf to cover her shaven head. They were exposed to the weather on this rocky island, and with the first chill Ikaros felt since summer began.

He wanted to give her his jacket. Why hadn't Reynard done that? (Of course, Reynard was not magically compelled to serve Calyx like a loyal dog.)

"Why didn't you kill her?" Ikaros asked aloud.

"Is that all you have to say?" said Reynard in disbelief.

"Seems relevant. She's your mark. Why isn't she dead?"

"Why are you helping her?" Reynard demanded, his voice thick with anger. "Blood and endless, what's going on with you? All of you? You don't think I deserve to know?"

"Ask the Black Raven," Ikaros hissed back, and oh. He was angry too, but not at the man in front of him. "He allowed this to happen. I told you back at Cask and Barrels:

four of us were given the same mark. We didn't get into this merry dance without him leading us here."

"That's impossible," Reynard said. "I don't know what your game is, but I trust our god. Would he have given me the ship? Would he have let me take your precious Petal out from under your nose with a shadow portal, if he wasn't on my side?"

"We're supposed to be on the same side," Ikaros grated. "If you didn't have some doubts, Calyx would be dead on the deck of the *Silken Hare*. You're questioning this. You have to be."

"Perhaps you can't handle the Black Raven having a new favourite," Kaldoran snarled. "It's always been you, hasn't it? We looked up to you, me and Bors. We were kids when we signed up, and you were — the Hand. You made it all look so easy, so *meaningful*. We hung on every word you said."

"I'm aware," said Ikaros. They'd grown out of it, thank the nameless ancients, somewhere between the ages of twenty and thirty. The kids who came up in service to the Black Raven always grew up into allies and colleagues eventually — the ones that survived. It was always a good day when the fresh meat stopped looking at him like he'd stepped out of a scroll of epic murder poetry from ages past.

(They never stopped looking at Valeria like that, of course — Mardi was the first priest in two generations who managed to treat Valeria like an equal, rather than a terrifying gorgon.)

"What did the Petal promise you? What did she pay you?" Kaldoran went on, fuming. "I've had you watched for days. How long have you been bent, Ikaros? Ready to sell your loyalty outside the Raven's service?" His voice trembled on those last words as if he was only just holding on to reality.

"Oh," said Ikaros softly. "This is about Bors."

Ikaros had been the nearest, when Bors the Stave was stabbed through the eye by his own mark, a paranoid city judge who got in a lucky blow. Ikaros had been summoned by the gladii, to take the body of the Stave back to Raven's Gate. He'd been the one to break the news to Mardi, and to Reynard.

Mardi, numb with grief, forgave him for being the messenger. Apparently, Reynard Kaldoran never had.

Seven months had passed since. Ikaros should have noticed that one of his colleagues — one of his *friends*, really, was still burning with resentment. When you stopped noticing things like that, it meant that you were slipping too far from basic humanity. It was easy enough to do, when the decades slid past faster than they should, and your body never altered.

"So what is this?" Ikaros said quietly, dangerously. "You want to kill Calyx in front of me to show me how good you are? Want to make some kind of performance out of it, so the Black Raven will like you more? That isn't our way, Bow. Neither is letting all this personal shit get in the way of your job."

Reynard was weeping now, tears wet on his cheeks. "Personal shit?" he raged. "I'm still grieving our friend, who has been gone five minutes. He was like a brother to me. And you didn't wait a month before fucking his wife."

Ah.

"In my defence," Ikaros started to say, but he should have known it was far too late for reason.

The Bow flew at him, a curved scythe-knife in each hand.

Ikaros hadn't bothered to arm himself. He usually had a few weapons in the general vicinity, but he wasn't known as the Hand for nothing.

They fought hard and fast, darting in and out, Ikaros keeping distance from the knives, Reynard dodging what direct blows he could.

Ikaros fought with his whole body, hands and feet and forearms, snatching knives where he could, hurling them to the rocks. Reynard wasn't as fast as Valeria at finding more blades within the folds of his coat.

Painfully, step by step, Ikaros pressed him backwards, their boots slipping on the rough rocks. Blow after blow. Ikaros got one in for every four that Reynard dodged; was slashed bloody once for every nine swipes that Reynard made.

One smack in the mouth was particularly satisfying; Reynard spat blood and kept fighting. Ikaros kept pushing him, taunting him.

A fourth knife hit the rocks.

Ikaros was grabbed from behind, and it was only when he saw Reynard caught up in the same wild, tangling green vine that he realised it wasn't his opponent who had seized hold of him. It was Calyx. Of course it was Calyx.

She shimmered with power, with that foreign magic of hers, all colours. The vines she had used to snare them both were growing wildly out from between the rocks. Nothing had grown on the Cauldron for decades. Centuries, probably.

"Enough!" she declared.

Ikaros felt a wave of magic blanket him. The bond between them had been strained before because of the distance; because of his failure to protect her. Her magic wrapped around him now like summer and shaderoot and warm tea all mixed together.

It felt sweet. Blissful. It made him want to laugh out loud.

"Should have killed her when you had the chance," he confessed giddily to a bewildered Reynard.

Luckily, the bond read the warmth of his tone instead of the words he was saying, and gave him the benefit of the doubt.

(Damn it, he was wrecked by this woman.)

"How are you doing that?" sputtered Reynard to Calyx. "The Black Raven shrouded you. Cut off your magic."

"Your god is losing his touch," said Calyx, chin high, eyes gleaming with confidence. "Or perhaps he's not as fond of you as you think he is." She was marvellous.

Ikaros had to get a grip, instead of mooning over the Petal of the Imperium like he was a pageboy with a crush. "Start by telling her who hired us, Bow. All four of us. I know you have worked it out."

Reynard looked furious. "A client that none of us can afford to offend," he snapped back, struggling against the impossible vines.

"The King, or the Thirteenth Treasure?" pressed Ikaros. "It's either them or her family back home, and I don't think somehow that the Black Raven would be quite so amenable to foreigners smashing through temple protocol."

Calyx looked startled, as if it had not occurred to her that Ikaros had thought all this through quite so carefully. For a moment, the vines fell slack.

The Bow of the Black Raven screamed, a howl that was more prayer than protest. Black feathers poured out of his mouth like a swarm of bees, swooping around Ikaros and Calyx.

Behind them, the feather ship folded in on itself like a crumpled piece of parchment. Mardi and Valeria, both armed with knives and crossbows, fell out of the shadows as they vanished, both women rolling on the rough surface of the rocks.

(Oh, that was where they had been hiding. Smart.)

The remains of the ship of shadows hovered over them all for a moment, a threatening cloud of the Black Raven's disapproval.

"I didn't kill the Petal on your little barge," Reynard Kaldoran yelled into the storm. "Or Mardi, or Valeria. I always planned to kill you all right here, in this sacred place, under the auspices of the god you betrayed."

He said 'god' but Ikaros heard 'friend.' There was that anger again, bubbling under his skin. "Start with me," he roared, and ran at Reynard, letting his fury carry him forward.

He felt Calyx's magic tugging at him, trying to drag him back, but Ikaros had momentum on his side. It was, after all, a very small island.

The Hand of the Black Raven slammed into the body of the Bow of the Black Raven, throwing both of them backwards, and over the edge.

Into the River Divine.

20. Up into Owl's Gate

Not good enough.

Dio paced the deck of the *Silken Hare*. It was only minutes since the Cauldron had disappeared from sight behind them, and he was already feeling a twisting ache in his gut.

By the time an hour passed, he could no longer pace. The cramps in his stomach turned into waves of agonising pain in his chest that ebbed and flowed, sometimes almost tolerable, sometimes incapacitating. Even when that pain eased, the night-bloom tattoo on his collarbone felt raw, like someone had been pricking at it with the edge of a blade.

"We should go back," said Nimue when she found him curled up against the wall of Calyx's cabin. "You need to be with them."

"They didn't want me," Dio said sharply.

"That doesn't matter." She didn't deny it. "My mother's bond wants you there."

Some gladius he would make, if he let his hurt feelings and a bit of blinding pain keep him from his duty. "Your *mother* wants you safe."

"I can take care of myself."

He made a dry, pained sound.

Nimue looked unimpressed. "You're not going to do a very good job of protecting me if you keep shouting with pain all over the place."

"Who's shouting?" Dio was doing an excellent job at keeping his mouth shut when the pain was at its worst, *actually*.

"Your face," Nimue said. "It does the shouting for you."

"We promised we'd wait for them under Owl's Gate," snapped Dio.

"That's three hours away."

"I'm aware," Dio said with gritted teeth. "Please leave me to my heroic restraint."

Nimue huffed, but she left him alone for a while.

The pain eased, an hour or so from their destination. Dio didn't mention it to Nimue; didn't want her worrying that it meant something worse had happened. He couldn't be sure that it was bad news for Calyx. It didn't feel like she was dead...

Nimue came up to him after a while, prodded at his chest with suspicion. Of course she had noticed. "You don't seem as troubled."

"Perhaps that means they're fine and they're following us," said Dio, managing a smile.

Nimue was quick to assume the worst. "We have to turn around."

"We can't," Dio admitted, laying his head on his knees.

A dull ache lingered in his bones, but that was a holiday in comparison to everything else he'd felt surging through his body today. "The captain has his orders, to sail for Owl's Gate regardless of anything you or I have to say about it."

Nimue rolled her eyes. "You didn't trust yourself to stay on task?"

"Ikaros didn't trust me," Dio bit out.

Nimue scrunched down next to him, not seeming to worry about sitting on the damp wooden deck. As royals went, she was a good sport really. "I hate this."

"I hate it more," said Dio.

She bit her lip, glancing upriver. "Perhaps we could slip away while no one's watching."

Dio followed her gaze. "I wouldn't..."

The body of a dark-haired man in black thumped on to the deck out of nowhere, in a rain of black feathers. River water cascaded off his featherbrace jacket. His eyes were closed.

"That's not Ikaros," yelped Nimue. "Not the Bow, either. Is there another one?"

The unconscious man looked entirely like a priest of the Black Raven. His long dark braids spread out on the deck, as soaking wet as his clothes. His face was a gothic portrait of beauty at rest. His collar was thick with black feathers.

He was, quite literally, the man of Dio's dreams.

"Aodhan," Dio breathed.

Owl's Gate was a majestic white temple that stood astride the width of the river, with ancient archways underneath that allowed ships to pass through on their way to and from Phoenix Burning.

This was the largest centre of healing and surgery outside the cities of the Divine Kingdom.

The arches were adorned with elaborate, grotesque stone carvings of owls, owls, more owls. There were ridges and plinths built strategically into the stonework, so that real owls could nest and hover here, at the temple sacred to the worship of the god who wore their face.

There was a protocol for dealing with an unconscious patient brought by boat. Healers swarmed the barge, tossing Aodhan into a sling between two porters, then carrying him up into one of the towers that formed the lower half of the Gate.

Dio and Nimue, leaving the *Silken Hare* in dock, were escorted at a more civilised pace up a narrow, spiralling staircase, and into a high-ceilinged hall. The windows were arched here, with marble shapes partly covering some of the glass. Natural light still streamed through from the late afternoon sun.

There were more owls inside the hall, perched on rafters, gazing down at the visitors.

"How do you know this man?" Nimue asked Dio in the brief period that the two of them were left alone, standing in front of the glass windows with the view of the busy River Divine sprawled out beneath them. "Are you collecting priests of death?"

"Not intentionally," Dio protested. "It's a long story."

"We're so terribly busy right now. However will you find the time to explain it all?"

A ginger-gold owl swooped along the corridor, gliding with immaculate precision to land on the window ledge in front of Nimue. A silver name tag hung from its neck, proclaiming that its name was Atticus.

"Birds do behave very strangely in this kingdom of yours," said Nimue, startled.

Atticus the owl leaned in, with what could only be described as a threatening expression.

Nimue took one step back.

"I thought you studied diplomacy," said Dio.

"I didn't finish my studies yet!"

Atticus took to the air again, swooping along the hall with the implicit invitation to follow.

Dio took Nimue's hand, all the better to drag her along with him. If following this owl meant postponing the question of how exactly he had met Aodhan, then all the better.

"We can't treat him," said the knight of the Bright Owl, folding his arms across a stocky chest. He was middle-aged, with a shock of silver hair and eyes that had clearly seen a lot of hard choices over the decades. This wasn't one of them. He hadn't paused to think when he set eyes on the patient, merely stepped back and refused.

Dio felt his chest tighten painfully. It was not the bond, or the distance from Calyx — he could feel her, she was *fine*, moving in their general direction — no, it was anxiety about the strange, pretty man from his dreams. Lying on the narrow bed, Aodhan looked grey and unwell. He had still not awoken even when dragged from the barge to this blinding white temple of healing.

"Why can't you?" Dio protested. "What's wrong with him? Is he going to—" Surely knights didn't give up on patients this quickly, not without trying *everything* in their power.

The knight was irritated by being questioned. No compassion in sight. "We don't have permission to heal this one. You shouldn't have brought him here."

"I give you permission," Dio said immediately.

"Ha!" Apparently this was funny. Dio probably shouldn't hit the man, but he was sorely tempted.

Nimue took over, clearly trying to prove that her diplomatic training was useful for something. "Can you explain why you won't treat him?"

"Can't," the healer corrected automatically. "Not won't. It wouldn't do any good. Not here. Not him."

There was something in the way he spoke, a combination of awe and distaste, as if he couldn't wait to move on from this particular patient. Dio hadn't seen the man touch Aodhan, not once.

"Why?" he asked, one more time. "One of your knights healed a priest of the Black Raven in front of my eyes, so don't tell me this is some kind of religious constraint."

The healer put up a hand to stop Dio's righteous flow. "This is not a priest," he said impatiently. "And I wouldn't worry too much about him dying, if I were you."

"What is he," Nimue pressed. "If not a priest?"

The knight of the Bright Owl looked surprised they didn't know. "He's a god, of course. And he's not ours. So I'll thank you to get him off the premises."

21. Underwater, Somewhere Else

Even the water tasted like flowers. It should be salty, this far south. It was roses and violets in his mouth. Ikaros had forgotten what anything tasted like except for Calyx, her magic, her intrusive bloody bond pushing all manner of floristry up his throat, over his tongue.

He was drowning, he realised, as a secondary sensation. Mouth full of flowers, choking. Water everywhere, dark and impossible.

He had lost track of Reynard Kaldoran, after shoving him into the River Divine and falling along with him...

Nothing to see down here but water, a wavering pattern of light, and...

This was what dying felt like.

He'd known he would get here eventually.

Death marked Ikaros when he was born, a pale shaded scythe-knife splayed across his right palm.

Death tempted Ikaros when he was eight years old, a street kid with no hope and no future. Bright-eyed and merry, Death ran with the other boys, pretending to be one of them, playacting at being human.

After Death left him alone, Ikaros marked his wrists up to the elbows with hopeful cuts, calling to the Black Raven to shelter him.

Death did not come.

Ikaros offered himself to Death when he was thirteen, a wayward youth standing on a bridge, staring into the swirling waters of the River Divine.

The Black Raven took the form of a bright-eyed boy with a wicked smile, the same age as Ikaros. Long dark hair in braids that fell to his waist. He sat on the edge of the bridge, shifting his weight back and forth like this was a game.

Like he wanted to jump too, just to see what happened.

"Take my oath," Ikaros demanded, not for the first time. He'd burned incense in every raven shrine in the kingdom to earn this encounter. It wasn't going how he had expected.

The boy with the long black hair tipped his head back, laughing in the sunshine. "Jump with me," he said. "We'll go together."

"Don't try to fancy it up," said Ikaros, and held out his arms in entreaty. "Take my service." *Take me*.

"You can serve me without killing for me," Death reminded him.

"I don't do anything halfway," promised Ikaros.

Death leaned in, and kissed him on the mouth. He tasted like honey cider and fresh bread. "We'll see."

In the week that Ikaros turned fourteen, he missed too many meals. Got sloppy. Almost bled to death after a street robbery went wrong. Woke up to find Death sitting on the edge of his bed.

(A real bed, clean sheets. Never mind the god in his lap, this was the real miracle.)

"Let's see how good you are with your hands," said the bright-eyed boy, making it sound kind of dirty.

An hour later, Ikaros had his hands wrapped around the throat of a flour merchant in the depths of his store cupboard. A thick-set man; he took a long time to die.

"I can do better," he said to Death, afterwards. The scythe-knife tattoo he had been marked with at birth was darker now, nearly black. He couldn't stop staring at it. This meant he belonged with someone.

"I hope that's true," said his new master, who still looked like a carefree youth.

They sat on another bridge together, passing an apple

back and forth, bite for bite. It was the best-tasting thing Ikaros had eaten in weeks.

"Why did he have to die?" Ikaros asked. "That mark. What did he do?"

Death raised an eyebrow. "What do you think he did?"

"Some terrible crime, I spose. Did he desecrate a temple? Or say bad things about you? Did he beat his wife?"

No one knew why Death took some sacrifices, refused others. All that they knew was that he chose. He chose, and his servants killed, and someone paid.

And it was *sacred*.

"Would that make it easier for you?" mused Death. "To know he was a bad man who deserved his fate at your hands?"

Ikaros snorted. "It wasn't hard."

Ikaros was twenty when he first met Valeria, the Blade. It wasn't unusual, that so much time had passed before their paths crossed. There were dozens of priests of the Black Raven, and they didn't exactly hang out at the same taverns at the end of a work day. The younger priests were encouraged to live in the temples, to work in pairs when the job was dangerous (one to take the mark, one to back them up), to learn the names of the hand-maidens and other support staff.

The older priests, the veterans like the Whip and the Sword and the Blade, they kept themselves distant from the temples. No one knew where they lived, when they were not serving their god. (They were always serving their god.) If you saw one of them, then they weren't on duty, because no one ever saw them when they meant business.

Legends, all of them.

Ikaros was occasionally paired with Scylla back then — the Dart. It made sense for a close-fighter to be matched with a distance weapon. (They were all weapons; he knew that now. Tools of their master.) Scylla was obsessed with Valeria the Blade, collected all kinds of rumours and clues and fragments of poetry about the older woman.

The Strix job was Scylla's, with Ikaros as backup. Neither of them were expecting trouble, not from a soft mark like Gussie Wenting, a scoundrel who had married and abandoned seven wives across the kingdom — hardly a surprise that someone had finally scraped together enough coin to beg the Black Raven for justice. It wouldn't be a shock if it turned out the wives had banded together to pay the coin...

The job went wrong. It all went wrong. By the time it was over — the worst job Ikaros had ever seen — Gussie was dead, along with his eight surprise bodyguards. So was Scylla. There was blood soaking into a hotel carpet, and most of it belonged to Ikaros.

He hadn't seen his god's face in years. Didn't expect him to come now, to answer the prayer of a dying priest.

As Ikaros lost consciousness, the last thing he saw was the window of the hotel room, black with feathers, and the shape of a woman stepping out of the shadows...

"You're the Blade," he murmured, hours later, as the Knights of the Bright Owl worked to save his life.

The beautiful woman gave him the coldest expression he had ever seen. "You owe me a new featherbrace," she informed him. "I'm never going to get all your blood out of mine."

The first time Valeria took Ikaros to her bed, six months after they first met, he found thirty-nine knives concealed within her clothes.

The water didn't taste like flowers any more. It didn't taste of anything. Ikaros could not feel Calyx and her threads connecting to him. That probably meant he was almost gone...

Ikaros was twenty-two when he considered retiring. His girlfriend Layla laughed at him. "What, you think you're going to move in on the Wombat, pour ale for the rest of your life? This isn't your world, love."

"You're giving it up," he said stubbornly. "Why can't I?"

Layla was a cleric of the Silver Hawk, a foot soldier of the god everyone else knew as War. For a short-statured woman, she wielded a mean axe. But she'd always meant to return to her father's tavern after a decade of war service, retire gracefully while she was still alive.

"I'm ready," Layla said, patting him on the shoulder. "My god and I, we're done with each other. But you, dear heart. You're never going to be done with yours."

Ikaros thought about that, two weeks later, when he strangled a sailor in Mermaid Bay and felt the warm benediction of the Black Raven cross his brow like a kiss.

He thought about it again months later, when he saw his baby daughter, cradled in Layla's arms.

They don't need me. Better off without me.

Ikaros was twenty-four when he married Valeria for the first time. It lasted three years. It never stopped being a white-hot disaster.

Ikaros was thirty when he married Valeria for the second time. When it was good, it was good. When it was bad...

Well, the stories exaggerated. They only nearly burned a city down once.

"How long have you been doing this?" asked Mardi Morency, new recruit to the Black Raven — smart as a button, good head on her shoulders. Dark eyes alive with enthusiasm. She ignored her fellow novices, trailing instead after the older priests, hungry to learn what made the legends so good at their work.

Ikaros was one of the legends now.

"I can't remember," he said, then counted in his head. "Twenty years, give or take."

(This conversation was twenty years ago.)

"You must be good at what you do."

"We all serve as best we can."

She seemed impossibly young, but she had turned eighteen before she joined the temple — Death didn't take kids as young as Ikaros had been, not any more.

"How will I know?" Mardi asked him. "Which weapon is mine. What kind of priest I'm supposed to be?"

(She wouldn't be the Needle for another year but oh, by then she would have earned it.)

Ikaros remembered how it had felt, to become the Hand. To feel part of something so much greater than himself. His name was a weapon; he was a weapon. All was right with the world.

"You'll know," he promised Mardi. "You'll feel how right it is, in your bones."

"That new girl," said Valeria, when the two of them met in the only tavern of a town too small to even have a name. "The Needle."

"She's been in service with us for five years," said Ikaros. "I know you know her name is Mardi."

"She keeps asking me questions. Talking to me."

"She probably wants to be friends." It had come as a surprise to him too, but Ikaros thought it was best to be open to new experiences.

"Why?" asked Valeria, baffled.

"Because you're a wise old mentor," he told her sagely. "She wants to drink your experience like sucking juice out of an orange."

"Fuck you. Do you think I need friends?"

"If I knew what you needed, we might still be married."

Valeria laughed at him. "Last I checked, we're still married."

(Marriage between priests was forbidden now, had been for years. If Ikaros and Valeria got another divorce, it would be *forever*.)

Ikaros raised his eyebrows at her now and smirked a little. "Want to get a room?"

Bed was what they were best at together. They'd known each other's bodies intimately for decades (on and off) and knew exactly how to move, to touch, to ravish each other.

The last time they tried to make a go of their actual marriage, it was just after they'd been hired by a husband and wife at a masked ball. The husband hired Valeria to kill his wife's lover… and the wife hired Ikaros to kill her husband.

(They found this out later, or perhaps they simply guessed the most obvious customer? It was not as if they were ever told who paid for the mark to die.)

With the deaths due for midnight (to court maximum drama), Ikaros and Valeria were stuck at the blessed ball for hours, joining in the formal dances and making intense eye contact across the room. Daring each other to be the first to make a move.

Of course it ended up in a cloakroom, Valeria scratching bloody lines down Ikaros' back as he fucked her against a wall, the iron boning of her wide skirts nearly strangling him in the process.

He tore her dress; she held him between her thighs, hands clenched in his hair, until he made her come twice more with his mouth alone.

They killed both men at midnight, shattering the lanterns to perform their sacraments in darkness. Then they took themselves off to Valeria's nearest house (she owned several) to take a shared bath by candlelight, reminding each other of every possible way they could bring each other pleasure.

They played at being husband and wife for another three months after that, but by the end of it they were throwing wine glasses, flirting with other people, and making each other miserable.

Friends was fine. Colleagues was good. Even *husband* and *wife* were fine as long as they were fond names they gave each other, attached to no expectations of married life. Ikaros trusted Valeria more, knew her better, than nearly any other living soul in the world.

But he shouldn't be married to her.

He probably shouldn't encourage her to make other friends. She'd damage them, sooner or later.

"The Needle seems robust," he said as a final word on the subject, fifteen years ago. "She can probably take you."

Valeria laughed.

Ikaros awoke, out of the water. Spat night-bloom petals from his salt-wet mouth. He was in a cave. A dark cave, waist high in river water. He couldn't see a single candle or lantern anywhere, but light flickered eerily against the domed, craggy ceiling.

The next thing he spat out was a mouthful of black feathers.

"I know you're here!" he yelled, hearing his voice bounce back in a mournful, mocking echo. "*Death*."

When Ikaros was a child, he saw Death as a child.

As he became a man, Death grew broader shoulders, longer hair, a masculine swagger.

His voice deepened; it was rare to see Death in person. But his voice in your ear, guiding your hand... Ikaros lived for those moments.

He had not heard the voice of Death in... how long was it now? Six years? Twelve?

Twelve years ago was when the Stave and the Bow came bright-eyed to Raven's Gate as a package deal. Two young men, friends as close as brothers, eager to serve. Ikaros hadn't taken them seriously at first. You couldn't pay attention to every recruit.

But Valeria saw something in Bors, the Stave. Picked

him as backup for her missions, as an excuse to teach him a thing or two. She would laugh in your face if you called her a mentor, but...

Mardi had also been charmed by the Stave, reluctantly at first.

Bors was steady. There was a calmness about him that was soothing. Ikaros stopped resisting his friendship once he realised that Bors was capable of sitting quietly in a tavern for hours without speaking. (Truly, what more could one want in a companion?

When Bors and Reynard worked together, they were magic. The Bow and the Stave. One, frenetic and fast-talking. The other, calm and quietly wicked. They planned jobs more intensely than anyone else — did their research. Rumour was, they always *knew* who had paid their coin. Considered it part of the process.

Honestly, Ikaros had assumed they were a pair in bed as well as out, until Bors and Mardi became... well, a far better argument for marriage between priests than he and Valeria had ever been. Not that they were allowed to take that particular sacrament...

It didn't matter now. Bors had been dead for months, leaving behind an angry best friend and a not-quite widow. The child he longed for would have no father. The retirement he planned would never come.

No one gets out alive.

Mardi would. Ikaros would eat broken glass to make it happen.

But he had to be alive himself, to have any chance of helping her.

"Death!" he yelled in the cave. The forbidden name, the one word that a priest of the Black Raven never spoke aloud, because it was the name of their god, too sacred to speak. "What the fuck have you done?"

No one else would speak to their master like this; Ikaros had always seen things a little differently, and the Black Raven humoured him. Had always liked to pretend that they were equals. Friends?

That was what was so disarming about the beautiful bastard.

A man stood on the rocks, veiled in shadows. Ikaros waded towards him. "Am I dead?" he demanded. "After all of this. You let Calyx take us. You let Bors die. You've betrayed us over and over. What the hell do you have to say for yourself?"

For a moment, Ikaros had a flicker of a doubt that this was the Black Raven. From behind, in the darkness it could still be Reynard. A hood covering his long hair, the tailored shape of a featherbrace with all its patterned embroidery...

Soaking wet, Ikaros made it up the rocks, seized the arm of the man in black. Who turned, wild-eyed and bare-faced, and threw himself sobbing into his arms.

God, after all.

Ikaros held the trembling figure of his master. If the Black Raven wanted comfort, he'd chosen the wrong priest. "What is wrong with you?" he asked gruffly.

Gods weren't supposed to cry.

"I'm broken," Death gasped into his neck, adding more

wetness to Ikaros' clammy skin. Genuine tears, hot and searing.

Ikaros patted his back awkwardly as if this was a baby novice, devastated after their first kill. "Worse things happen at sea?" he ventured. It was one of the things Layla used to say, when they were young and stupid together, trying to figure out what their life might look like with a baby in it.

(Before they figured out together that hers would be better without Ikaros in it.)

Death made a sound that was half laughter, half misery. "I'm not really here," he sobbed.

"No," Ikaros agreed. "I'm not here either. I'm drowning in the River Divine. My only consolation is that that little fucker Reynard is drowning too."

Death pulled back. He had never looked less otherworldly. There were shadows under his glorious eyes, tear-tracks on his skin. "Do you remember?" Death asked Ikaros. "When we were children together. Do you remember my other name?"

"We were never children together," said Ikaros flatly. "I was an old man at eight years old, and you were a divinity pretending to be a child so I wouldn't run away from you."

Death quirked a small smile at that. "Would you really have run?"

"We'll never know."

"You remember, though. The name you gave me, before you knew who I was."

Ikaros sighed. "I always knew who you were, dear heart."

Death blinked those pretty eyes of his. Ikaros, as always, was easy for him.

"Aodhan," he admitted. "You wanted a name. I gave you one. Don't tell me you still use it?"

"Sometimes," said Death sadly. "When making new friends."

Ikaros rolled his eyes. Death — *Aodhan* looked impossibly young. Ikaros himself had never felt so old in his life. This felt less like a religious experience and more like an intervention. "Who do you have your eye on? Fresh meat for the temple? I'd sort out your handmaidens first, there's been a major balls-up in administration..."

Aodhan's tear-rimmed eyes looked apologetic.

"Oh," Ikaros breathed. "Fuck you. You did all that deliberately, didn't you?"

Aodhan raised himself up on his toes and kissed Ikaros on the forehead. "Don't die," he murmured. "You're needed, love. I need you."

For the first time in a very long time, Ikaros was afraid. There was something final in the voice of the god he had followed for more than forty years.

"Right back at you," he whispered into the darkness.

So much darkness.

His mouth filled with salt-water and petals.

Death came for Ikaros, one more time.

22. Beneath and Inside Raven's Gate

Raven's Gate was even larger and more imposing than Owl's Gate, with four archways across the breadth of the river, and thousands of ravens carved into its black granite outer walls. That was a lot of beaks, when they were all pointed directly at you.

Dio had sailed under Raven's Gate many a time, but never had any particular reason to enter the largest temple of death in the kingdom. Not until now.

It was evening when they had first arrived hours ago: lanterns lining the gate, candles flickering. It was still dark outside, but Dio had lost track of how late it was.

He and Nimue were being ignored, which was far better than the first few hours here, when they had endured an intense and scrutinising interrogation by a matron who reminded Dio of his aunties. Mavadian's large and spiky black headdress proclaimed her to be something of an authority figure around here.

Being ignored was far better than being glared at by this terrifying woman who thought he was some kind of criminal — until Nimue mentioned they had recently been travelling with Valeria the Blade, Ikaros the Hand, and Mardi the Needle. At which point, Death's Auntie lost complete interest in Dio and Nimue, confident that whatever nonsense was going on here with the unconscious Aodhan, it was absolutely Ikaros' fault.

Dio was not going to argue with her.

He hadn't seen Aodhan since he and Nimue, assisted by a couple of low-ranked Knights of the Bright Owl, delivered his limp body to the priestesses.

And now, they waited, in a small chamber with only one window. One narrow bed, which neither of them were calm enough to use.

They waited, and waited.

Plenty of time for Dio to agonise over the fact that his mysterious dream boyfriend was a god — and not just any god. The Black Raven himself. The god of death.

(He would rather think about literally anything else.)

"Do you think we're prisoners?" Dio asked Nimue at one point.

She gave him a scornful look for thinking anything else.

"Is my mother still approaching?" she asked, every hour or so.

"Soon," he said. And: "Closer, now."

Finally, he put a hand to the floor and saw clover sprouting between the slate tiles. That was confirmation, if he needed it — the warmth of his night-bloom tattoo and the overwhelming feeling of rightness had been his first clue. "She's here."

"Oh," said Nimue, overwhelmed with relief. "Finally."

They waited.

Calyx did not come for them.

Pain blossomed in Ikaros' chest. The ground was unsteady beneath him, with the familiar shift back and forth that told him he was in another bloody boat.

What he wouldn't give to be on dry land.

He opened cracked, salt-encrusted lips, and felt cool, fresh water pour over his face, his chin.

"Steady, sailor," said an amused voice. "Mind how you go."

Ikaros' eyes snapped open. That was a mistake, because the salt and sticky residue from his sore eyes had gummed his lashes together.

That soft voice 'tsked' above him, and the fresh water rolled blissfully over the top half of his face next, soaking his hair and eyebrows. Gentle hands wiped his eyes, and his mouth.

He opened his eyes properly, and found that his head rested in the lap of his wife. "What happened?" he croaked, his throat too dry to make much of the words. He could taste blood on the inside of his mouth.

Valeria scooped another cup of fresh water from a bucket nearby, and held it close enough for him to sip. "What do you think? We rescued you. Did you think we wouldn't?"

Ikaros looked around, wincing as he moved his neck. He'd done some damage there — bruising down his back, by the feel of it. His fingers were too stiff. His chest burned from the inside out, as if someone had beaten the saltwater out of his body. How long had he been unconscious?

This was not the *Silken Hare*. No, it was Death's vessel, the ship of feathers and shadows, though the high mast had disappeared somewhere. It was shaped more like a barge, wide and flat. Still black, still edged with live ravens with their beady little eyes.

It was late — the early hours of the morning, though still dark.

Lying on his back, head cradled against Valeria's thighs, Ikaros saw up, up, beyond the boat. Raven's Gate hung above them, the mighty arch of spirals and carvings and more ravens.

"Reynard?" he asked.

"Not dead, either," reported Valeria.

Ikaros nodded. Good. For the best, probably.

"He woke up before you," she added. "Stormed off to state his case to Mavadian and the others up in the temple."

Oh. Less good.

"Do we have to move?" Ikaros asked.

Valeria's fingers swept through his hair, and she scooped another cup of that clear, fresh water against his lips. "Not yet, my love."

The owl brought word of the dying god.

After Valeria had dragged Ikaros' body out of the river, forcing the saltwater out of his lungs with her bare hands... after Mardi and Calyx worked together to drag Kaldoran to the rocky shore — and Mardi knocked the other priest unconscious when he tried to fight them.

After all of that.

Calyx stood at the prow of a ship. The green shoots and flowers she had sparked during her capture had changed the magic of the black shadow-ship. It liked her now. Reshaped itself to make her more comfortable: she preferred a barge to a yacht.

They were already heading south-west down the Coronis branch of the River Divine, when the owl came.

She was small and tawny, with a flecked coat and deep black eyes. She swooped around the shadow-ship, wings spread wide, then glided down to perch near Calyx.

A bronzed name-plate hung from her collar: Zenobia. She carried a twist of paper with the message. Calyx recognised her daughter's hand instantly.

Leaving Owl's Gate, moving on to Raven's. Captain agreed given the emergency. Tell Valeria we're taking a dying man to the temple. His name is Aodhan.

Valeria, reading over Calyx's shoulder, started swearing wildly.

Mardi, resting on the deck between their two unconscious colleagues, looked up with mild interest. "What's going on?"

"The Black Raven," said Valeria angrily. "He's manifested human again. And this time he seems to be dying."

Mardi let out a deep and heavy sigh. "You can be the one to tell Ikaros."

Of all the buildings that Calyx had seen along the river journey of the last several days, Raven's Gate was the most intimidating, especially at night. Its high and shadowy arches resembled a fortress, rather than a place of healing.

(They had sailed under the place of healing, carrying their wounded men past Owl's Gate and on through the long night.)

"You're sure about this," Calyx said to Mardi.

Valeria was to stay behind, keeping an eye on Ikaros and the Bow, neither of whom had woken after their near-drowning.

"This is the only way you'll get your answers," said Mardi Morency.

Mardi had stolen a jacket she referred to as a 'feather-brace' off the unconscious body of Reynard Kaldoran, hanging it up to dry over the last few hours. It was still damp and crusted with salt, but Mardi wore it anyway, buttoning it all the way from her neck down to her pregnant belly, where she let it hang loose.

Calyx knew armour when she saw it. Her own clothes were wrecked, but she took a moment to use her magic to clean the ragged silks, and press the linen stemma so that it fell in the traditional pristine column from throat to ankle. Back at the Imperium, ladies often used magic to transform their outfits into grand, majestic statements of power, fashion, beauty. They were not accustomed to using magic for laundry — they had people for that.

Before she stepped off the boat, Calyx passed a hand over her scalp, reducing the stubble to a smooth, clear surface. She was ready.

Mardi led the way up into the central arch of the temple. So many stairs and spirals. Finally, the two of them strode across a long gallery, lit with lanterns. Priests and hand-maidens gathered here, watching the newcomers with a curious eye.

Dio was nearby. Calyx could feel him. With all four of her bonded servants close, her power flared up, brighter than ever. She could do this.

A matron in a spiked black headdress swung out of a nearby room, facing down Mardi with all the scorn and disdain of a governess telling off a wayward pupil. "Needle," she said. "What have you done?"

Mardi lifted her chin. "I'm here to resign my service, Mavadian."

The other woman glowered at her. "You think you're worthy of an honourable retirement? You, who have failed to dispatch your most recent mark? She's standing here in our master's halls. An insult to all that we are."

"It's a little more complicated than that," said Mardi.

Calyx stepped forward, catching the matron's eye. "Mavadian," she said, her voice ringing out with what her sister always called 'palace tones.' The voice you used when you wanted everyone at court to hear what you had to say. "I hear you are the senior representative of your god in this temple."

"I am," said Mavadian, her own voice raised and formal. "Your presence here is unwanted, Petal of the Imperium."

"Oh," said Calyx with a small smile. "So you do know who I am. Tell me please, how it is that four of your master's servants were all sent forth to murder me at the same time?"

Whispers started up among the onlookers.

Mavadian's own expression of triumph faltered. "You do not know our ways," she declared.

Mardi scoffed. "This is not our way, Mavadian. This is no one's way. Where is our god? Perhaps Aodhan can explain."

Mavadian looked scandalised. "That name is not for your mouth, traitor."

"Traitor?' demanded Mardi, louder than before. More people were coming to watch their performance. Handmaidens appeared in doorways, staring with open curiosity. Several priests in those black featherbraces joined the crowd. "I was sent honestly and honourably to end this woman's life as sacrifice to the Black Raven. I accepted the mark. And then I learned that Ikaros the Hand, Valeria the Knife and Reynard the Bow also accepted that mark."

A louder rustle of whispers occurred at the naming of Ikaros and Valeria.

"You are mistaken," said Mavadian, standing taut and still. "Such a thing could not happen. Your mind has been warped by this foreigner's magic tricks."

Mardi leaned in, furious. "I'm not the one who has been warped. This happened on your watch. Explain it, or I take my concerns to a higher authority."

"Higher than me?" Mavadian scoffed.

Mardi raised both hands and clapped them above her head. Black feathers spiralled out of thin air, landing in her dark, curly hair. "Your pride is showing," she said. "I think you've forgotten what it means to serve the Black Raven."

There was a shout from behind them, and a scuffle. The gathering crowd of priests parted to let Reynard Kaldoran through. He was ragged and miserable, in soft shirt sleeves. There was a cut over his eye, and he hobbled as he walked. He had armed himself anew — he now held a crossbow loosely at his side, with a knife in the other hand.

"Mardi Morency has broken the covenant!" he screamed. "She has accepted an oath of loyalty to a master other than ours."

Calyx turned, though she was uncomfortable having a

creature like Mavadian at her back. "She accepted nothing," she said scornfully. "I bonded her against her will, out of self defence. Would you like me to do the same to you?"

Another disturbance broke out, at the far end of the hall. An elderly hand-maiden, all in black, with a thick apron covering her robes, pushed her way through. "Mavadian! The visitor has gone."

"Gone?" said Mavadian furiously. "What visitor?"

"The one we cannot name aloud," said the newcomer, looking desperate.

"How did he get out? He's dying."

More mutters and whispers broke out among the gathered priests, handmaidens and the rest of them.

"Will someone," roared Reynard Kaldoran, staggering forward on the verge of collapse. "Tell me what the blood and endless is going on around here!"

Dio lay on the bed in the small chamber, very still, not sleeping. He'd tried picking the lock several times, but none of his old tricks would budge it.

Nimue had not moved from the window, though there couldn't be much of a view out there. It was all lanterns, early morning river traffic, and ravens.

You could not escape the ravens. Nested as they were, all around the outside of the arches, they filled the air with croaking, grating noises. It made Dio want to scratch his skin off.

"Something's happening," Nimue murmured. "My

mother's magic — other magic. This temple is full of it. It all feels bad. Wrong."

Dio could not feel anything, except the settled comfort that came from Calyx being so very close by. "What should we do?"

Nimue turned, and the shadows moved with her. She had wings again, or at least a faint outline of wings like the green shapes that had taken hold of her at the Eye of the Basilisk.

"I think," she said, staring at the way the wings moved with her body as she shifted back and forth. "The River Divine is calling me."

"Resist it," urged Dio. "We have enough magical demands on us right now."

Calyx was directly above them, in the temple. He could feel her. Why wasn't she here? Why had she not come for them?

"But I think," said Nimue, biting her lip. "I think I can use its magic to get us out of here."

"That seems like a terrible idea."

Something heavy thumped against the locked door of their cell.

Dio jumped and stared at it. "Are you doing that?"

Glowing purple tendrils slipped through the keyhole.

"Are those night-blooms?" Dio yelped.

The door shook, and shuddered again.

"The river wants to help us," said Nimue, with a beatific smile on her face. "Everything's going to be fine. We don't need my mother to rescue us. It's my turn."

Ikaros was barely on his feet when the owl came upon them, circling around the deck of the shadow-barge. This owl was enormous, with high tufts above its ears, and deep orange eyes. Its feathers were mottled, cream and ochre.

Valeria reached up her arms to welcome the damned creature, who cried out in approval and landed at her feet. Its nameplate read: Artemis.

"A message from Ulwen," said Valeria, unfolding the scrap of paper from behind the name plate. "She says the temples are in chaos."

"All of them, or just ours?" Ikaros asked, eyeing the imposing black shape of Raven's Gate over their heads.

"The Bright Owl has stopped answering prayers up and down the river."

"That's not good."

"Ulwen also says she's heard about disruption in the temples of the Lark of the Hearth. Across several provinces, but mostly in the temples along the river."

Artemis the owl hooted at them, and made no move to leave. Ikaros tried shooing it, but got an orange-eyed glare for his trouble.

"We don't have any food for you," said Valeria. "The *Silken Hare* should be moored nearby, they always have a soup pot on the fire..."

The temple door swung open, and a bedraggled man burst out. He was barefoot, bare-chested, clad only in a pair of black larkflax bags, like a sailor. Dark, wet braids hung down his back.

Ikaros felt like he had been punched in the chest. "Speaking of gods who don't answer prayers."

"Oh," breathed Valeria. "I'd forgotten how pretty he is."

"I hadn't."

Aodhan, the Black Raven, god of death, staggered towards the shadow-barge. The ship, recognising him, shivered in anticipation. "I need you to take me to Phoenix Burning," commanded Death.

Ikaros' body tightened as the bond magic resisted the command. "We can't leave here without Calyx," he said.

Aodhan leaped from the temple steps to the deck of the black shadow-barge, using what little strength he had left. He stumbled forward, teeth bared, facing off against Ikaros. "Are you mine or not?" he demanded.

Ikaros felt that familiar sensation of flowers curling inside; his body rebelling against their presence, their taste. "Opinions are divided," he choked. Flowers rose on his tongue.

There was a cry behind them. Dio came running out of the temple. "There's something wrong with Nimue," he yelled.

Vines and leaves burst out of the door behind him, dark green and lush. Night-blooms, larger than Ikaros had ever seen them, flowered fiercely on those vines. Black, purple petals, lit up with bright, glowing stamens.

This wasn't Calyx's magic. Ikaros felt none of the familiar pull. Not even the night-bloom tattoo on the side of his neck responded to the otherworldly presence of these flowers.

The river, though. The river responded. The waters swelled beneath them, lifting up the shadow-barge like this was the ocean, tossing them back and forth.

Dio scrambled on to the deck. He gave Aodhan a wary

look, as if they were long-acquainted. "Are you doing this to her?"

The Black Raven gave Dio a dismissive look. "I don't care about the daughter."

Dio's face flashed with anger. "She's my friend, Aodhan! You can't pick and choose who you care about."

Interesting. Since when was young Dio on personal-name terms with Ikaros' god?

"He's a deity of the Divine Kingdom," said Valeria. "That's literally what they do."

"We need to go, now," said Aodhan in an urgent tone. "The divine magics of the kingdom are in crisis, Ikaros. I need your service."

"We can't go without Calyx!" protested Dio.

Aodhan gave him a pitying look. "I really thought *you* understood me."

Green kept pouring out of the door of the temple — leaves and shoots and tendrils and Nimue. Nimue was green. Green light streamed out behind her, like wings.

The river water ran up the steps towards the girl, lapping up to touch her feet.

Aodhan looked shocked; stunned. It couldn't be good, when something was so extraordinary that it surprised a god. He blinked, and looked away. "We're going now," said Aodhan. The shadow-barge shivered at his touch, breaking away from its moorings. Black ropes slithered free of the dock.

Ikaros tried to move, to throw himself overboard, but the barge dragged them away. Away from his mistress and her bond.

Pain blistered in his stomach, in his veins. Ikaros screamed, and violets flew out of his mouth. Blood, flecked on the petals.

He could hear Valeria screaming, too far away for him to reach. Dio's cries of pain mingled with hers.

Darkness swamped Ikaros again, and he fell into it.

Calyx, standing in the upper gallery of the temple, surrounded by priests and hand-maidens all in black, felt the magic coming before she saw it. Leaves and tendrils threaded through the doorways, along the polished floors. They burst into flower: night-blooms with stamens that glowed brightly, despite it being clearly morning outside the windows.

"More foreign magic!" exclaimed Mavadian in disgust.

Mardi gave Calyx a wild look. Calyx shook her head. "It's not mine." She could feel it, the heavy pressure of the magic closing in around her. It felt familiar. "I think it's the river," she started to say.

Reynard Kaldoran barrelled into her, knocking her to the floor while remaining on his feet. Mardi drew a long, needle-sharp blade to defend Calyx. Reynard pointed the bolt of his crossbow between Calyx's eyes.

"One of you kill her!" screamed Mavadian. "Then we can make sense of this mess."

Mardi slid into Reynard's line of sight, blocking him from where Calyx lay on the floor. "You already shot me once. Think you can do it again?"

Calyx felt the bond magic twist inside her. The golden threads stretched and pulled... "Mardi, they're leaving," she gasped. "Ikaros, Dio, Valeria. They're moving away from me."

"So," she heard Reynard say. "I only have to kill one of you to get to her."

The windows shattered. Glass rained in upon them all. Calyx rolled, pulling up her stemma to shield her head and face. When she uncovered herself, she saw her daughter.

Nimue stood on the ledge of an arched window. Bright green wings spread out behind her, fluid and liquid. Magical. Dripping with river water, and river magic. Nimue glowed brightly, like an emerald. Like the waters at the Eye of the Basilisk.

Her whole body shuddered, and she fell forward. "Mother," she gasped.

Calyx scrambled to her, practically knocking Mardi and Reynard aside to reach her daughter. "Nimue."

Nimue was full of magic, pounded flat by magic. She shook with the effort of holding so much power within her slender frame. "They've gone," she gasped. "The Black Raven took all three of them with him."

Calyx swept her daughter into her arms, holding her. "It's all right. We'll find them. It will all be —"

Nimue fell apart into a burst of emerald-green water, swamping the polished floor.

Calyx stared blankly at her own empty arms, then down at the river water soaking into her stemma and silks.

Her daughter was gone.

23. Down the Coronis

"I'm sorry," said the voice of the god. He didn't sound sorry.

Dio opened his eyes, and stared into the face of Aodhan. He felt like an idiot. Keeping his secret, flirting with the mysterious night-time prowler with the dreamy eyes. He had suspected Aodhan was dangerous, but he'd assumed a mild, sexy kind of danger.

Not end of the world, smite-you-where-you-stand kind of danger.

Dio groaned as he came fully awake. His body twisted in pain. Calyx's absence was a knife in his gut.

Aodhan stood at the prow of his shadow-ship as they swept on down the Coronis branch of the River Divine. The ship had changed, since the Cauldron. She was lower in the water, a stockier shape. Instead of the high masts, there was a mound that almost looked like a cabin, except that it had no doors or windows.

This vessel was no less otherworldly for being a barge instead of a sailing ship. She was still shaped from shadows and feathers, pulled whole from the underworld, or wherever gods kept their miracles. Nothing about this shadow-barge was real.

Aodhan — his pretty eyes and his pretty words. They were not real, either.

Dio had never really had to bother about the gods. As one of those rare people born into this land without a tattoo that told him which of them to follow, he'd been free of expectation. He'd spent hours in the smaller, less reputable temples of each of the gods, learning useful facts about the various divinities that might help on his gladius exams, but never felt especially drawn to one over another.

No service he had ever attended had warned of gods sneaking into his dreams to make out with him. Even now, Aodhan smiled to see Dio awake, as if he thought him a friend, an ally instead of a hostage.

Dio sat up with some difficulty. "You took us away from her," he accused.

Aodhan shrugged. "I needed you more."

Dio saw Ikaros and Valeria lying on the deck, both still out cold. Ikaros was in rough shape, banged up as if he had been in a fight recently. He was shivering in his sleep. So much for the protection of the divine.

"If you didn't want us to be tied to Calyx," said Dio furious. "Why did you let them take her as a mark?"

"You're presuming a lot," said Aodhan. "Who says I allowed any of this to happen?"

Dio sat up. "If you didn't," he said slowly. "We're in a lot more trouble than I thought."

Aodhan huffed at him. "Only just figuring that out, are you?"

Past Raven's Gate, they were in the final approach to the city, steadily moving towards Phoenix Burning. The city lay ahead of them: a marvel of deep umber stone, curving domes dotted with bright terracotta tile, and high golden spires, built at the mouth of the Coronis.

In full sunlight, the city looked afire. This early in the morning, it gave off more of a quiet, warm glow.

They were not at the city yet. There was still the Court of Miracles to pass through; a final gauntlet.

The river should be wider here; certainly, it had been widened, many times, by grand lords with armies of workers at their command. This last stretch of river before the city dock had long been reserved for religious transports only. No boats, ships or barges were licensed to be moored along this end of the Coronis unless they were affiliated with the gods.

And yet.

Somehow, over the decades, the river had thickened with permanently moored houseboats, temple vessels and other less official floating structures webbed together with canvas and netting. Each of them claimed some form of religious affiliation, though they were well known to be a hotbed of strange magics, sex work, gambling and crime.

This was where you came if you wanted to disappear, whether for one night or for a lifetime.

When you sailed the slow pass through the Court of Miracles (there was too much traffic on the river to take this last stretch quickly, no matter the time of day), you kept one hand on your coin purse and the other on a scythe-knife, just in case. It was said that the only way to be sure of your safety was with a priest on either side of you.

A colossal joke, then, that Dio was on a barge approaching the Court of Miracles with a god at the helm, and a pair of (unconscious) priests along for the ride.

"Are you feeling okay?" he asked Aodhan. The look of extreme bafflement that he received from the god in response made him feel daft for saying anything. "You were dying a few hours ago," Dio added defensively. "It's not weird to ask."

It was definitely weird to ask.

"I am not myself," said Aodhan after a moment, still giving Dio that odd look, like he had asked him to strip naked and sing. "There is something wrong with the kingdom. Has been wrong since she first stepped over the Isthmus from the Imperium. Even then, she is the symptom, not the cause of my distress."

"What did Calyx ever do to you?" Dio asked impatiently.

Aodhan gave him another of those odd, half-humorous looks. Frustration warred with amusement on his beautiful face. "Not Calyx," he said. "As it turns out, *she's* not the problem. And I am a fool."

Calyx was still in shock when she left the temple, with Mardi — and Reynard Kaldoran of all people — trailing behind her. She could not believe that Nimue was gone. Her magic still hummed with her daughter's presence.

No, there was something else going on here. Calyx was going to find out what.

The shadow-barge was no longer moored beneath Raven's Gate. The Black Raven had taken it along with Ikaros, Valeria, Dio. The *Silken Hare*, however, was exactly where Calyx expected it to be. (Hoped, at least, not expected. None of the crew were under her thrall any longer, not since she released them from her bond to save them from Kaldoran and his miracles. She had only four servants left under her bond, and only one of those servants remained at her side.)

She had paid them, at least, for the entire journey, and they were still willing to complete the contract despite no magical compulsion to do so.

The captain looked troubled as he welcomed them aboard. He rubbed absently at the pale tattoo that marked him as one of the Black Raven's chosen from birth. "Have you prayed lately, priest?" he asked Mardi.

Mardi shook her head slowly.

The captain nodded, as if that was what he had expected. "You might want to try it," he advised.

Reynard Kaldoran hesitated before joining Calyx and Mardi on the barge. Calyx gave him an impatient look. "Do you want answers, or do you want to kill me?"

"I absolutely want to kill you," he said in a mutter. He had made no move to do so since his last attack upon her person in the temple.

Calyx waited.

"I want answers," Reynard admitted reluctantly.

"Then come aboard in peace," she said. "We'll find our people, and your god. Ask him if you're supposed to kill me."

Reynard hesitated, and then he stepped on to the deck of the *Silken Hare*.

"Not sure if this is a good idea," Mardi said in a low voice.

"Oh," said Calyx. "It's very, very bad."

She did not have time to nurse the finer feelings of assassins. She had a daughter to... no, not grieve. She might feel numb in the chest, but that was not what was happening here.

Calyx had a daughter to find.

"Nimue," said Dio, not quite believing it. "What has Nimue to do with anything?"

He liked the girl well enough, but it had never occurred to him that she was important. The impression he got was that Calyx had dragged her into all this like a spare piece of luggage.

Aodhan looked exhausted, which was the opposite of reassuring. The god drew a cup of water from a barrel and sipped from it, wandering near the crumpled figures of Ikaros and Valeria, who lay breathing shallowly, lips flecked with blood. Someone had dragged them closer together.

"Nimue," said Aodhan, "Is the beginning of the end for the Divine Kingdom. I don't know if she's part of some plot the Imperium have against our country, or if it's all —" he waved a hand, as if searching for the words.

"Accidental?" Dio asked. "Coincidence?"

"Destiny," said Aodhan, his mouth curled up in distaste. "The inevitable end of all that we are."

"The end of the Divine Kingdom?"

"Of the gods." Aodhan shook his head slowly. He walked back and forth on the deck, circling the prone figures of Ikaros and Valeria as if they were mere inconveniences. Furniture. "I really thought it was the mother."

"You thought — you knew they were coming?"

"Everyone knew they were coming!" declared the god of death. "The end of the gods was written into the sacred codex hundreds of years ago. *The seed of the house of flowers will be one with the river. The divine shall rise as the gods fall to dust.* The Divine King thought it was him, old fool — or his line, if he could breed magic into any of them. That's why he invited her here in the first place. That's why he put the clause in the marriage contract to make your Calyx sail the river without her own people at her side — hoping to give destiny a kick in the pants. That she'd sail into the city, marry his son, and hand him all the divine power he's ever wanted."

Dio stared at Aodhan. He had been a prize fool, hadn't he? Listening to him felt like a betrayal of Nimue, of Calyx. "It was you," he breathed. "It wasn't the Divine King or the Thirteenth Treasure who marked Calyx for death. Who broke all the rules of the temples to send four priests against her. You probably wanted to blame them — but you're the one who did it. And you... failed."

Aodhan gave him a wavering, weak smile, and coughed into his hand, his whole body shaking. "And haven't I fucked myself over," he said, blood shining on his teeth.

The *Silken Hare* slowed along with other river traffic as the river narrowed to the width of a canal.

You could see the glowing orange-gold towers of the city in the distance, looking like something embroidered at the heart of a tapestry, utterly unreal.

Here, it was all bustled-together punts and pontoons built upon each other, on both sides of the river. This was a city all on its own: dozens, maybe hundreds of floating houseboats stitched together haphazardly with roofs made of silk and tarpaulin. Calyx stared in fascination.

The air was rich with scented oil, the odours of frying food, and sweet, sticky fruits for sale.

"Where do we alight?" she asked Mardi, since the captain was busy with his crew.

"Not here," Mardi said immediately. "Too dangerous, unless you're in the market for a miracle, or you have stolen goods to fence. We'll follow the Coronis all the way to the city wharf."

Reynard Kaldoran hovered like a black cloud nearby, glaring at everyone who came near, and yet making no move to attack Calyx. She stayed close to Mardi, regardless. Calyx's last remaining servant. Her only protection.

Mardi stood on the deck with one hand resting thoughtfully on her belly. Calyx' own pregnancy had been so very long ago, and yet she recognised much of herself in this woman. Waiting, alight with anticipation for the next chapter of her life to begin. For the baby to be in her arms. Terrified, too. Everything would change, in ways that no one could predict.

At least Calyx had been cushioned by the comforts of a palace at this stage of her pregnancy, not roaming a magical river with threats at every turn.

"Who was Nimue's father?" Mardi asked in a soft voice.

Calyx glanced at her in surprise. "What does that matter?"

"I wondered if he was from around here, or descended from someone connected to the River Divine. A river god, for example."

"Is there such a thing?"

"There used to be, when the world was young. Before our kingdom was limited to our five great gods, and the

Divine King. They were the nameless ancients back then: deities all over the place, bursting out of nature. Spring and summer gods. Mountain and river gods. The sun and the moon. All of that. If you listen to the old songs, the nameless ancients spread their seed to any mortal who would have them. Families often have odd little traditions or stories trailing back that far. Most of my kin have never left the banks of Lake Lamia because a lake spirit once promised protection to my ancestor. Other families follow the river, or celebrate good fortune at specific times of year. Everything strange or unique in any given province can be explained by a tale about some god fucking a mortal he shouldn't, or making a promise he shouldn't, or turning a nymph into a tree."

Calyx did not know whether to laugh. Mardi's tone was deadly serious. If only this new river affinity of Nimue's could be so easily explained. "Nimue's father, my husband," she confessed, "Was Graykirc Wilder. A solid, dependable knight trained in the House of Steel. A noble warrior. He was a younger son from the ruling family of the principality of Iorvigal, to at least nine generations. He had no ancestors from the Divine Kingdom that I know about."

Nothing so interesting as a misbehaving god in Grayk's family line, at least not that she'd ever heard about. The best thing she'd ever been able to say about her husband was that he was kind — which was not nothing, but he'd showed as much interest in his young wife as she had offered in return: it amounted to very little over the handful of years they had shared.

"Oh," said Mardi thoughtfully. "Well. Perhaps they have river spirits in Iorvigal, too. I don't know much about that part of the world."

Calyx breathed out slowly. It wasn't just her. "You

don't think Nimue's dead." Not if Mardi was entertaining some notion of a divine bloodline.

"I don't see how she can be," said Mardi. "Not with power like that at her fingertips. I've lived my whole life around the River Divine, all kinds of wild magic, and that — what I saw at Raven's Gate was immense."

Calyx groaned. "Power isn't everything. I'd give up all my magic, every mote of it, to know Nimue was safe."

Mardi nudged her with an odd smile. "I don't think you're going to find the answers you need at the palace. We should probably take a detour first. What you need is a miracle."

Behind her, Reynard Kaldoran made a scoffing sound, but he did not speak up to disagree.

Ikaros dreamed of Nimue.

He shouldn't spare her a second thought. He had enough on his plate. Torn between his bond to Calyx and his service to the Black Raven… what did a foreign child princess matter?

But here he was, dreaming again, and Nimue was the only person here.

The girl sprawled on a large green chair — a throne, Ikaros supposed — in an echoing hall with no other furniture. It all looked rather palatial.

Nimue's head was freshly shaven. She wore one of those odd formal garments that Calyx preferred — the stiff fall of linen at the front, soft layers of silks underneath (deep blue and green, fairly obvious symbology). The ensemble looked like a marble column standing in front of a fountain. (Or a river.)

Usually when he dreamed like this, it was all about Death. So he had a fair idea what he was dealing with.

"Nimue," Ikaros greeted her. "Or am I addressing someone else?"

She smiled warmly at him, and there was no trace of the child he had talked with on the barge. "You know who I am, Ikaros," she said in her melodic voice. "I'm the River Divine."

24. On the Left Bank of the Court of Miracles

"Why would I need a tattoo?" Calyx protested as Mardi hustled her along a makeshift corridor that hung, in canvas and rope, between one of the pontoon temples of the Court of Miracles, and another. Along the way, they passed booths and stalls all selling arcane jewellery, charms and herbal remedies.

"It's a tradition," Mardi replied. "It's one of the oldest forms of magic. If you want to find your way back to Nimue, the ink-speakers are your answer."

"Ink-speakers," Reynard muttered behind them, easily keeping up with his long legs. "They're barely even priests."

"Not everyone useful is a priest," Mardi said, looking lighter than she had in the whole time Calyx had known her. "I've been meaning to come here myself," she added to Calyx. "It's good luck for a coming child, to ink the first letter of their name on your skin."

"Oh," said Calyx, only half-joking. "So this is *your* errand."

Mardi's eyes flashed. "I believe in this, Calyx. If Nimue can be found, we'll find her."

Calyx ached for her daughter. "I don't want to leave the river, if she's..." part of it. It seemed impossible. But she felt Nimue's presence in the water, she *did*. She had not realised how much magic was contained in her daughter until she was gone, but now she could feel her everywhere.

Mardi stomped one foot on the canvas bridge. "The river is still beneath our feet. We won't go far."

Calyx's shaven head and bright white stemma drew eyes everywhere they crossed the left bank of the Court of Miracles. At Mardi's suggestion she had added a silk shawl to cover her arms from the bright sunshine, but it did not stop the staring. No one approached them, which probably had more to do with Mardi's featherbrace than anything else — the locals knew a priest of death when they saw one.

Finally they reached a bright red houseboat covered in a wide tarpaulin covered in familiar designs: night-blooms, drawn in that same thick-lined style as the marks that had flowered on the skin of Ikaros, Valeria, Mardi and Dio when she laid her bond upon them.

Calyx still did not know why her magic had manifested in that particular shape, to that particular flower. Servants she pulled under her bond usually wore a gentler mark: the soft pink outline of a single petal, near their wrist or ring finger. It didn't pay to be more intrusive than you had to be.

"Ahoy the *Ink-leaf*," Mardi called as she stepped on board. "Anyone home?"

A handsome, long-legged man covered in red-and-gold

tattoos emerged from within. He wore a burnt-orange tunic over baggy green sailor pants, brighter clothes than Calyx was used to around here. A bird wing, brighter red than the other art on his skin, covered his chest, spread wide across his clavicle.

"Dear heart," he said warmly, embracing Mardi with such enthusiasm that Reynard, behind Calyx, let out an impatient huff. "Look at you, you're enormous! Ready to name that child of yours?"

"Ready to commit to a first letter, at least," said Mardi, smiling all over her face. "Calyx, this is Yain. Abbot of the Blazing Phoenix." Another kind of priest, after all. Not of death, or healing. Calyx remembered that *phoenix* represented art and creativity. She wondered what it meant, that the nearby city was named as it was. Phoenix Burning was to be her home soon, and she knew so little about it.

The ink-speaker looked Calyx over thoughtfully, then dipped his head in something like a bow. "Petal," he said. "Aren't you magnificent." His gaze slipped past to Reynard, and he smirked a little. "Bow. Finally going to let me mark you up?"

"Not today," grated Reynard.

"You win some, you lose some." Yain turned back to Calyx, eyeing her bare arms. "Always happy to meet a new canvas."

"She has a lost child to find," put in Mardi.

"Ah, that's less happy news," the ink-speaker said with some sympathy. "Lucky for you, I'm the best in the business. Let's have a look at you."

"It can't be that simple," said Calyx, a short while later. Mardi and Reynard were waiting for her on the deck, as she consulted with Yain in some degree of privacy — privacy enough, at least, that she was willing to remove her stemma and silks, show him more of her skin than she'd ever bared for a stranger (apart from Ikaros, she remembered with a shiver). "You write her name on my arm and that's enough to bring her back to me?"

"It's not nearly that simple." Yain circled her, and she could feel his eyes on the scars that marked up her back. "I see you have your own experience with words on your skin."

"Family illness," Calyx said shortly. "It causes lines of poetry to appear on your skin in times of... upheaval."

"If such a thing were common, it would put me out of business," Yain said in a tone that sounded teasing enough, though there was a wary undercurrent.

"My mother died of it."

"I'm sorry to hear that," he said, as if he said such a thing ten times a day. "But it's not an illness, my dear. That sounds like a curse."

"Does it matter what we call it? I've had the lines incised from my skin by a surgeon, whenever I can. The trouble with poetry is you can't always tell how long it will be. But if you don't catch it early... my mother died with a completed sonnet on the back of her thigh. It took half a year to appear, one line at a time."

"You are a wonder," said Yain, and his fingertip shivered

against the most recent of Calyx's scars. "I want to stare at your back until the next words appear."

"I'm hoping it will be years before that happens," she said tartly.

"You'll be living nearby, though," he noted. "If you're to marry our Treasure."

"How did you know that?"

"You're a legend, my dear! Stories have been flooding down the river of your exploits. Our royal bride, come to heal the kingdom with her flowers and her magic." He whipped around, eyes fixed on hers. "Promise me. Next time you find a line of poetry on your skin. Bring it to *me*, not those butchers of the Bright Owl."

"And will you keep me alive?" Calyx said sharply. "Or study me like an exhibit?"

"I'm very talented," said the abbot of the Blazing Phoenix, eyes dancing. "I can do both things. First things first. Let's find your daughter."

Five letters, traced on to her forearm, spelling out her daughter's name in pale grey linework. *Nimue*.

"Blue, I think," said the ink-speaker. "If she's at one with the river."

"Green," murmured Calyx, thinking of the Eye of the Basilisk.

"As you like."

It was still ink at this stage; no needles brought into play. An outline to work with.

"I thought you didn't believe in that part of the story,"

said Calyx, leaning back into his soft chair. Sitting down had been a mistake. Sleep was calling her home.

Had she properly slept, since she first set foot in this kingdom? Since she first started her long pilgrimage down the River Divine? Calyx was exhausted, and she had barely got started.

Everything will change, at Phoenix Burning.

"I believe everything my clients tell me," said Yain gently. "That's what makes the miracles work."

Needles darted in a light, compelling dance across Calyx's skin. It didn't hurt, not exactly. It felt like something she could sink into, and forget.

Voices murmured behind her, Mardi and Reynard, sounding furious at each other. Finally saying aloud whatever had been grating at them both over the last few days, or longer perhaps.

Calyx shouldn't listen. But she felt outside herself, as the sharp rhythm of the tattoo needle pressed into her arm. Nothing to do but float away...

"How could you do it?" demanded the male voice. "That's what I don't understand."

"Do what?" the female voice replied, on the edge of something dangerous.

"*Ikaros.*"

"Don't knock it until you've tried it. He's very good."

"Bors longed for a family. You were supposed to love him. And you threw yourself at Ikaros the moment he was dead. You let *him* give you a child."

"This is Bors' child. And mine."

"I can count months, Mardi."

"I don't owe you an explanation — no, don't pull that face, I *don't*. Still, I do want my child to know you, if you can restrain yourself from being a colossal arsehole by the time she gets here. So here's the short version: Bors and I took Ikaros to our bed over a year ago. We couldn't conceive on our own. This was our best chance."

A long pause. A silence that stretched.

"And you still — after Bors was dead."

"Why not? I'm still breathing, Reynard. I still want to be a mother. If Bors hadn't died when he did, this would be our child. We would have retired together. Married, finally. I loved your friend for a decade. Would you begrudge me this future?"

"Fuck. Now I do feel like an arsehole."

"Let me be the first to say: I told you so."

A long pause, and then a longer pause.

"Mardi, I'm sorry."

A soft, wry laugh.

"Oh, don't strain anything. Pour a libation out for my baby when she's born, and we'll call it even."

"To our god?"

"Ha. I don't suppose he gets many of those, does he? Perhaps you should pour one out to all five. Assuming they're still here by the time she..."

Calyx was not asleep. She lay back, eyes fixed on the red roof of the houseboat, half an ear on the conversation between

Mardi and Reynard. But she was also elsewhere. She was on the river. Half-caught by a dream.

The water ran underneath her, singing and shivering. She followed its path, out to the wide river, where the boats came and went. Over the city wharf, on her way to the palace.

The river water spilled up the steps, along streets, dancing up out of fountains. Calyx had seen an oil painting of this city, its palette of orange-red-copper glowing off the canvas. Black marble steps leading up into towers of gold. When she first saw it, she had thought: *that can't be a real place*.

Now she was standing in the central court of the palace, at the heart of a deep stepped amphitheatre. Water ran off every surface; pooled at her feet. Flowers floated on the water: rose petals and cherry blossoms and night-blooms, though it was the middle of the day.

Sunlight scorched the top of her head as she stood in bright white silks and stemma, waiting for her bridegroom.

He stood with his back to her, high on the precipice overlooking the amphitheatre. Wearing black, of course, because this was the Divine Kingdom and they'd never bleached cloth in their lives. He was hooded, in long black royal robes heavy with gold embroidery, jewels, and a feathered hem that swept the golden tiles.

Her child-bridegroom. The Thirteenth Treasure of the Divine Kingdom. Her future.

She ran to him, barefoot, her feet splashing in water every step of the way. The river was here, even at the heart of the palace, waters rising. At ankle height now, at knee-height, dragging her down even as she climbed the amphitheatre steps.

Calyx's clothes were wet and heavy. She released the

stemma, tore off the silks, let them be pulled away by the weight of the water.

She had nearly reached her bridegroom as the water rose to lap at her chin, at her mouth and nose. She outstretched one arm, grasping at his ankle.

The prince turned, looked down at her: a teenager with golden paint on his face and a cruel twist to his mouth. She writhed in humiliation as his eyes raked over her nakedness, and looked away. The river rose to engulf her. Calyx was drowning, and her new husband did nothing to stop it. As her fingers clenched more tightly around his ankle, he kicked her away.

Water swept over her head. Hands came around her body, holding her up until she could breathe again, sucking in a lungful of air. A voice growled words into her ear.

"I've found her. She's safe."

She knew that voice. *Ikaros.*

Calyx gasped, starting away. Her arm burned, but she couldn't feel the needles anymore. "Is something wrong?"

Yain stood over her, staring in dismay at his handiwork. "Fuck me," he breathed. "This has never happened before."

Calyx turned to look at her arm. Green words spilled across her skin, dotted with her own blood. It was not her daughter's name, though the grey letters were still visible beneath, where Yain had traced them. The new tattoo in deep emerald ink was six lines of a poem, wrapping around her forearm, deeply melded into her skin.

down, down among
the ghosts of flowers falling
she weeps
into the river
and the river
reaches up to take her hand

25. On the Right Bank of the Court of Miracles

Nothing like the sharp sensation of your wife's boot connecting to your lower ribs to wake you up from an unnatural sleep.

Ikaros sucked in air and stared up at Valeria.

She looked tired. Not old — she would never look old, not as long as she served the Black Raven. But her cheeks were hollowed, the scars across her face more pronounced than usual.

Calyx was somewhere nearby, though not close enough for Ikaros to feel safe. He inhaled, exhaled, and got to his feet. "What did I miss?"

They were still on the deck of the shadow-barge, moored on the right bank of the Court of Miracles — though 'moored' suggested such practical necessities as a ring and a rope. The shadow-barge did not require such things. It waited where it had been left, near a tangled assortment of dice-boats and drinking skiffs. The current moved impossibly around it, having no effect whatever on the boat.

By the looks of the sky, it was somewhere in the afternoon. A sunny day; they were both lucky not to have ended up sunburnt, left out in the elements like that.

"Why are we on this side?" Ikaros asked, surveying the busy river for any sign of the *Silken Hare*. It was odd to be docked on the right bank. Most inward traffic veered to the left, to avoid collisions. Perhaps the gods did not worry about such things as accidentally ramming mussel trawlers.

"They left us here," said Valeria. "The Black Raven has Dio with him, I suppose. Why else would he choose this bank of the river?"

The ancient Shrine of Tribute was located on the right bank, where the Court of Miracles kissed dry land.

"Fuck," said Ikaros. Aodhan had been looking at Dio like he was good enough to eat. He should have guessed why. "What do you think Calyx's bond will do to the boy if he swears service to a god after the fact?"

"Let's not find out," Valeria said impatiently. "Come on!"

Dio was burning up. His whole body felt aflame. He did not know if the pain was caused by his distance from Calyx or something else, but it was all terribly wrong.

Aodhan was terribly wrong.

The beautiful god had dragged him across the rocking, ramshackle pontoons of the Court of Miracles, from barge to skiff to bridge to deck, with all eyes on them. Every priest and pick-pocket in this whole benighted boat-village kept their distance, knowing danger when it streaked across their planking.

Aodhan was bleeding — not actual blood, but there was something vital leaking out of his body, whether it be power or miracles or some mystical god-stuff that held him together.

Feathers? Dust? The Black Raven was less than he had been. He became lesser with every moment of desperate flight.

When they passed by a ship selling fresh-cut flowers, the blooms wilted. When they passed a barge selling live river-crabs for the table, the creatures fell limply into their buckets.

Dio felt like he, too, was dying. Why else was his chest so tight, his fingers and toes so swollen, his stomach on the verge of bursting open...

Aodhan's fingers, clenched tightly around Dio's wrist as they stumbled together across the Court of Miracles, were so cold that they stabbed pain through his bones.

"Nearly there," the god muttered beneath his breath.

"Where?" Dio retorted. "Can't we just stop? Find the others. They'll help you."

"No," Aodhan snapped, squeezing Dio's wrist harder. "They don't want to help me. They're on her side now." His skin was practically grey.

I'm on her side. Dio didn't know if Aodhan meant Calyx or Nimue, but it didn't matter. Dio would choose to protect them, both of them, if he could. Gods could take care of themselves.

"Where are we going?" Dio asked.

"Shrine of Tribute."

"Why?"

Dio was genuinely shocked. The Shrine of Tribute was the only temple in the Divine Kingdom that wasn't sacred to any specific god — a strange choice for a deity in freefall.

Surely he'd want to be around his own hand-maidens, his servants. There was a temple to the Black Raven in the city, and Raven's Gate itself back along the Coronis. Those would be safe places where Aodhan could wrap himself in worship, build his strength.

Why this shrine? What was the point?

And then it rose in his head, one of the many random question-and-answer sets about the gods of the Divine Kingdom that Dio had memorised, in the hope they might come up on the next gladius exam.

At which shrine would both the Silver Hawk and the Lark of the Hearth swear a new acolyte to their service?

It was a trick question, inviting the student to fill the space with a double answer, naming a well-known war temple, along with one of the many popular temples for domesticity, love, protection and fertility. But the only one-size-fits-all answer was the Shrine of Tribute. It was the oldest, the first of the shrines from the early days of the new gods, when the five birds took the Divine Kingdom for their own.

The shrine was old, and small, and largely neglected by worshippers outside the Court of Miracles — hardly surprising, as no one wanted to be robbed on the way to service. But the shrine was a sacred space to all the gods, and the more old-fashioned mode of priest.

"Do you want me to be your *acolyte*?" Dio demanded, stumbling over the edge of a rope bridge. He swayed, glancing down into the dark river water below. (For a moment, he thought he saw a face down there, watching him.) "A servant of the Black Raven? Me?"

"I need you to be mine," said Aodhan. He wasn't nearly as attractive now, with this desperate look on his face, as if he was empty all the way down to his bones. Did gods have bones? "I need new blood, Dio. I need you."

Dio's stomach, already rebelling along with the rest of his body, lurched in another jolt of pain. Calyx's bond tugged at him. They would rip him apart, these two, without even trying. So much power, and he was stuck in the middle like a bone for two dogs to chew over.

"Why would you want me?" No one had ever chosen Dio. His aunties had passed him around like a parcel, none of them holding on to him for long enough to get attached. Even this whole mess — his involvement was an accident. Calyx's magic had reached out and scooped him up because the Bow had not reached the Blooming Cup in time.

He could so easily have missed out on all this.

"Loyalty," murmured Aodhan. "You're full of it. Brimming. Loyalty and life. You'll make a fine priest."

"Then why didn't you want me when I was born?"

It was Aodhan's turn to stumble. They were halfway across the rope bridge now, and the god was so shaken that Dio was able to wrest his arm back. Bruises like fingerprints flared up on his wrist. He rubbed at the painful skin angrily.

"What makes you think that?" asked Aodhan — no, the Black Raven. His eyes filled with a sadness that reminded Dio all over again how compelling he had been, when he was a stranger in the dark.

"None of you marked me as a baby," Dio snapped back. "No god chose me. I've been free of you, my whole life. Free to choose my own fate." Left alone. "What makes you think you can have me now?"

Aodhan's eyes glowed with dark fire. "I can have anything I want," he said. "Even you. Especially you. You belong to no one else..."

"No," said Dio, shaking his head. "I don't want to be your priest."

"Take my service."

"No," Dio said again.

Aodhan's voice rose up, rich and heavy and furious. "This is all you've ever wanted. A place. A hearth. To be chosen. Why give all your youth and spirit and fire to the gladius corps? They'd only waste your talents. I choose you, Dio Taurus."

It was awful, to have someone — even a god — look inside your heart and see you, so completely. And yet. Dio had changed over the last few days. He had found a purpose, even if it was accidental.

"I don't choose you back," he said stubbornly.

The god hissed, and something else fell away from him. A fine layer of ghost feathers, grey and pale. What remained of the Black Raven was weaker, a frail shadow of Aodhan. "You can't refuse," he said.

"Watch me," said Dio Taurus.

Death smiled a cruel smile. "You won't survive refusing me."

Dio had always wanted to be brave. What was his dream to be a gladius all about, if not that? Service, glory, courage. Pretending to be brave, right now, was the hardest thing he'd ever done.

"Let's find out," he challenged Death.

There were no priests or hand-maidens tending the Shrine of Tribute. It was a small stone hut on the edge of the shore, where the pontoons of the Court of Miracles gave way to a ragged line of damp tents. There was no sacred flame to be tended, or religious artworks worth stealing.

There was a plain stone altar, on which locals could leave any small offerings to the gods: ripe fruits, flowers and harvest nuts, the occasional nice-looking pebble.

Nothing worth offending the gods over, though the bunch of grapes balanced on the very edge of the altar were fresh enough to look succulent.

It was a while since any of them had eaten a meal.

"He's not here," Ikaros raged. "Where are they?"

Valeria turned her back on him, surveying the Court of Miracles — so many bridges, pontoons, awnings and banners, all decorated in bright colours. Chaos afloat. "They can't be far," she said. "Where else would they go?" Then she let out a noise like she'd been punched in the gut.

Ikaros whirled around, just in time to see a cloud of black ravens explode into the air, a little way from them. "Dio!"

Husband and wife ran across the Court, treading lightly on roofs and awnings, slithering across canvas and damp wood.

Finally they reached a rope bridge, soaking wet and swinging loose of one bracket. Dio lay there, looking wrecked, his chest rising and falling raggedly. Eyes closed. His body was soaked with water as if there had been a summer storm only seconds ago; they'd just missed it.

"Oy!" yelled a fortune teller in bold, brassy gold jewellery, with a small crowd gathered behind her. "This is you, isn't it? Bloody priests. We won't have you lot causing problems here."

"This is the Court of Miracles," Valeria snapped. "Don't you know a miracle when you see one?"

The fortune teller scoffed. "Keep your gods off our bank," she said. "We know the way the wind's blowing, and it's not for them."

Valeria frowned, as if about to continue the argument. Ikaros ignored them, scrambling on to the bridge. "Dio. Wake up."

The young man was lying horribly still, his body sprawled on the rope bridge. There was a mark on his face that had not been there before: a black scythe-knife emblazoned across his cheek.

"Ikaros," Valeria warned.

He looked down, and saw what she was seeing. Water dripped up the sides of barges and boats. It slithered along the rope bridge in narrow rivulets, wetting Ikaros' boots. Where it met the unconscious Dio, the water pooled and expanded quickly, forming a shape.

This all felt very familiar.

"The River Divine, I believe," said Ikaros.

The water shuddered, and resolved itself into Nimue. She was clad, thank the Blood and Endless, though the green tunic she wore was alarmingly transparent, and did not look any more solid than she was now. The girl leaned over Dio, brushing her mouth to the cheek that had been marked by the Black Raven.

Dio choked awake, as if they had caught him in the middle of a nightmare. Ikaros found himself breathing at the same ragged pace, matching the breaths of the young man. Beside him, Valeria pressed his arm, just to show she had noticed him caring about something (about someone), in case he thought he'd got away with it.

"Death!" shouted Dio, wild-eyed.

"So dramatic," chided Valeria. "We know who you mean, dear."

"He's gone after Calyx."

"But why," Nimue breathed, clutching at Dio's ragged, wet shirt. "He should know by now that it's me. I'm the problem."

"Oh," groaned Dio, rubbing his head. "He knows. He knew before you stepped in to save me. I can't believe you fought him."

"Sorry we missed that," said Ikaros.

"He was hurting you," Nimue said furiously.

Dio's hand slowed at his own cheek, touching the mark tentatively. "He's allowed to, now," he said, his voice sounding hollow.

"No," said Ikaros. "He is not."

Dio met Nimue's eyes. "He's going after your mother because it's the only way he can hurt you. He's terrified of you."

Nimue drew Dio to his feet, then outstretched both her hands. The rope bridge underneath them untied itself, glistening with water, steady beneath their feet. Water poured up to form a more solid railing and, to Ikaros' alarm, something that looked like a sail.

"No," Ikaros said immediately. "We're not travelling on that."

"On the river, you mean?" said Nimue archly. "I know your prejudice, Ikaros. But I'm the only way you'll reach them fast enough."

"I think it's marvellous," said Valeria, and moved past Ikaros to step on to the bewildering structure of planking and magical liquid that was by no means a boat. Not by any definition. "Best miracle I've seen all day."

Ikaros groaned, and grasped the railing of Nimue's vessel of water. "I hate this," he informed them all.

They slid across the rooftops and canopies of the right bank of the Court of Miracles together, heading for the open water of the harbour, taking their miracle with them.

26. The Bower of Fountains

Three months ago.

Calyx, Petal of the Imperium, waited in the Bower of Fountains, a reception hall so beautiful that it hurt the eyes. There was glass everywhere: glass and marble and the babbling splash of secret fountains.

No flowers growing here, which might have made the space feel a little more like it belonged in the real world.

She had been waiting more than an hour, according to the majestic water clock in the far corner. That was to be expected. Just because the Empress summoned you did not mean she intended to make herself available.

Palace life revolved around the Empress: her needs, her wants, her schedule. Calyx did not envy Niniane's life — after all, she had no minute to herself in any given day — and yet Calyx could not help but resent that it could never again be easy between them.

They could never simply meet for mint tea and gossip as other sisters might. Even a private conversation between them had to be this: an exquisite location, a formal gown, and a long, uncomfortable wait.

Calyx was wearing pink today. Blush and fuchsia silks, nestled under her crisp stemma which displayed a spiralling arrangement of spring blossom to match the gardens outside.

If she had to stand alone in this cold rock of a room instead of out in the gardens where there was sunshine and life, at least she could bring the garden inside with her.

Several servants entered silently, carrying a table on which was laid a formal tea: pots of mint and lemon, rice cakes and salmon, thinly sliced cucumber salad (in the pickled glaze that Niniane loved, but Calyx had loathed since childhood) and sweet berry tarts.

Chairs followed, carried by more servants. Calyx hovered, knowing she could not sit at the table until her hostess arrived.

After they had all cleared out, Niniane breezed in, clad in her own formal stemma and silks, along with the gold clogs and torc that showed she had been meeting with actual important people (family did not count). She sighed and sat down heavily, rubbing her head. The clogs were kicked off for a moment, and she looked like any other woman who was having a hard day.

Now Calyx felt terrible for being annoyed at her sister.

"Well!" said Niniane, already tucking into a rice cake. She was rarely allowed to eat and drink away from the public eye, and always made the most of it, sending sesame seeds and lemon rinds scattering as she dove through a plate at high speed. "I suppose you're going to fight me on this."

"Over cucumber salad?" said Calyx, hiding a smile. "I wouldn't dare." She seated herself gracefully, and palmed a berry tart. "What did you wish to discuss?"

"I've arranged your marriage," said the Empress of the Imperium.

Calyx coughed. Her body froze up as crumbs of pastry caught in her throat; for a moment, she could not breathe. "What marriage?"

"You know how this works," sighed Niniane in a world-weary air only slightly tinged with malice. "You sent your daughter to the House of Velvet to be trained in diplomacy. Perhaps she should explain it to you?" Perhaps more than slightly tinged with malice.

Calyx had thought she was safe — that one loveless marriage, one child for the Imperium in a family rich with children was enough. (She had been prepared to fight, if this was Nimue's marriage on the table; Calyx's daughter would not be sold off as young as she was.)

The Imperium chewed through them all, in the end.

Just because she had not seen it coming did not mean it was not inevitable.

"Where am I going?" Calyx asked, after soothing her throat with a mouthful of mint tea. "Where are you sending me?"

"Phoenix Burning."

"I've never heard of it."

Niniane raised her eyebrows. "Really, Calyx. The Divine Kingdom is one of our nearest neighbours."

"That snake-pit? They hate women. Sister, they hate women with magic." The thought of it turned her stomach. "Who am I to marry?"

"The Thirteenth Treasure, son and heir to the Divine King. It's an excellent match."

"Do they know how old I am?"

"You're thirty, hardly hitting your crone years." The Empress mopped her mouth, already preparing for the next meeting. "Pack lightly. By the time all the contractual negotiations are done, it will be high summer over there."

"I am at the disposal of the Imperium," said Calyx, her thoughts boiling over in her head.

"Of course you are," said Niniane, avoiding her gaze. "I'm glad you're not being silly about this."

"I want Nimue with me," Calyx insisted, as the Empress rose to leave. Any minute now, servants would sweep in to erase all trace of this tea: table and chairs and lemon rinds and sesame seeds. Barely a handful of seconds to try for a negotiation.

"Do you think that's wise?" said the Empress, stepping back into her gold clogs. "She's halfway through her training. Still a child."

Too young to be left to the wolves of the Imperium without her mother to protect her.

"She's old enough to visit a foreign court," Calyx said, radiating calm and good sense. "I want her with me."

It had been a relief, when Nimue showed no exceptional talent at magic. It gave them a freedom she would not have been allowed, if her daughter was one of the family's more valuable resources.

The Empress pretended to consider, as if she had not anticipated this request already, and made her decision ahead of time. "Oh, I suppose so," she said after a moment. "She's quite far down the list of marriages to arrange. You can send her back when I need her."

"She's always wanted to travel," Calyx said, with a grateful smile. "And what better diplomatic practice than witnessing her mother's marriage to... what was his name?"

"The Thirteenth Treasure of the Divine Kingdom," said Niniane, rolling her eyes. "Honestly, Calyx. It's a good thing *one* of you has diplomatic training."

27. In the Harbour, Not the City

Calyx stumbled out of the ink-speaker's cabin and into the bright morning, distancing herself from Yain's hasty apologies. She couldn't think about the family curse now. Couldn't think about the strange magic that had turned her intended tattoo into something else…

She found Mardi and Reynard standing to attention, surrounded by armed guards. City gladii, she realised. They were dressed lightly, as was everyone in this kingdom, with bare legs and sandals. Even their armour was barely there, featuring a breastplate of blood-coloured leather, and a skirt of leather lappets covering some but not all of their meaty thighs.

Beneath the red leather, layers of amber and orange tunic hung in points to give the impression of flames. These were the armed forces of Phoenix Burning, ready for action.

Their captain, the only one wearing a plumed helmet, lowered his sword and stood to attention. "Great Petal," he said politely. "The palace are expecting you."

"Indeed," said Calyx, not in the mood for tact or diplomacy. "Are we so very overdue?"

"You were expected to arrive yesterday."

"It's been quite a voyage." One she had embarked upon with no assistance whatsoever from the palace. Was it the Divine King who had lost patience with her, or the army of servants and bureaucrats who worked for him?

"Allow us to escort you directly." The captain of the gladii gave Mardi and Reynard a suspicious look. "This is not a respectable area of the city."

"On the contrary," said Calyx, layering her tone with a little more frost than necessary. "Everyone has been so kind. You may escort me as far as my ship, Captain. I prefer to arrive in the city aboard the *Silken Hare*, as planned."

She knew the importance of a first impression. She could not afford to look weak as she came to meet her new life.

"That means further delay," the captain protested. Clearly he had not spent enough time around royalty if he thought his opinion was desired.

Haughty tones were required now: Calyx stared down her nose at him. "I'm hardly dressed for my first palace reception," she said, pulling her silken shawl more tightly around herself. "Mardi, Reynard, with me."

Her education might have prioritised magic over diplomacy, but Calyx had spent her whole life in the Imperium. She knew how to play the Grande Dame to get her own way.

The small cohort of gladii escorted them across the shabby and ramshackle collection of boats and bridges (or floating rat nests) that was the Court of Miracles, to where the *Silken Hare* was berthed. It was immediately evident that the men expected to come aboard for the final leg of the Petal's journey.

Calyx stood her ground, waving her assassin companions aboard. "The Divine King was very clear, as was my marriage contract," she informed the captain. "No armed forces of this kingdom or of the Imperium to be provided for my protection on this voyage down the River Divine. I would hate to void our agreement after coming all this way."

"You have entered the bounds of Phoenix Burning, Great Petal," protested the captain.

"Have I? The harbour is not the city." With the power of polite demurral on her side, she slipped aboard. "Meet us at the city wharf!" she called with a wave. "For a more formal introduction between the Petal of the Imperium, and the city of Phoenix Burning. I look forward to it."

Mardi stood watching in amusement as the crew unmoored the barge once more, leaving the armoured gladii standing on a pontoon at the edge of the Court of Miracles. "You can't put it off forever," she noted. "Sooner or later, you'll have to set foot in the city." She gave Calyx an odd look. "Was Yain not able to help you?"

Calyx checked that her shawl was in place, hiding the poetry that had got the better of the ink-speaker. "You might say that."

"I'm sorry."

Calyx pressed her lips tightly together. "You're right," she said. "Nimue or no Nimue. I can't put off my arrival any longer." Her magic felt useless. Perhaps the wife of the Thirteenth Treasure could do what the Petal of the

Imperium could not, and find her daughter. "Onward to Phoenix Burning," she called to the captain of the *Silken Hare*. "Let's get this over with."

The River Divine widened here, emerging from the clutter of the banks of the Court of Miracles to form a harbour that ran around the city, presumably meeting the ocean at some point out of sight. Ahead lay the city wharf, and then the city itself. Phoenix Burning rose up in golden spires from a series of wide steps of dark granite leading from the water. The combination of shapes and colours did not quite look like a bird aflame, but it made a good stab at it.

So close now. Calyx's new life was about to begin, no matter what poetry exploded across her arm. A life with a time limit was still a life, and she intended to live it for as long as she could.

"Mardi," Reynard said in a warning voice.

"What now?" Mardi said, then let out a gasp as she turned around.

Calyx turned her back on the city of false flames, following Mardi's gaze, and saw Death rushing towards her.

Death's ship, at least.

It looked like a black cloud, whipping across the harbour, avoiding every other ship on the water. Ravens, Calyx realised as she stared into its depths. This was cloud of ravens, all wings and beaks and shadowed fury. The cloud moved like a ship — like a swift yacht on the wild ocean, tacking sharply to catch the winds here and there.

Behind Death, something pale and bright began to build... water, glowing with light. A tidal wave on a river? Calyx could not wrap her head around what she was seeing. Shadows and water, coming right for her.

She saw Mardi wrap her hands helplessly around her belly, not knowing how to protect her baby against this new threat. She saw Reynard Kaldoran, a crossbow at the ready, realising too late that his weapons could do nothing. In the final moment before the collision, the man hooked one arm around Mardi's shoulders, pulling her close to him.

The cloud of ravens hit the *Silken Hare* all at once. Darkness wrapped around them like a cloak along with a sound of screaming wood, splintering. There was a wild whir of feathered wings, a shiver of cold closing in around them. Calyx heard the captain calling out to his men, and then she heard nothing but the groaning, creaking of a barge breaking apart.

The deck exploded gently under her feet like someone had dropped a wineglass, and somehow slowed the scatter of shards.

Calyx flung out her magic in all directions, but the pressure of the angry god and his miracles, the darkness of the black feathers, muffled her connection to her own power.

Calyx fell.

Cold immersed her: the water of the River Divine. Cold, wet, underwater. Buried alive, deep.

No. Calyx would not allow this. She had been so close. She hadn't sailed the length of this damned river just to drown in the last few feet of it. She lashed out underwater, feeling for something, anything that would connect her back to her magic.

It was day, but when she opened her eyes under the deep and murky water of the river, she saw night-blooms glowing.

Ikaros did not have time to worry about the precarious method Nimue used to transport them across the river; they were going too fast to think about anything at all. Their floating bridge skimmed quickly over the right bank and down into the harbour, lifted by an impossibly high wave that appeared in the centre of the otherwise still River Divine. They arrowed into the swarm of ravens that was Death's ship, closing in on the *Silken Hare*.

They were not fast enough.

Death smashed into the barge, and Nimue screamed so loud it seemed like all the water of the river rose up to amplify her pain.

Their floating bridge disappeared from underneath them, as Ikaros had always known would happen.

He lost Valeria and Dio in an instant. Nimue, clearly, could take care of herself.

The water was heavy and cold. Every time Ikaros struck out with a swimming stroke, he hit a piece of the broken barge.

He had only one consolation: the water tasted like flowers, and that meant Calyx was nearby. She had to be.

Ikaros swam into the chaos, into the floating debris and the hurricane of black feathers as his god fought the river (and the river fought back). He was driven only by the compulsion to find her, to save her...

He dove underwater, hoping this would give him some relief from the chaos. When he opened his eyes, though, he saw nothing but floating wood, churning feet, as the sailors swam to safety. He pushed himself deeper, deeper, and finally saw the reassuring purple glow of night-blooms. He had never seen them flowering underwater before, but he was used to botanical wonders when Calyx was nearby.

The tattoo on the left side of Ikaros' neck flared into life, hot and hungry.

Blooms billowed and blossomed underwater: the darkness lit up with her. He could now see Calyx floating below him, her eyes closed, her pale skin glowing like the stamens of the night-blooms. Tangled flowers and vines wove around her body, as if they might provide a substitute for breathing. Her silken clothes swelled and flowed, lifted by the water into shapes very like the petals of a flower.

Why wasn't she moving?

Ikaros kicked out wildly. He had never been a strong swimmer, but nothing was going to stop him reaching her. He had long since abandoned the idea that serving Calyx was a humiliation. What else was he good for in this world?

Through the thick, wild water of the river, Ikaros struggled closer, closer. Pieces of barge sank slowly around him, and his lungs burned for lack of breath. He was going to have to surface for air soon, but he was so nearly there...

Calyx's eyes snapped open and she stared at him through the murky, shadowed water.

Alive.

Ikaros grabbed for her, and she grabbed him in return. For a moment they clung to each other, the magic settling tightly around them both like a glove. Finally, he was *touching her*.

They kicked together towards the surface, and the night-blooms came with them, trailing in a halo around both bodies.

Ikaros burst up out of the water, gasping for air. Calyx

gasped too, flailing in darkness. He lunged for her, and she grasped him by the shoulders, hauling him in. The kiss was ugly; an ungainly piece of work. He could do better, but it had been a long day.

She kissed him back, wild and clinging, and they shared each other's breaths for a ragged moment or two.

It took longer than it should have done for either of them to notice that this was not the harbour of Phoenix Burning. They were somewhere else entirely.

28. "It's not exactly a place."

Calyx startled, wrenching herself out of Ikaros' arms as if he had burned her. She could not feel Nimue any more. She could not feel Dio or Valeria — it was as if the bond threads had been cut, though when she stretched her magic, she could still feel them there, just... distant. The connection was muffled, like it had been when she was swamped by the Black Raven and his powers.

"Where are we?" she asked.

It was dark, and they were both waist-high in water, but there was solid ground beneath her feet. The air smelled slightly stale, and her voice echoed against walls.

Ikaros let out a shaky breath, only giving the looming walls a cursory glance. "I've been here before. Not without him."

"Your god?"

"He should be here." Ikaros sloshed his way through shallower water, and reached back to assist her.

Calyx hesitated, but took his hand. She did not want to think about how warm his skin was, or how foolish she had been to drop all her restraint for one glorious moment of relief and desire.

She couldn't go around flinging herself at priests. She had a prince to marry. Her body had never been her own to share with others merely because she liked their dark eyes and sharp drawl and the line of their bearded jaw when they were turning away from her...

Calyx kept holding Ikaros' hand, even after he had led her up on to a small, rocky island. Her clothes felt heavy on her, sticking to her skin all wet and clammy. Her stemma pulled hard on her throat like it wanted to choke her. "Where are we?" she asked again.

Ikaros sighed heavily. "It's not exactly a place."

"I can see that."

As her eyes adjusted to the darkness, Calyx realised that this was a cave, but also that it was not in the best of shape. Dust drifted down from the curved ceiling. The rocks under their feet shifted around, as if shaken by unspeakable mysteries happening far below.

There was something strange about those rocks; unnatural. Or perhaps, too natural: the shapes of them, overlaid in patterns under her feet and again in the cave ceiling above, resembled the feathers of a bird.

It felt a little *too much* like a real place; even without Ikaros' warning Calyx would have suspected it was anything but.

"Last time I was here," said Ikaros, his hand pressing into hers — not quite a reassuring squeeze, but the ghost of a gesture as if he knew at least one of them needed comfort. "I was dying."

"How did that turn out for you?" she asked, more lightly than the topic deserved.

Ikaros turned his head slightly, still not looking directly at her. "You rescued me."

Surprised, Calyx gave a helpless laugh. "And where does that leave us now?"

Ikaros took a long, slow breath. "Utterly fucked," he said.

"It would seem so."

Finally, he turned to face her, their hands still joined. His eyes were dark and beautiful and if she had not already decided there would be no drowning today, she might have drowned in them. "Your daughter," said Ikaros. "Is destined to bring about the downfall of the gods."

Calyx's magic wanted him closer. No, *she* wanted him closer. But it was her magic that reached out first, wrapping itself around his upper arms. She had to get a hold of herself. "Is that a bad thing?" she managed to ask.

What could he mean? What kind of mythic nonsense was Nimue wrapped up in? *Let her have any destiny she wants, just let her be safe and alive.*

"Too early to tell." Ikaros looked a little wild around the eyes, and she wasn't sure if it was the situation — the near-drowning, his god, her daughter — or the pull between them.

Calyx had to think clearly. Had to take control of the situation. His warmth was not helping. She released his hand. "Where is Nimue now?"

"Where I left her," said Ikaros. He looked calmer, now they were no longer touching. "In the river. Why is there poetry written on your arm?"

Oh, that. Calyx's shawl was long-lost to the river. It had floated away, along with any sense that she had secrets to keep. "I'm dying," she said impatiently.

The cave shuddered around them. Fine dust fell from above. It smelled like wet feathers.

"My god might beat you to it," said Ikaros, glancing up. "Are you going to cut those out like the last lot? It seems to be a different poem."

"If I can find a surgeon who isn't distracted by the fall of the gods and can *follow instructions.*" Calyx placed cool fingers over the words; they were still reddish and hot to the touch. A real tattoo; the verses that appeared on her back were not usually so authentic. The pain only came when she cut them out. Still, she had no doubt that whatever made the ink-speaker put these words on her arm was connected to her family malady. No, not malady. *Curse.* "We have to get back," she said. "Nimue needs me."

"Nimue was holding her own, last I saw," said Ikaros dismissively.

Calyx seized his arm, pulling him closer to her. "You've seen her recently, though? She is alive."

Ikaros gave a short laugh. He didn't pull away from her touch. "Alive isn't quite the word for it," he said, covering Calyx's arms with his own warm fingers. "She's tapped into some arcane magic from the river. I suppose it runs in the family. Death is terrified of her. That's why he went after you."

The true name of his god; she did not want to think about what it meant that Ikaros was willing to speak it aloud. Did he believe in the fall of the gods? Was he on Nimue's side?

"Get me back to her," Calyx said, trying to make it a request, not a demand, though she could not help the way the magic thrummed between them now they were so close. "Ikaros, please."

His eyes darkened. "Last time I was here with the Black Raven, he released me with a kiss —"

Her mouth was on his before he had finished the sentence, and the rocks cracked open beneath their feet.

29. Death and the River Divine

One of the benefits of growing up on and around the River Divine since he was a lad was that Dio was an excellent swimmer. He'd never actually collided with a river barge from *above* before, nor witnessed a boat torn apart by an angry god, but he'd seen his share of disasters on the water in his time.

The crew of the *Silken Hare* reacted as Dio would have expected; they swam for shore, putting as much space as they could between themselves and the remains of their broken barge. Understandable, as the moon-jade chips used to fuel the ship should never be directly exposed to the magical waters of the River Divine... all sailors knew if that happened, you got the hell *away*.

(Mixing magics with magics was a renowned cause of historical disasters, though one might say that in this instance, that particular ship had well and truly sailed.)

Dio trod water, keeping an ear out for anyone in trouble. He surveyed the scene as best he could. He spotted Valeria a little way away, perched on a floating piece of the

Silken Hare's deck, as cool and calm as if she were reclining on a lounge in the middle of the Pandemonium nightclub.

There was no sign of Nimue, or the Black Raven. Ships all around them were circling, judging whether a rescue was necessary; or perhaps the various crews merely wanted a stickybeak at the last gasp of a vessel unluckier than they.

Dio wouldn't mind knowing more about *what the blood and endless was happening*. He swam in easy strokes towards Valeria.

"I hope you don't think you're clambering up on here with me," she said archly. "I just got comfortable."

"Can you feel Calyx?" Dio couldn't, and it was starting to worry him. The only mark on his skin making itself known was the new scythe-knife across the side of his face, which felt hot to the touch as if the god had used a burning brand to mark him.

"I don't think she's the one we have to worry about," said Valeria. Her eyes were strangely kind, sombre as she regarded his face.

A call rang out across the water, and Dio shaded his eyes from the sun as he turned. (The brightness was hitting the city at just the right angle to make its golden, amber, scarlet towers look as though they were aflame; a marvel to behold, but hardly the most important detail in this moment.)

Someone waved wildly at them from a small skiff; it looked like Mardi which suggested the shadowy glower behind her was the Bow.

"She's so resourceful," said Valeria in an approving tone. "I taught her that," she added.

Pleased as he was that Mardi was not dead, Dio was not sure that a skiff was any safer than the open water right now, not with what had happened to the *Silken Hare*. Apart from the debris floating on the surface, the water was oddly calm, considering...

A shape bulged in the river: at first it looked like a slow wave, or a large wing. Dio wondered if Nimue was up to her new tricks. But it was Aodhan who pulled himself up out of the water; a furious dark-eyed god dripping wet and hungry for vengeance.

Dio was reminded yet again that the type of person to whom he was attracted tended towards the dangerous. Something perhaps he should examine about himself, if he survived this.

Black feathers burst out of the water, forming a dark halo around Aodhan's bare-chested form. He clutched something dark and twisted in his hands — a shadow, or a cloak?

She lifted her head, and Dio realised to his horror that it was Nimue. She was wrapped in the god's dark power, bound by shadows. She looked crumpled; defeated. Her eyes were closed, her body limp. Only her pale face and bare scalp were visible, everything else had been swallowed up by Death.

"Fall of the gods," said Aodhan with a warm smile. "Not today, my dears."

The mark on Dio's face lit up, hot and raw. He felt himself tugged towards Aodhan, not with the desire he had felt when he was only a handsome man in the darkness, but something else. Something like Calyx's magical bond only deeper, set into his marrow.

This was how it felt, to be chosen by a god. Dio didn't like it at all.

"You're one of us, now," Valeria murmured, her eyes fixed on Aodhan.

Dio could not tell if it was awe or love or fear in her

gaze. Valeria had served the Black Raven longer than anyone alive, if you believed the stories. She wouldn't be coming to Nimue's rescue. Neither would Mardi, however kind she seemed. They were the Blade and the Needle: they had belonged to Death long before they belonged to Calyx.

Dio, though. Dio had loyalty baked into his bones, and he had never chosen to serve the god of death. He had been taken.

(Calyx took him too, but didn't mean to; he had chosen her back since then, over and over. He believed with all his heart that it was a choice. He hadn't fought her bond, as the others had; that mattered to him now.)

It was up to Dio Taurus to stop the Black Raven from hurting Nimue.

The river whispered around them.

Nimue's eyes snapped open.

Of course, Dio realised with a sinking feeling. She did not need him to rescue her. No one ever really needed him.

The cave of the Black Raven cracked, breaking apart in large, heavy shards.

There was a time in his life when Ikaros would have thought: *if my god dies, let me die with him*.

This was no longer that time, and he was no longer that priest.

He pressed Calyx close to his chest as they plunged once more into the dark and shadowy waters.

As the waters lightened, and the two of them coughed and spluttered once more in the open air — sunshine this time, an open sky over the wildly churned harbour of Phoenix Burning in the late afternoon — there were hands reaching for them both, pulling them to safety.

Ikaros found himself sitting in an over-filled skiff, water streaming from his featherbrace and hair, squashed in with the Blade and the Needle and the Bow, as well as Dio and Calyx. "What did we miss?"

"Where were you both?" Valeria asked in severe tones. "You can't have been underwater all this time."

The river rocked wildly below them, and Ikaros took that as a good enough reason to avoid the question.

Calyx squeezed Ikaros' hand tightly. "That's Nimue!" She had her magic back; Ikaros could feel it like a cool rain in the warm sunshine. Night-blooms bobbed up around them in the water, clustering around the boat; a strange sight to see them unfurled in daylight, already beginning to glow.

It was, indeed, Nimue. The girl floated in the air above the harbour, looking fairly serene for a person under siege by a god. Hundreds of black ravens hurled themselves at her, pecking and clawing without being able to get near her skin.

Death was the birds, and a dark cloud looming above the young woman, out of place in the azure sky. Death was below her in the form of Aodhan, bare-chested and shaking with rage as he poured everything he had against her.

Everything except us.

The River Divine, who had chosen Nimue as their avatar and champion, was not willing to go down without a fight. Naiads and water-sprites gathered in the harbour here, drawn from upriver. The sound of siren song was sweet on the air. Ashrays and grindylows, usually only seen where the river ran deep through the mountains, flickered on the surface of the water. Nereids lifted their long fingers up out of the river, reaching to Nimue, sharing their salt-water magic. Flora and fauna and all manner of in-between strange magical creatures were bobbing up out of the water, ready to serve their new mistress.

The river itself was thick with magic: it wrapped around Nimue like a cloak, and around Aodhan like a shroud. The battle was intense and hard to watch. The river was winning.

Valeria watched the scene, far too tense. She looked like she had taken poison already, and was waiting for the effects to set in.

"You realise," she said harshly. "If the gods fall, if he falls, we lose everything."

"Not everything," said Ikaros, his fingers tangled in Calyx's.

Valeria's eyes blazed at him. Anger at first, then something a lot like pity. "Have you forgotten?" she murmured. "She's not yours. Her magic is making you feel this way." Pain shuddered through her body, and she coughed up a whole camellia, petals spraying across the bottom of the boat. "You're only proving your point," she snarled at Calyx, who looked taken aback.

As if she, too, had forgotten that Ikaros was in her magical thrall. That he was not hers in any way that was honest.

Slowly, he let go of Calyx's hand.

The god of death called his birds to him and they flocked to his body, enhancing his power even as the river savaged him from all sides. Calyx had seen magical battles before, but nothing as intense as this; nothing as primal. No one in the thick of it was human, except her daughter, and the river seemed determined to use Nimue as if she was another of its mythic inhabitants.

The Black Raven no longer looked like a man. Water engulfed his skin, sticking to him, unmaking his shape until there was nothing left but shadows and feathers. "This is not our time!" he screeched into the air.

Nimue spoke in a voice that was not her own. Calyx knew her daughter, and this *was not her*. "I am the future. The river will take back this kingdom. The end of the gods is coming. But it doesn't have to be today. Clean up your house, raven. Tidy your temples. Stop fighting the inevitable."

He roared at her with what was left of his mouth. "The only thing inevitable is death!"

Nimue-not-Nimue raised one perfect eyebrow. "Not so nice on this side of it, I imagine."

Death screamed. Shadows and water and feathers sprayed outwards in one last burst of power against power.

And then, it was over. Nothing remained of the Black Raven but feathers, floating on the surface of a remarkably still river.

Nimue was gone, too.

Calyx scrambled to her feet, wildly rocking the boat. Ikaros put his hands on her, pulled her back down, half in his lap. "Have faith," he growled into the side of her neck.

"There," called Dio, pointing.

A figure cut through the water. Nimue had always been a strong swimmer, dipping in and out of the various pools of the palace gardens in the Imperium. Always busy and active, so very alive. Nimue reached their boat quickly, and her face came up from the water, smiling with exhilaration.

Calyx's heart had started beating again. This was her daughter. None of the river's otherworldly power touched her now. Nimue looked human; normal behind those bright eyes of hers. Calyx let out a sound, strangled and painful, reaching out.

Dio was nearer, and hauled Nimue up out of the river. She clung to him for a brief hug, all wet silks and rivulets, then laughed impossibly and crawled across the skiff full of too many people to reach her mother.

Calyx sobbed as Nimue climbed into her arms like she was a tiny child. "I thought I'd lost you."

How could she have ever imagined this would be a safer choice than leaving Nimue at home?

"Is he dead?" asked Mardi, one hand on her belly, eyes on the black feathers that floated on the water. "Can he die?"

"We'd know," Reynard said roughly. "We'd feel it."

"I don't know what I feel right now," said Mardi.

The bond threads connecting them all to Calyx were brighter than before. Stronger. That suggested the connection between the priests and their god might be weaker. Not that it was gone.

"If he is dead," said Ikaros with a wary look in Valeria's direction. "We're in trouble."

Valeria whipped her wet hair back, unbothered. "It takes more than that to kill a god. Even a god of —" *death*, she did not say.

After a moment's embrace, Nimue was already pulling back from Calyx, her eyes bright and wild. "What now?" she demanded.

They all looked at each other.

"Correct me if I'm wrong," said Ikaros in a scathing sort of voice. "But I believe there's supposed to be a royal wedding."

Calyx looked around. They were surrounded by boats, barges, ships, each with crew standing on deck, staring at the scene of the wrecked *Silken Hare*. She and her protectors were visible from the city wharf, where a cohort of gladii were waiting for her to step into her future. More armoured men lined the wide black steps leading up to the city, as if every soldier had come out to watch the show.

So many people had seen what happened. Did they understand its significance? Did they know what Nimue had done?

How could Calyx protect her daughter in a court where she knew no one, trusted no one?

Nimue leaned in, her forehead gently bumping against Calyx's — an old move they had not done since she was a child.

"There's no getting out of it now," said the daughter with the diplomatic training.

The Petal of the Imperium sighed. "I suppose we did come all this way. They'd be offended if we turned around and went home."

30. Phoenix Burning

It was a short distance across the harbour. Dio and Reynard took the oars. All eyes were on the small, overloaded skiff as it approached the wharf. Calyx could not pretend that she did not stand out, with her shaven head and wet pink silks. She had managed to straighten her stemma, though it was heavily waterlogged.

"Surely," murmured Ikaros, now sitting a respectable distance away; a fine trick when they had seven people crammed into a boat designed for four or five. "A Petal of the Imperium is allowed to use magic on such occasions."

Of course she could. Of course she should. *Be careful what you wish for, Ikaros.*

The Petal of the Imperium stepped on to a concrete pier of the city wharf, her daughter at her side. She wore layers of teal and green silk underneath a crisp linen stemma which displayed a magical pattern of ivy winding around a marble column. The daughter wore lilac silks, with a linen cap to cover her shaven head, and a pattern of violet petals decorating her own stemma. Both wore gold sandals. Every inch of the fabric of their garments was dry as a bone.

(Magic was useful for so many things, but one could never discount the everyday value of being able to instantly dry, restore and re-decorate clothes in an emergency.)

Behind them came the retinue: three priests of death in tailored featherbraces over black larkflax. If you looked closely at the beaded patterns on their jackets, you might see the shape of night-blooms woven in dark thread against the black. Dio, beside them, wore a similar arrangement, though Calyx had given him a long silk coat in the style from her homeland, as green as the river at the Eye of the Basilisk.

Reynard stood back from the group. Calyx had fixed his clothes too, and created a new featherbrace from empty air since Mardi had taken custody of his, but he refused to stand with the others. "I think you've forgotten, Petal," he said in a cold air. "I have no bond forcing me to serve you."

Calyx faltered. She had not forgotten, and yet — he was right, she had not given it a thought. She had dressed Ikaros, Mardi and Valeria like dolls, assuming they would be willing to come with her.

She hadn't exactly given them the choice.

The thought of entering this city alone, marching up the black steps of Phoenix Burning without this deadly retinue at her back, was terrifying. She could not face the Divine King and his Thirteenth Treasure without them. Could she?

I will release you once we are safe, she had promised

Ikaros. *You will do everything you can to protect my daughter, and to keep us both alive until we reach Phoenix Burning.*

Here they were, at Phoenix Burning. Were they safe? Would they ever be?

The captain of the gladii stood at the foot of the city steps, waiting for Calyx to cross the pier and join him so that he could take her to her husband. Her future.

"I don't know how to do this," she murmured. She had watched her sister transform into the cold, calculating, effortlessly pristine Empress without having the faintest idea how she did it.

Calyx had always felt safe in her comparatively low status within her own family. Could she stand as the wife of a royal heir? Be a queen to a future king? Could she protect her daughter inside that palace? (Even if Nimue was an avatar of the river, or some kind of prophesied god creature, she was still vulnerable... wasn't she? Certainly she was still a child.)

What happened when the god of death recovered his strength and moved against them? What if the rest of the gods joined in for good measure?

(What if Ikaros and Valeria and Mardi took his side? Surely if they had the freedom to choose, they would support the god who gave them purpose and ageless long life, and...)

"We'll be with you," said Dio, in a low voice, stepping forward. "You won't be alone."

Calyx looked at him gratefully, warmed by his presence. "If I released you from the bond, you'd still stay, wouldn't you? Join my honour guard?"

"Of course!" Dio Taurus said, as if she'd given him a gift.

Behind them, someone cleared their throat.

Calyx braced herself and turned to face Valeria, Mardi, Ikaros. Ikaros most of all, staring blankly at her like he had never put his mouth on hers in a cave. Like he had not been her companion and partner and protector during this long voyage down the River Divine.

Ikaros, who served her only because she had forced a magical bond on him.

It was Valeria who spoke. "Are we joining you, Petal?" Her voice was icy, but no flowers emerged from her lips. She was not fighting the magic.

Calyx could not risk dropping the bond now. Could she? Just because Reynard Kaldoran had been convinced (somehow) to leave her un-murdered did not mean that a newly freed Ikaros or Valeria or Mardi would not instantly finish the job, as soon as they were able.

Even — especially — with their god in ruins. They had served the Black Raven their whole lives. They had only known Calyx for a matter of days.

"I don't want to walk into that palace without you," she said helplessly. "All of you. I need you."

"Then you have a choice to make," said Ikaros. "Tow us in your wake like you dragged us down this river — or drop the bond, and let us decide whether we *want* the job you appear to be offering."

Calyx had been so busy worrying about whether the assassins were likely to kill her — it had not occurred to her that any of them but Dio would serve her willingly. "Would you do that?"

Valeria scoffed. Mardi stood very still. Ikaros looked pained.

"I don't know," he admitted. "*I don't know*."

Nimue shifted at Calyx's side. "Mother," she murmured. "There really is only one way to find out."

The captain of the gladii had grown impatient. There was the sound of marching feet behind Calyx. She was out of time.

At least, she thought in one desperate moment. *If Ikaros strikes me down where we stand, I won't have to marry a boy barely older than my daughter.*

There was only once choice she could make, and she made it. The scent of night-blooms filled the air around them as Calyx, bathed in sunlight, cast her magic.

The threads snapped. The magic fell away. And for the first time in this kingdom — for the first time in her life — Calyx had no magically-bound servants in her thrall.

It felt a lot like being naked.

Calyx breathed, standing on a pier with four assassins and a volunteer in front of her.

"I am Calyx of the House of Flowers," she said, by way of introduction. "Petal of the Imperium, and betrothed of the Thirteenth Treasure of the Divine Kingdom. I invite you to join my retinue, to advise and protect me while I live here, at Phoenix Burning."

"She'll pay a good wage," Nimue added. "And you can sign a fair contract of employment."

"Madam," broke in a voice behind her: the neglected captain. "You cannot supply your own retinue. You agreed —"

"I agreed in my betrothal contract to bring none of my own people from the Imperium, and to expect no armed protection from the palace while I travelled down the River Divine," Calyx flung behind her. "That journey is over. I am, I believe, free to offer employment to citizens of this country." She turned back to the others: Dio, already stumbling towards her. Reynard Kaldoran, already turning away.

Ikaros, Valeria and Mardi returned her gaze with interest.

"Will you join me?" Calyx asked.

And waited for their reply.

Dio did not have to think about it; he felt stripped bare without the bond, and he was well aware that Death's mark still lay upon him. Here, he could serve and protect. Belonging to Calyx's inner circle (in a freaking palace!) was as significant an honour as wearing the blood-red armour of a gladius. More, perhaps.

His aunties would be delighted.

Dio went to them, and Nimue hugged his arm, somehow proud of him, though it was the easiest decision he had ever made in his life.

Of the death priests, Dio was astonished that Valeria moved first. She circled Calyx with caution. "I've lived a long time," she said. "This is interesting enough that I want to see it played out. But I won't be caged again."

Calyx sounded startled. "That's fair," she said.

Mardi moved next. "We need to discuss maternity arrangements. Likely, I can only sign a short-term contract."

"Understandable," said Calyx. "Though I'm sure the palace provides childcare options. We'll have to look into that."

The captain of the gladii looked like he was about to explode all over the city wharf. Dio hid a smirk, not envying him his job.

Then it was just Calyx and Ikaros, staring each other

down. The Hand of the Black Raven, and the Petal of the Imperium.

"You made the right choice," said the priest of death, flexing his hands as if he expected to be using them in the near future.

Calyx's smile was incandescent. "I know," she said. "How are you going with yours?"

"Still thinking about it," Ikaros muttered.

"Do you need more time?"

"How long have you got?"

Behind them, the captain of the gladii threw up his hands in impatience.

Calyx gave Ikaros a thoughtful look. "Why don't you come along to the palace with us? You can let me know your answer when you are ready."

Dio watched Ikaros. The other man was as tense as a crossbow ready to loose a bolt. Bit by bit, the tension went slack.

A choice was made.

"Peachy," said Ikaros, letting out a long breath. "Come on, then. Let's do this."

END

Calyx, Dio, Ikaros, Mardi and Valeria will return… in ***City of Petals Rising***, coming first to the Sheep Might Fly podcast in 2024-2025.

This novel was created with the financial support of the author's frankly extraordinary Patreon backers. If you'd like to join this exclusive club, you are very welcome to visit patreon.com/tansyrr

Also by Tansy Rayner Roberts

SPARKS & PHILTRES

Gate Sinister

House Perilous

Land Glorious

THE CREATURE COURT

Power & Majesty

The Shattered City

Reign of Beasts

Cabaret of Monsters

TEACUP MAGIC

Tea & Sympathetic Magic

The Frost Fair Affair

Spellcracker's Honeymoon

Lady Liesl's Seaside Surprise

Have Spirit, Will Duchess

This Enchanted Island

BELLADONNA U

Unreal Alchemy

Holiday Brew

Practical Witching

MUSKETEER SPACE

Musketeer Space

Joyeux

Castle Charming

Castle Ever After

Gorgons Deserve Nice Things

Love & Romanpunk

Merry Happy Valkyrie

Splashdance Silver

Liquid Gold

Ink Black Magic

NON-FICTION & ESSAYS

Pratchett's Women: Unauthorised Essays

From Baby Brain to Writer Brain: Writing Through A World Of Parenting Distractions

It's Raining Musketeers

AS EDITOR

Mother of Invention (with Rivqa Rafael)

Cranky Ladies of History (with Tehani Croft)

Adventures Across Space and Time: A Doctor Who Reader (with Paul Booth, Matt Hills & Joy Piedmont)